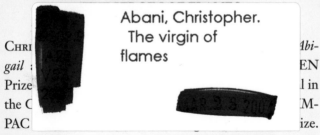

Abani, Christopher.
The virgin of
flames

CHRI ... *Abi-*
gail ... EN
Prize ... l in
the C ... M-
PAC ... ize.
His other honors include a PEN Freedom-to-Write Award,
a Prince Claus Award, and a Lannan Literary Fellowship.
He teaches at the University of California, Riverside.

Also by Chris Abani

Novels
Masters of the Board
GraceLand

Novella
Becoming Abigail

Poetry
Kalakuta Republic
Daphne's Lot
Dog Woman
Hands Washing Water

THE VIRGIN
OF FLAMES

Chris Abani

PENGUIN BOOKS

PENGUIN BOOKS
Published by the Penguin Group
Penguin Group (USA) Inc., 375 Hudson Street, New York, New York 10014, U.S.A.
Penguin Group (Canada), 90 Eglinton Avenue East, Suite 700, Toronto, Ontario, Canada
M4P 2Y3 (a division of Pearson Penguin Canada Inc.)
Penguin Books Ltd, 80 Strand, London WC2R 0RL, England
Penguin Ireland, 25 St Stephen's Green, Dublin 2, Ireland (a division of Penguin Books Ltd)
Penguin Group (Australia), 250 Camberwell Road, Camberwell, Victoria 3124, Australia
(a division of Pearson Australia Group Pty Ltd)
Penguin Books India Pvt Ltd, 11 Community Centre, Panchsheel Park, New Delhi - 110 017,
India
Penguin Group (NZ), cnr Airborne and Rosedale Roads, Albany, Auckland 1310, New
Zealand (a division of Pearson New Zealand Ltd)
Penguin Books (South Africa) (Pty) Ltd, 24 Sturdee Avenue, Rosebank, Johannesburg 2196,
South Africa

Penguin Books Ltd, Registered Offices:
80 Strand, London WC2R 0RL, England

First published in the United States of America by Penguin Books 2007

10 9 8 7 6 5 4 3 2 1

Grateful acknowledgment is made for permission to reprint an excerpt from "Sunday
Morning" from *The Collected Poems of Wallace Stevens*. Copyright 1923 and renewed 1951 by
Wallace Stevens. Used by permission of Alfred A. Knopf, a division of Random House, Inc.

PUBLISHER'S NOTE
This is a work of fiction. Names, characters, places, and incidents either are the product of the
author's imagination or are used fictitiously, and any resemblance to actual persons, living or
dead, businesses, companies, events, or locales is entirely coincidental.

LIBRARY OF CONGRESS CATALOGING-IN-PUBLICATION DATA

Abani, Christopher.
    The virgin of flames / Chris Abani.
        p. cm.
    ISBN-13: 978-0-14-303877-1
    1. Street art—California—Los Angeles—Fiction. 2. Artists—California—Fiction. 3. East
Los Angeles (Calif.)—Fiction. I. Title.

PR9387.9.A23V57 2007
821'.914—dc22   2006051570

Printed in the United States of America
Designed by Ginger Legato

For
Mark, Charles and Gregory
Athos, Porthos and Aramis

also
Harold Pinter and Musa Farhi

There are singular people who appear like
metaphors somewhere further out than we
do, beckoned, not driven, invented by belief,
author and hero of a dream by which our own
courage and cunning are tested and tried; so
that we may wonder all over again what is
veritable and inevitable and possible and
what it is to become whoever we may be.

—Diane Arbus
Harper's Bazaar

acknowledgments

Blair Holt, who saw it even when I didn't and who pushed me to places hard but revelatory. Percival Everett, who can never quite escape the deluge of pages and whose friendship sustains and guides; Cristina Garcia, who never seems to run out of generosity; Walter Mosley, who continues to give and never wants anything back; Brad Kessler, Bridget Hoida, Jonathan Speight, Allison Umminger, Carol Muske-Dukes, Junot Diaz, Parissa Ebrahimzadeh, Peter Orner, Gabriela Jauregi, Titi Osu, Helene Igwebuike, Maurya Simon, Ishita Roy, PB Rippey, Wendy Belcher, Kachi Akoma, Steve Isoardi, Jeannette Lindsay, Emily Raboteau, Angie Cruz, Ron Gottesman, Russell Banks, Tara Ison, Tayari Jones, Elias Wondimu, Sara Mayinka, and Richard Russo—for reading and friendship. Alma Lopez, for letting us use her amazing print for the cover. Kathryn Court and Alexis Washam—for believing and for guiding this book to print.

My family, always: especially Stella and Daphne.

The divine Ellen Levine. There are no words.

The terms "Goodoo Dolls" and "The Ugly Store" are copyrighted by Jeannette Lindsay, and are used with kind permission.

Several drafts of this novel were written in Marfa, Texas, while I was on a Lannan Writers Residency. Thank you for the support and for everything you do for daring and engaged literature.

All the bookstores—independent and otherwise—that never get thanked.

For everyone who fills my life but who isn't named—thank you.

THE VIRGIN
OF FLAMES

I want to prove that Los Angeles is a practical joke played
on us by superior beings on a humorous planet.

—Bob Kaufman
Unholy Missions

this is the religion of cities.

The sacraments: iridescent in its concrete sleeve, the Los Angeles River losing faith with every inch traveled. A child riding a bicycle against the backdrop of desolate lots and leaning chain-link fences, while in the distance, a cluster of high-rises, like the spires of old Cathedrals, trace a jagged line against the sky, ever the uneven heart of prayer. The inevitable broken fire hydrant surrounded by an explosion of half-naked squealing children bearing witness to the blessed coolness of water. World-weary tenements and houses contemplating a more decadent past, looking undecided, as if they would up and leave for a better part of the city at any moment. A human silhouette on a park bench reading a book. Junkies hustling the afternoon. And out of sight, yet present nonetheless, the tired bounce of heat-deflated basketballs against soft tar. And a dog. Old, ancient even. And curious.

two

White.

Black sat before the mirror applying paste to his face. Face paint really, but it was thick like wallpaper paste. Too thick maybe, but when he was mixing it, he thought it would take that much to cover his complexion. It would also help the mask to harden with a sheen he could paint over: rouge cheeks, blue eye shadow, and really black eyelashes. But for now, he had to get the right shade of white. There were three cups of the stuff in a row in front of him in varying degrees of brilliance. He studied his face from several angles, imagining in that pause Miss Havisham sitting in front of a mottled wedding cake in a mottled wedding dress, both of which were the color of the paste on his face, an aging ivory that recalled the musty smell of empire in decline, a sad color really. Whose empire he had no idea. Probably something he had seen in a movie. He wiped it off, suddenly filled with an inexplicable overwhelming melancholy. The thought of Miss Havisham depressed him, made him think of being caught forever in the moment of desire, in the eternity of the bacchanal unable to consume or be consumed by it.

"Fucking sad," he muttered at his reflection. "Jesus!"

He picked up the second cup and applied the contents slowly to the left side of his face, marveling in a childlike manner at the way mirrors reversed the world. On the wall next to the mirror, a letter-size color sketch of the Virgin of Guadalupe on black paper gazed at him. It was a close-up of her face, which was a brilliant white, the color he was trying to match. It was pinched into sorrow by red cheeks and a wash of blue for her shawl. He wanted to paint a mural of her. To capture all the bittersweet emotion of being the Mother of God. Since he was broke he couldn't afford to hire any models, which was why he was sitting in front of the mirror trying on face paint. He intended to dress up as her and use himself as a model, painting a more detailed cartoon from his reflection. That would be the study he would transfer onto any wall he could find to use as a canvas. But whatever difficulty getting the face paint right posed paled in comparison to getting the rest of the costume together. For her robe, he had appropriated his landlord's wedding dress from the cleaners across the street. While trying out the dress, which was several sizes too small and which he had to adjust at his sewing machine, he thought that the contrast of his dark hands and feet against the white of the dress and his face made for an interesting play.

While he waited for the contents of cup two to dry, he turned to look at the wedding dress hanging from a hook on the door like a ghost, all of its ectoplasmic sadness oozing everywhere. Having acquired the dress, he had bought a blonde wig for his hair, though it was hard to tell what color Mary's hair had been. In all the pictures a shawl covered her head. But since Jesus was painted with blonde hair, he figured it made sense. He didn't want to admit that there was the element of subversion in this choice, that somewhere in the back of his mind he actually thought of her more like Marlene Dietrich. Whatever he decided to do with the hair, he hadn't solved the problem of the blue shawl. Should be easy enough, he thought. Turning back to the mirror, he smiled, the paste pulling his lips into a grimace. This is the right shade, he wanted to yell, but was afraid of cracking the still drying surface.

Without trying the contents of the third cup, he painted rouge cheeks onto the hardening mask of his face, and blue eye paint in a shadow around the eyes. Finishing, he leaned back. He looked beautiful, he thought, thinking at the same time how odd it was that he would think that. But then so many odd things had been happening since he took on this project, not least of which was the fact that Angel Gabriel, sometimes in the shape of a fifteen-foot-tall man with wings, sometimes as a pigeon, had taken to stalking him.

Leaning against the wall of the room that he used as an easel was a rug of rice paper. Unsnapping the elastic binding, he laid it out on the floor in a crinkled eight-foot spread. He sat on the stool by the workbench and lit a cigarette and studied the paper. This was how it always began for him. Almost imperceptibly, but with a snap of the wrist that could only be deliberate, Black sent a small ember spiraling into the air. It landed on the paper, and he sighed happily as it made a small hole with a charred black lip. This too was part of his ritual. Finishing the cigarette and stubbing it out in the bowl of bone-black pigment on the worktable, he got up and circled the paper the way Ali would circle the ring to psyche out his opponents. Finally he stopped and lay down backward, the paper crackling under him as it moved to allow his weight to spread out into the weave. With his eyes closed he made a paper angel, then rolled about on the paper, making sure that his body touched every inch of it. He believed that this way, his body was one with the paper and that when he painted he could conceptualize very accurately the dimensions needed. He made all his models do it. Again, it was ritual. Getting up, he dragged the paper over to the wall and stuck it there with masking tape. Now to paint, he thought.

His cell phone rang.

Bomboy wanted to meet.

He would pay for lunch.

"Lunch? I am about to work. Can't come out to play."

"I need help. What will it take?"

"I need rent money, puto."

"I'll give you two hundred bucks for your time."

"I'll be there soon."

Black paused by the door. He didn't want to clean his face until he was sure he could duplicate the shade of white. Fuck it, he thought, pushing a pair of sunglasses on as if they would somehow detract from the grotesque carnival of his face, I am an artist.

He pulled up in front of Bomboy's building, an apartment block Bomboy said used to be the Langley Hotel, on Normandie and Eighth, and which still had, on the roof, an old penthouse where Cary Grant had lived. This whole area, just one block east of Wilshire and heading downtown, used to be the best of Los Angeles in the twenties and thirties, Bomboy bragged.

The penthouse was in dire need of renovation, and was inhabited mainly by pigeons, but it was all there: tennis court (its chain-link ball stop leaning drunkenly into the Santa Anas), an empty swimming pool and the four-bedroom penthouse. Black rang Bomboy on his cell.

"I'm here."

"Come up to the roof, man."

"Why? I'm hungry. Come on down, cuño."

"Come on up. I have some good weed."

Black sighed and headed in.

"The blood of Jesus!" Bomboy said when he saw Black's face. "What's that shit?"

Black shrugged. "Project I'm doing. Couldn't afford a model."

"Project of what?"

"Virgin Mary."

Bomboy laughed. "You look more like the undead in a Japanese horror movie," he said.

Black ignored him and taking the proffered spliff, he took a hit. On the roof, lounging back, legs dangling over the empty pool, they smoked pot and watched planes fill the sky.

"Where is my money, puto?" Black asked finally.

Bomboy shook his head and counted out the two hundred dollars.

"As promised. I thought we were friends, Black, where is the trust, eh?"

"In God we trust. So what's up?" Black asked, stuffing the two hundred dollars into his back pocket.

"Oh, nothing much. It's just that I need to buy some fake papers. I want to travel back home soon. To celebrate the peace."

"Home?"

"Yeah, Rwanda. I miss it."

"Fake papers?"

"You know, on Alvarado."

"Well, if you know where to get them, why do you need me?"

"To speak Spanish. Those guys don't speak English."

"How long have you lived here and still don't speak Spanish?"

"Speak any African languages?"

"Whatever, chingado."

"That's rich chingado to you."

"Still a chingado."

They smoked some more.

"Say, Black, what are your plans exactly?" Bomboy asked after a while, lighting up again.

"Plans?"

"You know, for life. I mean you are a grown man, not getting any younger, no offense, and yet you are still leeching off of your friends."

"You invite me over to insult me?"

"No, not insult," Bomboy said. "But you know we Africans are very ambitious and progressive. I'm just thinking of you."

"So ambitious you're working in a butcher shop, güey."

Bomboy laughed.

"You are vexed. I am sorry, but I don't work in a butcher shop. You know I own that abattoir. Because of me, five people have jobs. I also live in a nice place and drive a Lexus, so don't even compare yourself with me."

What Black couldn't voice because the pot was making it hard to concentrate, but which filled the air around him with the thickness of smoke, was his fear of simply disappearing like the planes overhead, into the endless sky, forgotten by some distant watcher on a roof somewhere.

"Well, I guess you are a better killer than me."

"Oh, is that supposed to hurt me? You may be older than me, Black, but you are still a small boy. I found myself in an unfortunate position and I did what was necessary to survive. You on the other hand, you my friend, are becoming a joke."

Black was silent. He looked out at the empty pool. The last time he was here, a young man had been lying at the bottom, gun drawn, body riddled with bullet holes, his blood vainly trying to fill the concrete hollow. He and Bomboy still smoked their bong by the body that day, knowing it would take the police a couple of days to get to the dead banger. Nobody knew who shot him, or why. Nobody cared. Only the pigeons, and Cary's ghost, and they weren't talking. There were a lot of ghosts around the old parts of Los Angeles, same as in any city. It was just that in Los Angeles, the neon lights and the new buildings distracted one's vision. But Black knew if he looked closely, they would be there, crowding in, singing, begging, crying and dying all over again, every night.

"Feed me, shithead," he said, getting up.

Bomboy struggled up.

"You are going like that?" Bomboy pointed to Black's face.

"I came here like this."

"Please wipe your face," Bomboy said, passing Black a handkerchief, indicating the white makeup.

Black shook his head, refusing the handkerchief.

"It's okay, I've got wipes in the car," Bomboy said hopefully.

Black just smiled and shook his head. They headed for Langers. On Seventh and Alvarado, the deli was a favorite. They both ordered the pastrami sandwich and waited impatiently for the food to arrive, doing their best to ignore the stares Black's face was getting. It certainly had a few of the waitresses talking, and the head chef even came out from the kitchen to see this character.

"Shooting a movie?" he asked. " 'Cause nobody told me. If you're shooting a movie in here, we've gotta be paid."

"No movie, sir, my friend is an artist and this is just an idea he is playing with," Bomboy said. "We just came in for some lunch."

"Can't he speak for himself?" the head chef asked.

Bomboy shrugged.

"He's a mime."

The head chef sniffed.

"Well, in that case he can't complain."

Laughing, he returned to the kitchen.

"Why do I embarrass you, darling?" Black said. "Mime?"

"Do you have a better idea?"

"You could say that I am your girlfriend."

"That's not funny, my friend. That is just preposterous."

The food came and they ate fast and noisily, without talking, appetites fueled by the pot. Finishing, Black wiped his mouth and said:

"Now, pay up and let's go."

"Okay, but you're still taking me to Alvarado. Like I said, I need to buy some new papers. You know, license, green card."

"How many identities have you had, man? How many lives have you got?"

"Nine."

"Okay, but ándale, hermano."

Bomboy put down the toothpick he had been using to root around inside his mouth. He picked up the bill and examined it for a minute.

"Sure," he said, getting to his feet and heading for the cashier.

At the intersection where most of the deals for fake IDs in Los Angeles were made, Black walked up to a man leaning against the wall of the 7-Eleven. Speaking rapidly in Spanish, Black gestured toward Bomboy. Nodding, the man asked for a photograph. Black turned to Bomboy and interpreted. Bomboy handed over the photograph. Then the man pulled an inked stamp pad from his pocket. It looked like a prop from the set of an archaic post office, like the one from his childhood memories, where tired and bored-looking workers inked heavy brass seals before slamming them down wearily on brown envelopes.

"What's that for?" Bomboy asked.

"Fingerprints," Black replied. "For the green card."

"But it's a fake. The moment they scan it, it will come up fake. Why doesn't he use his fingerprints? It won't make any difference."

"Does he look like the kind of guy who would do that? It's just to make the ID look real. Come on, 'mano."

The man with the stamp pad stood patiently through this conversation. With a cough, he flipped the lid open and held it flush with his body, out of sight to anyone more than a couple of feet from him.

"Come on, you're making me nervous, pendejo. This place is crawling with undercover cops. Let's do this and go," Black said, looking around.

"Looking like that in this neighborhood, I think the police are the least of your worries," Bomboy said, extending his hand. The man grabbed it roughly, pressing the right thumb deep into the ink. Releasing Bomboy's hand, he pocketed the stamp pad in one fluid motion and produced a piece of photographic paper in its place. He pushed Bomboy's thumb onto it firmly, and then let go.

"Fifty dollars," the man said.

"Pay him," Black said.

"How do I know he'll come back?"

"Okay. Pay me later," the man said, clearly not in the mood to argue and indicating for the first time that he understood English. "Come back in twenty minutes." He melted away so fast that the only proof that he had even been there was Bomboy's inky thumb.

"Now what?"

Black was smiling. It was nice to see the usually confident Bomboy so out of his element.

"Now we wait in that McDonald's over there. Drink a cup of coffee slowly and come back in twenty minutes."

They crossed the street and while Black fetched the coffee, Bomboy made his way to a table at the back. He yanked a handful of tissue from the dispenser on the table and tried to wipe the ink off his thumb. Black returned with two coffees. The hot bite on his tongue caused Bomboy to wince.

"What's wrong with you?"

"Hot coffee."

"All the *bad* things you have seen and a little hot coffee has got you acting like a pendejo."

Bomboy mumbled something under his breath. From the window, they could see that the guy they had spoken to had returned to his spot, leaning against the wall of the 7-Eleven.

"Our guy is back. Let's go," Bomboy said, getting up.

As they were about to cross the street to the 7-Eleven's parking lot, a quarter on the sidewalk caught Black's attention. It was brand new and shining. Was it a good luck omen? He considered it thoughtfully.

"Hey, what's the delay?" Bomboy asked, foot poised over the edge of the curb.

Black ignored him and bent down for the money. As he straightened up, he saw several police cars pull into the 7-Eleven's parking lot. He and Bomboy stood on the sidewalk across the street and watched all the loitering men, including the one with Bomboy's green card, being arrested.

"Shit. LAPD," Bomboy said. "Shit, fucking shit! And that guy has my picture and fingerprint on a fake green card."

"It could have been worse," Black said, staring at his reflection in the window of a car parked near them. The blue lights from the cop cars, also reflected, flashed across the white sea of his face.

"You're right. It's good to have someone to watch over you."

"Yes," Black said, his voice dull, glancing about for Gabriel. "Someone to watch over me."

three

Yellow.

Not canary but vibrant nonetheless, Black's dilapidated Volkswagen bus. Nicknamed the Blackmobile, it was his home away from home, cluttered as it was with books, dog food, clothes and a sleeping bag. The windscreen was steamed up. At night, winter in Los Angeles was like winter everywhere else, except for snow of course. But with temperature drops between ten and thirty degrees as day fell to night, it was still cold. He shivered and thought at least the rain isn't too bad yet. Before he turned the key in the ignition, he reached out and touched the bobble-head Alsatian on the dash. Black loved dogs but had a long and complicated history with them, somewhat shamanic and somewhat desperate. He dropped his hand from the plastic toy and turned the key. The engine coughed a few times and then, as it banged into life, Black leaned his head back and howled. There was something decidedly feral about him.

As he waited a few minutes for the engine to heat up, he lit a cigarette and reached into the glove compartment. He pulled out Randy Newman's *Land of Dreams* on eight-track, and selected "I Want You to Hurt Like I Do." It reminded him of his mother. Fuck, he thought, fuck it all, as he pushed harder than necessary against the accelerator, ignoring the looks from the patrons outside The Ugly Store, tearing off in a squeal of tires, the old van shaking from the effort.

He followed the flood bed of the Los Angeles River, but instead of fingers of water fanning into a delicate delta, this flood bed was scarred and then zippered over with railway lines. Only the slight levee running by the road proved there had been a river here once. Black's journey, from the Pasadena of his early childhood to the East Los Angeles of the rest of his life, seemed guided by this river and its ghosts. He cut through downtown, to San Pedro Street and then across to the 10 West, heading for Santa Monica. A circuitous trip, but less traffic: in Los Angeles, to go the long way round was sometimes the shortest path between two points. It was a quantum thing.

When he got to Santa Monica, he parked in the pier lot. He got out of the van and stood awhile staring through the space between the slats into the water below. He spat carefully, aim perfect. Turning, he headed for the beach. He never bothered locking his van. There was nothing to steal from it.

It couldn't be more than a few minutes past nine and the boardwalk was crowded, though the sounds grew fainter as he made his way down the sand. In the floodlit parking lot to the left, teenagers made out in cars with open doors, pumping out loud music. Some, in groups, like gaggles of half-naked geese, lounged on top of parked cars, or on the floor passing joints or drinks. Parked at the edge of the lot was a police car, content to watch for now. The homeless spread along the sand in the dark like an infestation of ants, Black thought. He knew they came here to escape the dangers of downtown LA. He changed his mind. They didn't look like an ant infestation, more like melancholic whales beached so long they had shrunk to dark forms half their original size and had forgotten how to swim. Something in him wanted to minister to them, to save them. He could do that. He did it for dogs already, so why not people? He knew all about being lost. All of his own melancholy was wrapped up in this desire. He remembered the time he bought an on-line reverend-hood from the NewWineChurchofGod.com.

It had been simple enough. He downloaded the six-page church theology, charged the fifty dollars administration fee to his credit card, clicked the OK button, and waited for the dialog box that would announce his ordination, as promised, in gaudy gold letters. But his laptop had difficulty downloading the Flash document. Something to do with Active X Controls, the error message informed him. He liked the sound of that. Active X Controls. It sounded liturgical.

Irritated, he had stared at the white dialog box with the red X in the corner. It stared back, like a blind cornea with red stigmata. The vocal section of the document was unaffected, though, and a strangled robotic voice that reminded him of Hal from *2001: A Space Odyssey* said: "Congratula-tionsyouhave been ordained apastorat The NewWine Churchof God . . ."

In the ghostly glow of the notebook's LCD screen,

it had almost been possible to believe that it was the voice of God. After that everything else had seemed rather anticlimatic: the gold-trimmed certificate in its imitation rosewood frame, the complimentary CLERGY car sticker and the dog collar.

He turned away from the homeless; they didn't need him. He glanced at the luminous dial of his watch; it was nearly ten. He looked up and saw a woman standing at the edge of the water. She was graying, with a gentle face and a dignified air. She seemed unaware that little tongues of surf were licking at the legs of her business suit, wrapping themselves around the leather briefcase in the sand next to her, gently moving it further out to sea with each surge. Her sadness seemed absolute. He was riveted, as though she and he were the last people left on earth. He wasn't attracted to her, but to her absolute aloneness; this was what had drawn him to Sweet Girl. He wanted to approach her, this stranger on the beach. He wanted to save her. He knew he could do it. He could make up the rituals.

"Good evening," he would say, holding out his hand.

The woman would smile and take his hand in a shy shake.

"This way," he would say, leading her closer to the water's edge. With his heel, he would draw a square and in its middle, a circle, both in the sand. He would ask her to take off her top and kneel in the circle as he stood before her. He would reach down to the sand, pick up fistfuls and pour them over her head. The soft light would be reflected by the silicone and it would look like she was being showered in glitter. He would say: *This is our body. The one true home.*

Feel the fall of it. Feel the wind carry it. This is the ancient way. Do this in memory of us. Don't forget.

Then, dusting off his hands, he would bend her head, first back then forward. Washing it gently with the salty water of the ocean, fetched in his cupped hands, with the tenderness of a woman washing a child in a long-ago gathering of shadows. *This is water,* he would say. *This is mother. The path. Taste the salt of it. Feel the flow. This is the ancient way. This is dread. This is freedom. Do this in memory of us. Don't forget.*

Then pulling her to her feet he would point her to the water and say: "Go," pressing pennies into one palm, cowries into the other. "Go, throw the money in the sea, one palm for the new coin, one for the old, pay for your sins. Then place something precious to you on the sea's lip, set it free on the water of life, set your heart free, this is the ancient way."

Instead, he approached her, this stranger he wanted to pull back from the edge of that dark body heaving in the night, and said: "I think your briefcase is getting wet." But she didn't hear him. Without another word, he climbed back up to the pier with its lights and Ferris wheel and crowds and fishermen. He bought a hot dog and a cola. Sitting on the wooden rail of the pier, feet dangling over the darkness below, he ate quickly and putting the can to his lips, he drained it in one gulp. With a loud exhalation he crushed the can against his head and sent it skipping over the waves. Large drops of rain began to fall as he lit a cigarette. Match held defiantly into the wind, he smoked, wishing he could see Sweet Girl again. The rain grew heavier and he jumped down and ran for the Blackmobile.

He settled into the van, starting it and watching the single blade try futilely to wipe water from the windscreen. His obsession with her had led to him following her in the past. But he had stopped that. It wasn't healthy. I'll see her tomorrow, maybe, he told himself, but not tonight.

Tonight it was raining.

four

Incendiary.

Black thought as he watched Sweet Girl walk toward the stage. He knew all eyes in the room were riveted on her. She looked at him as she passed and smiled thinly, the lacy fabric of her top teasing his cheek. He opened his mouth to speak, but she was gone, already climbing the three steps up to the stage.

She paused for a moment, hands above her head, fingertips trailing on the ceiling, which was mirrored, waiting for the jukebox to start. He liked this moment best. The pause between when the stripper came on stage and the music started. In that hush everyone held their breath, even the other strippers, every face marked with something like lust. That pause held everything for Black, who as an artist, a muralist, saw everything as whole—texture, silence, sound, color and image. The expectation was elastic, a bubble spreading out into the room. And when it burst, the dancer would have them. Or not. Just as it became unbearable for

Black, the first notes of the song started and he let out his breath in a shudder.

Slow, slow, almost languid, Sweet Girl began to move to the music. Eyes closed, lips part open, front lower teeth visible, face turned up to the light, to the mirrors. The feeling was worship. Then she smiled and her eyes opened. Chin still up in worship she looked surprised to see herself in the mirror. Smiling she traced her forefinger over her lips and then with aching slowness, the tip of her tongue flicked over it.

Everyone in the room was looking up. Not at the elevated stage, but at the mirrors on the ceiling. Seeing Sweet Girl see herself as if for the first time. Feeling all of it spilling from her eyes. The smile on her face, a phantom, a ghost of a thing, emerged as she examined her wet fingertip. Reaching up she traced her face in the mirror, leaving a snail trail of dampness. In his seat, Black moaned softly as though she had touched him.

Faces, the audience's, like globular stars, filled the clear sky of the mirror. Sweet Girl selected a face from the many hanging there. A man. About fifty, balding, nostrils flared in excitement above a dirty moustache: a shaggy dog of a man. Sweet Girl looked directly into his eyes hanging there in the mirror, holding him in her smile. Then like the slow drip of new honey, she shimmied out of her diaphanous top. And as it slowly fluttered to the floor it was his release. Another face. A woman. Alone. This look wasn't performance. It was lingering. Sweet Girl's nose curled slightly, as though the smell of the woman was in her, held, just a moment too long, then gone. Another. A thin rake of a man whose eyes held all the fire his body couldn't. With the same forefinger, Sweet Girl teased one reluctant bra strap off, then the other. Without taking her eyes from his, she reached back with one hand and released the clasp, the other holding on to the mirror, pinning the man's face to one spot. A casual shrug dropped the bra to the floor and Sweet Girl danced back and kicked it forward, the bra landing just short of the stage lip. The move, though clearly practiced, held ease.

All this time, Sweet Girl was still looking up, and Black wondered how come she didn't get a crick. Spinning around slowly in her panties and plastic-cone pasties hard like arrow tips, there was a stillness about her. As though she was stationary and the mirror was a wheel of fortune. Stopping at Black's face, she smiled. Then looked down. Straight at him. He felt self-conscious, but in that masked way that men who are over six feet tall and weigh about two-fifty have learned. She cupped her breasts with both hands and held them up as though in offering. Black felt his own hands, delicate and incongruous given his weight, sliding up his sides, stopped just short of his own plump chest by her teasing smile. No one else noticed. They were all leaning forward intently. Black hesitated. Was Sweet Girl mocking him? As he watched, her tongue snaked out to its full length; six inches from root to tip. Like a thing with a life all its own, it strained downward toward her nipples. Black pushed away from her, the spell broken. He got up and walked to the bar, noting that it was just past seven p.m. For a moment he wondered what it said about him that at seven on a weeknight evening he was in a strip club. He knew Bomboy Dickens, who was nursing a drink at the bar, would say: We are lucky, that's what it says; in that thick accent that was like a gel over everything he said, making it seem more authentic.

Black watched him for a while, realizing for the first time the difference between him and Bomboy. Black, as a painter, lived in a world of composition—shade, angle of light, perspective—one in which things blurred into one another even as they stood out in sharp relief; Bomboy, on the other hand, lived in a world of statements—often contradictory, but no less rigid and clear each time.

Bomboy was still leaning against the bar, where he'd been since they arrived together a couple of hours before. He was drinking Guinness from a pint glass, and in his shiny black silk shirt, starched linen trousers, mock-croc shoes and black hat he looked out of place. No, Black corrected himself as he approached, Bomboy was out of time. Or as Bomboy would have said: anachronistic. Sitting on an empty bar stool, Black waited for the generously proportioned barmaid stuffed into lingerie several sizes too small to come over to him.

"Hey, Black. What happened? I thought that one is your favorite?" Bomboy asked, gesturing vaguely with his drink toward the stage and Sweet Girl.

"Whatever," Black mumbled. "Hey!" he said, banging his palm on the bar top to get attention. The barmaid didn't look up from her cell phone.

Bomboy turned to look at Black and the barmaid.

"Cool your temper," he said. "Do you want Guinness?"

"Why would I want Guinness, cabrón?"

"Guinness, my friend, is the truffle of alcohol. Truly decadent but packing a velvet punch to floor you."

"I'm fine," he said. "Hey! Puto!" He banged on the bar top again.

The barmaid looked up and was about to return to her conversation when Bomboy caught her eye. He nodded in her direction and she came over.

"Yes?" She pointedly ignored Black.

"Give this man anything he wants," Bomboy said, slapping a twenty down on the bar.

"What does he want?" she asked Bomboy.

"Black?"

"Jack Daniels."

"You heard him. Keep the change."

She slammed the glass down in front of Black without asking if he wanted water or ice, turned, smiled sweetly at Bomboy and walked back to the corner and her cell phone. Black downed the drink in one gulp.

"That is serious drinking," Bomboy said. "Be careful when you drive the Blackmobile."

"You worry about *your* car."

"I don't have to. It's a Lexus," Bomboy said, unable to keep the smugness out of his voice.

Black looked at his empty glass and tried to get the barmaid's attention again. It wasn't working.

"God, I hate that bitch," he said.

"Easy."

"I hate this place."

"How can you hate this place?" Bomboy asked, with a two-armed gesture that spilt the thick malt Guinness everywhere. "How can you hate Charlie's?"

Charlie's was a down-home strip bar on Manchester and Crenshaw. It wasn't seedy as much as it was run-down: the floor covered in carpet so old and worn that it looked like a pattern in the floor. Walls covered in faded wood paneling. A couple of pool tables listed dangerously by the door, and it was unclear if the table legs were uneven or if the floor just sloped that way.

The semicircular stage, with a mirrored ceiling, jutted

six feet out, next to the pool tables, and was bordered by an ornate rusting six-inch-high metal frieze. A row of chairs fringed the stage, leading away from a second row set around small tables. Behind these there were two doors— one led to the men's toilet and the other to the ladies' and the dancers' dressing rooms. Next to the dressing room door, a smoked one-way glass panel looked into the club— Charlie's office. Beside it, a jukebox hugged the bottom lip of a slope that led up to a bar with twelve stools. On the wall opposite the bar, a few gaming machines lounged, blinking tiredly. To the left of these were the couple of booths reserved for lap dances.

Charlie, an aging ex-dancer in her sixties, loved to hug the patrons tightly, fondling their penises with one hand while the other cupped her mouth as she flicked her tongue in their ears, asking in a husky voice if they liked older women.

Charlie's was to stripping what the run-down St. Louis Rib Shack on Crenshaw and Adams was to food—they were both a little rough around the edges but, boy, didn't they serve the best stuff. Deep in the heart of South Central Los Angeles, the clientele were for the most part black, and the occasional white patron got as many curious stares as Juju Bee, who could shoot Ping-Pong balls from her labia across the room to land in a chosen patron's lap.

The song changed. Smokey. "Ooh, ooh. Baby, baby." Black turned back to the stage, to Sweet Girl. She looked directly at the audience now, though she wasn't focused on anything, on anyone, just the room of men; a general sweep. But the look itself was specific, as though what lay before her was water, and she mad with thirst from weeks in the desert. Black moved on the bar stool, the vinyl cushion sticky from sweat. He swallowed hard, throat suddenly dry. Without taking his eyes off Sweet Girl, he reached for the empty glass in front of him, knocking it into a crash. No one turned to the sound. No one spoke. In Sweet Girl's world, the men only saw what she wanted them to. But she looked straight at Black. Laughed. The sound low in her throat, like breath blown over an open bottle's neck. Then she turned away.

He followed her gaze. It lingered on parts of her body. First her hands, running palm open down the sides of her torso, from her breasts to her waist, flowed, like water, like a lover's embrace. Her eyes followed her hands, and her smile was part schoolgirl innocence, part naughty. Down to breasts taut and dimpled from implants, across her hard stomach, to lean, athletic, almost muscular thighs. And then her hands pulled at her skin deliberately yet reluctantly, as though the pleasure was in the wrongness of it. Her head drooped in sweet decline, hair hanging over her face.

And then Sweet Girl was looking directly at him. Her hands were on the move again, traveling to the shadow of where a breast's curve swept up to her armpit. He followed her eyes down to her crotch and then into the dip, and as she came up, her legs flashed open for just the briefest moment, but long enough for everyone to imagine they saw more than they did. Mouth open, her tongue licked her forefinger again. Black's tongue licked his dry lips, as he stared at the glistening tip of that finger. Never taking his eyes from it, he followed its plunge, down to her clean-shaven pudenda, and then with the trip beat in the song, Sweet Girl swung round just as the tip of her finger slipped from view under her thong, and then her backside was jiggling like two tambourines in the hands of a revival Baptist minister in the throes of spirit. Then the song ended.

"I like the way that girl makes herself open to love," Bomboy said, turning back to his bar stool.

"You know she is a man, right?" Black said.

"That girl? Come on, stop playing."

Black shrugged and turned back to the bar to try to get another whiskey. He could understand Bomboy's disbelief. Even though he had known Sweet Girl was a transsexual who, though generously endowed in the bosom courtesy of surgery, still had her penis, he couldn't stop thinking of her as a girl. It was the only way Black could accept his desire for her. Noticing Black trying to get the barmaid's attention again but not succeeding, Bomboy stepped in.

"Black, you don't know how to deal with women," Bomboy said, summoning the barmaid as if by magic. "You are either too soft or too hard. Gently, gently, eh?"

This time, Black paid for six glasses. He lined them up.

"Ah, Black. This is bombastic drinking," Bomboy said.

Black toyed with asking Bomboy why he never shut up. He thought better of it and began to throw the drinks back with considered deliberation. Thinking about Sweet Girl with each swallow. As she walked among the audience thanking the men for the tips, Black got up and left.

Outside, night held the promise of rain.

i**ggy naked.**

Except for underwear and the pair of buffing pads on her feet. She danced across the floor of The Ugly Store's café in wild abandon, the metal loops on her back clanking in time to the music, watched with interest by a stuffed moa, an ugly ostrich-like bird from New Zealand that was now extinct. All along one wall a huge canvas covered in text was stretched. It was Black's most unusual mural to date and the only one on an indoor wall. A little plaque at the bottom announced: *American Gothic: The Remix*. Moving back and forth across it, Iggy's shadow looked like a moth beating against a screen door. Black watched for a while, then retreated to the hallway in the back with the staircase that led to the rooms above where he lived, and lit a cigarette.

Several boxes were piled high against one wall, their tense line broken by the lazy lean of a ladder. Next to them a mop listed in its bucket, waiting out the day. Everything was wrapped in the smell of incense and food. It was like coming home: everything in its place, everything familiar. Black walked through a door marked *Shiva* and pissed. He glanced up as he washed his hands. The faint light from the hall reflected in the mirror above the sink carved his face unevenly into the background. Black was dark enough to be black, yet light enough to be something else. His hair was long, limp and unkempt, and shadowed his forehead, deflecting light onto his spreading nose and the one-inch scar on his right cheek. He put his finger to the scar, traced its uneven keloid-lividness.

He had done it to himself, cut deep with a pocketknife to keep from going off the 4th Street Bridge that night, carving himself into visibility, he said. To fill the emptiness inside: a deep well, he said. That night had been the lowest point in his life, as he freely admitted to anyone who would listen, though he never gave details about why.

Long ago Iggy had asked him:

"Was it the cut that kept you from going over?" Her tone as gentle as the fingertip she ran over the scar, until bumps goosed his skin.

"No. It was the dog," he replied, reaching down to fondle the ear of the smelly black-and-white mutt that had followed him everywhere until it died.

When he got out, he walked through the door that led into the shop, and ran straight into an eight-foot-tall evil-looking statue of Anubis, the Egyptian god of the dead, carved in a solid dark wood that could be ebony. Its oversized overbite, embedded in a head that was several sizes too big for the body, overshadowed everything around it. He moved past it quickly.

"Black?"

He kept quiet. He didn't know why. He wasn't exactly

looking at her. He was still smoking, standing in the shadows of the three floor-to-ceiling shelves crammed with bric-a-brac.

"You can't hide. Might as well come out," she said.

"I'm not hiding," he said, emerging from behind the shelves heavy with broken toys, voodoo dolls, fetishes from Java, Africa, New Zealand, Australia and Papua New Guinea, sour-faced-Annies (dolls with heads made from desiccated apples, that looked like the shrunken heads of cannibal cultures), and flowerpots that could only look at home on a balcony in the lower sixth circle of hell. "I just didn't want to interrupt you. Especially since you seem so naked."

"It's nothing you haven't seen before."

He shook his head, suppressing whatever sarcastic comment he was thinking, and walked over to her. He always had to fight the urge to rub his hand over her shaved head. Reaching out he touched one of the metal rings hanging from her back instead. No matter how often he saw them, they looked painful. As a fakir-psychic, she suspended her body in midair from meat hooks in order to induce a trance. Black still thought it was a strange practice for a lapsed white Jew from East LA, but she'd had a lot of success with it as she now had a celebrity client list. The Ugly Store had one rule and that was that to gain entry, clients had to be scarred. Psychic scars, mental scars, and general eccentricities were welcomed, but as it took some time and observation to determine these, visible scars were like gold and guaranteed an appointment. He'd seen Jennifer Garner and Uma Thurman in line scratching desperately but discreetly at their faces to ensure entry.

At first Iggy had just driven the meat hooks under her skin, believing her first teacher, who told her that the skin would callus and form strong straps, like leather. But the promised calluses never formed. Instead her skin began to tear. So on the advice of another teacher, she had the special stainless steel loops made and threaded under her skin. Three on each side of her spine, all along the back. When she had a client, she connected the metal loops to hooks hanging by chains from the ceiling, directly over her tattooing chair. By using a remote control device, she was able to hoist herself up to the desired height.

Black could only imagine what she must look like to the client who was lying back in the chair looking up at her eyes: one green, one purple. Did she look like a bald, white, demented broken-wing bat? And what of her skin, stretched into big pimples like a fetish cushion pulled by the hooks attached to the loops on her back? A witch from the Middle Ages about to be flayed?

Once in a trance, Iggy divined a shape and began to create an intricate tattoo on the client. While the needle danced over burning flesh, she would sing the prediction in a droning monotone that matched the needle's buzz. The results varied, ranging from a single black dot, small geometric shapes and flowers, to the one that covered a client's entire back. It all depended on how long the client had been coming to see her. For squeamish clients, she offered a henna alternative so that they could reverse the designs, but though she never said anything about it, Black could tell from her eyes that she disapproved of the no-pain-wanna-gain clients.

Iggy reached for a robe draped over the back of a chair and wrapped herself in it. Sitting on the chair, she crossed first one leg, then the other, untying the buffing cloths. As she looked she caught sight of the moa and Anubis.

"Gosh," she said. "Those two are the twin towers of Ugly."

He had heard it before. Many times.

"They set the tone for the rest of the store," he said, sitting down and turning off the boom box playing loud merengue. She reached forward, snatched the cigarette out of his hand, took a drag and then stubbed it out.

"Hey!"

"Smoking is bad for you," she said.

He looked away from her as she fixed her eyes on him; the two different colors disconcerted him. She smiled, stood up and walked over to the bar in the corner. She pulled a bottle of brandy from under it and splashed some into a couple of glasses.

"Why don't you get the pygmy to clean?"

"Ray-Ray is not a pygmy. He's a dwarf."

"Yeah. Whatever. Legs too short, eh?"

"Black!"

"Am I right?"

"Yes," Iggy said, laughing.

"So are you bringing those drinks over or what?"

She walked back, jingling the whole way, and put a drink down in front of him.

"Mazel Tov."

He downed the brandy and grimaced, even though he didn't need to. He set the glass down and pulled his shirt away from his body. He hated when it clung to him. She watched but said nothing.

"So where've you been?" she asked instead.

"Out."

"So not working then?"

He shrugged. His painting was all he really cared about.

"Ah. Strip club or hooker?" she said.

He laughed.

"Some things never change, love."

"Well, actually they do," he said, thinking of the recent but persistent appearance of Gabriel.

"What?" Iggy asked. "What has changed?"

"I think I am hallucinating," he said.

"Why do you say that?"

He didn't want her to think he was going crazy, so he hesitated.

"Black?"

The need to know if he was crazy or having a real visitation overcame his fear.

"Well, I have been seeing Gabriel recently."

"Gabriel?" she asked.

"The archangel."

"Wow."

"Yeah."

"Is he beautiful?"

"I don't know. He scares the shit out of me. Sometimes he's fifteen feet tall with huge wings, other times he's a pigeon."

"A pigeon?" she asked, laughing.

"Look, forget it."

"No, no. Tell me."

He finished the brandy but said nothing.

"Is there any reason why you would begin to see Gabriel now?" Iggy asked.

"No. Not that I know of."

"Well, he's the angel of annunciation. So maybe you are going to get good news. Or maybe, you just wish really hard that you would."

"I'm not imagining it," he said.

"Of course not, darling," Iggy said. Her tone was soft, like felt rubbing against a freshly shaven chin. He liked it. Liked her.

"There is of course the question of ghosts," she said.

"Ghosts?"

"Well, yes. Everyone is attended by ghosts," Iggy said. "What matters is whether we begin to attend to them."

"How do you mean?"

"With some people, the ghosts are transparencies, barely visible as they hover around, sit at the table next to them and so on. They are particularly hard to see in bright sunlight. Sometimes, when memories are revisited, there is a flickering of light and shadow, image and text across them, and for a moment they flare up and then vanish."

"So are you saying that ghosts are our memories?"

"Ghosts are the things, the shapes we make with our memories," she said.

"Ah. So if some are light like . . ."

"Like well-worn lace drapes blowing in the wind."

Black smiled.

"Yeah, like that. Then what are the other ghosts like? The ones we attend?"

"Like thick black lines drawn in a notebook. They are visible, brooding dark clouds that we drag around with us like reluctant sulky children. We feed them and they grow big and their haunting dominates our lives. We love them and we hate them and we are always measuring them for a coffin, yet we cannot let them die."

"Why?"

"Madness, my friend. Madness."

"So why do we do it? I presume that you mean that we, you and I, attend our ghosts?"

"Of course we do. That's how we make art. We are the lucky, the haunted."

"How do you know that's not all bullshit?"

"I don't really know."

Black sighed, relieved he wasn't going crazy after all. He was an artist and this is what artists did.

"However," Iggy began, her eyes sad. "They must remain ghosts. In your case Black, they have crossed over. They have come looking for you."

He shivered.

"Gabriel?"

"I don't know. Gabriel might be a good guy, you know, a spirit guide, who is trying to protect you from the haunting. I don't know."

"He is scary."

"Yep," she agreed. "That's what angels are. Scary. Listen, I'm going to turn in soon," she said.

He nodded and got up.

"Good night," he said, turning to leave.

"Going to the spaceship?" There was a chuckle under her words.

"Yes."

"Maybe Gabriel's up there."

"To scare the shit out of me?"

"No, to reveal it all to you."

The spaceship, which Black had built, was a squat metal blimp-like shape that hunkered above The Ugly Store like a half-deflated balloon, tethered by a forty-foot rusting metal pole. Swaying in the wind, it looked like a rotting cocktail sausage speared on a browning toothpick.

"A giant suppository," Iggy always said.

"It never flew," he told anyone who cared to listen.

"That's so Black," Iggy would say, meaning both the spaceship and his announcements; and it was. The spaceship was his desire, in a sense, to become a thing of his own making. With an Igbo father and Salvadoran mother, Black never felt he was much of either. It was a curious feeling, like being a bird, he thought, swaying on a wire somewhere, breaking for the sky when night and rain came, except for him it never felt like flight, more like falling; falling and drowning in cold, cold water. When he felt the water rise, he would morph.

"I'm a shape-shifter," he told Iggy once.

And he was, going through several identities, taking on different ethnic and national affiliations as though they were seasonal changes in wardrobe, and discarding them just as easily. For a while, Black had been Navajo, the seed race: children of the sky people, descendants of visitors from a distant planet. That was when he built the spaceship. It was the ethnicity that best suited his personality, their language the most like his memory of Igbo. But he gave it up because he never mastered the steely-eyed and clenched jaw look he saw in films. Besides, he didn't like being a sidekick and after a while it felt like every Indian on TV or in the movies was Tonto. Except, of course, the crazy one in *One Flew Over the Cuckoo's Nest*. He liked him, wanted to be him, but he couldn't stay angry about anything long enough. Maybe he was Tonto after all. Fuck that, kemo sabe, he'd thought.

Iggy understood. He knew people often said that—I understand—and it meant, Don't tell me any more, I can't hear you. But Iggy, he knew, really did. Time flies, he thought, time flies and you never know where it has gone. He was thirty-six with nothing, except a spaceship that didn't fly and a bunch of paintings on the walls of the river to show for it. Murals of Montezuma at his local McDonald's buying a Big Mac; mermaids draped on red couches, sometimes with legs and a mighty python wrapped around their waists and dangling down between their legs, sometimes with fish tails, with eyes of passion and fire, eyes that could undo a man. There was one of Charlie Chaplin as the Tramp heading off into the concrete horizon. In another, an Aztec priest held a young man bleeding to death while a car, gunfire spitting from its windows, sped away into the city. An Indian woman holding a gun and wearing a purple scarf stared defiantly from another. Hieroglyphs that he had created and whose meanings remained a mystery even to him ran between the murals like frames. It seemed that as fast as he could paint them, the army engineers (who'd built and maintained the river wall) covered them up; the army and the bloody city council. But somehow there were still many that managed to escape, and sometimes a homeless person riding a bicycle or pushing a cart down the channel from a distance looked like part of a painting, as though they had come to life; part of the river's memories and dreams.

The only way up to the spaceship was via a rickety metal ladder welded onto the side of the forty-foot-high rusting metal pole that the spaceship was impaled on, and Black stood on the flat roof psyching himself for the climb. It was cramped inside the spaceship. Made from salvaged and hammered metal and boards, it was about nine feet long, sloping down to two portholes at either end, each wearing different colored glass: green and purple. In that pinch there was only about a foot of headspace. It was spotless inside, with interior walls painted a warm yellow. The ceiling was only five feet high at its highest point, where it opened up into a skylight. The only way he could see any of the view without hanging out of the open door was to poke his head out of the skylight; like coming up for air. Of course there was always Gabriel to worry about, since the archangel had taken to roosting on the spaceship's roof.

In the muted purple light of one porthole, cramped into the small space, stood an equally small altar. He loved altars. Always had. This altar held a burning candle, an incense censer smoldering with hot coals and frankincense, a statue of the Virgin of Guadalupe and a representation of his totem, a small but lifelike dog. And behind the altar, scratched into the wood of the ship were the words: *Just Fly Away*.

"What is this spaceship thing?" Bomboy Dickens asked him once. "Why is this monstrosity so important to you?" Bomboy had a way of blurting out the thing everyone was thinking but was too polite to say. He also loved words like *monstrosity*, *capacity*, *tantamount* and *awesome*.

"It's my soul," Black said. And he meant it, though the word *yearning* would have been more appropriate. Of course if hard pressed Black couldn't say what it was exactly that he yearned for. The nearest thing he could say was that he didn't want to be himself. Or maybe that he was looking for who he should be. But he had no idea who he wanted to, or should, be.

As Bomboy had moved about inside it, the spaceship rocked.

"It is unstable, this soul of yours," he had said.

"Fuck you," Black said, afraid that Bomboy was right, even though he knew that some of the bolts and screws holding the craft to the four-foot-wide platform it was landed on were loose. As he bent over the candle to light the cigarette, the craft tipped ever so slightly. Shit, still haven't fixed that, he thought, blowing smoke out of the open skylight. There was something in the way he held his cigarette. Something that pointed to a wish unfulfilled, perhaps.

He paused by a pin board leaning against the sloping wall, next to the altar. It was divided into four diagonal grids by strips of colored ribbon and pins. With the long tapered forefinger of his right hand, the hand holding the cigarette, he scratched the side of his nose. Smoke curled up like a wraith around his head as he bent to examine the source of the itch in the grimy window. For the briefest moment, he was startled, as if a stranger was gazing back at him.

Blowing smoke at his reflection, he straightened, scanning for Gabriel, before pushing his head out of the skylight. He felt a wet splat on his head and looked up. Rain. He ducked back inside and looked at the squared-off board. In the middle was a watercolor of the Virgin of Guadalupe, the edges of her face blotting into what could be a blue shawl, or perhaps just another Los Angeles twilight. He pressed his fingers in a kiss to his lips and laid them on the painting.

"My muse," he said. Breathless. Remembering the night that had inspired the painting. The apparition of the Lady reflected on the wall of a small house in East LA. Like everyone present, he hadn't believed the rumor at first. Even when he saw it, he was still searching for the trick, the illusion. He was skeptical until the woman whose house it was, opened and closed the Venetian blinds several times without disturbing the apparition.

The Virgin was important to the people here. Not only as a symbol of the adopted religion of Catholicism, but because she was a brown virgin who had appeared to a brown saint, Juan Diego. She was also a symbol of justice, of a political spirituality. He had watched every year the procession to her, her effigy carried high through the streets of East LA starting from the corner of Cesar Chavez, held up, aloft, like a torch. That procession had been an annual event from the thirties, Iggy told him. He knew she had grown up here, the daughter of Jewish immigrants who had moved west in the twenties, but that was all she ever revealed about her childhood to him. The Virgin appeared here often, to reassure her people no doubt. In the Winchells donut shop on Fourth and Soto, hovering in the window for the longest time, transforming the tasty local treat into the most sought after cure for every ailment and malaise. In the law office of Tomás Alarcón, who was the most expensive and dishonest immigration lawyer in the whole area, but who, since the night he saw her shadow burned into the glass frame of his office door, had taken to not charging for his cases, accepting only whatever donations his clients could manage. His office soon became a rowdy barn when people paid him in goats, chickens and sometimes fish. And even though he fell behind on his rent, his Chinese landlord, though not a believer, was afraid of the black burn of Tomás's eyes and so didn't evict him.

Rumors of these apparitions spread by word of mouth and fast. The news was wrapped in Big Macs and passed over counters, it filled buckets of KFC, was whispered in the hush of washing machines in the Laundromat, passed out on the street between passersby and even between the dealers and their clients. Black heard it from Bomboy who heard it from Pedro who owned the taco stand opposite The Ugly Store.

The rest of Black's board was covered in photographs, about thirty of them. Some were glossy, some grainy and fading on plain paper. The grainy photos had been taken by the cheap camera in his cell phone and run off Iggy's printer.

There were only two subjects.

One was the Virgin. Statues, paintings, murals, posters, anything he came across in his travels of East LA; and he came across many. Each photo had a white name tag under it, labeling: 1st Street Underpass; Emil's Mobil Station— South Wall; Underpass to INS building—Los Angeles Street; St. Sebastian's—forecourt; Immaculate Heart Cemetery, tombstone—Breed; Rosa's Panaderia—Cake.

He lingered over photos of the second subject, stroking the glossies sensually and rubbing hard on the grainies, the cigarette held carefully away. These photos were of a young woman. In all the glossies she was dressed in variations of the same urban clothes: velvety sweats; pants; big shirts that drowned her, or small tummy-riding tight ones with faux-leather laces running halfway up the sides; sneakers; too much makeup; hair dark, near natty and streaked with blonde highlights. Beneath these, the labels read: Mercado—Flower Street; Westside Pavilion Mall—Pico; Kung Pao's—Chinatown; Payless—Jefferson & Hoover.

In the grainier shots, the same woman was naked. Or nearly naked. In lingerie. In a bra and panties. Panties and pasties. Plastic-cone-shaped pasties. Standing. Moving blurs. Squatting, facing the camera, eyes smiling, tongue licking her lips. These labels read: Charlie's—May '03; Charlie's—April '04; Charlie's—Aug '04; Charlie's. Charlie's. Charlie's.

"Sweet Girl," he said, under his breath, and it was a song.

b**lue.**

This Los Angeles half-light as Black sat, feet dangling, in the open door of his spaceship above Cesar Chavez and The Ugly Store, staring out at the vista of downtown, smoking a cigarette. His left hand, the hand not holding the cigarette, was stroking the dirty plastic of what looked like a Catholic scapular on a leather thong around his neck. It wasn't a scapular—one of those peculiar small squares of brown cloth with images of Jesus and the Virgin attached, and sewn under plastic for longevity—even though it did itch like a scapular and though there was a photo in it.

He hadn't been able to admit it to Bomboy, but Black was feeling a little lost. Bomboy's bluntness had a way of hitting things squarely on the head: he wasn't getting any younger and his life had no clear direction.

"Fuck," he said. He was still stroking the scapular that wasn't a scapular. The photo it held was of a young child, maybe three or four years old in a white dress. Faded as it was, it was hard to tell if the child was a boy or girl. The photo was pressed against an envelope with a name written on it in slanted penmanship. Obinna; *his* name, the one he'd had in another life. Black liked it up here. It was high, his perch, and he remembered maybe a time when he had flown a kite as a boy, his heart soaring with the cheap colored paper—or maybe not. He was having trouble these days separating the real from the imagined. Like the words he could hear now, as clearly as if someone stood next to him, voice soft on the blue light.

Don't Forget Me.

But the words were in a different language, all music. Echefulam. A language he hadn't heard since his childhood, but one he knew was Igbo, as sure as if he had been born to it. And he had been. His father had been Igbo. At least that's what he had always told Black. It was all so vague. He had only been seven when his father, Frank, was drafted into the army and sent to Vietnam from Caltech where he had been doing postdoctoral research in the newly developed rocket propulsion lab that was subcontracted by NASA. His father had been so proud. Not to go to Vietnam, but to be working for NASA on a space project. Black remembered that much. Remembered his father coming home drunk one night, walking into his bedroom and waking the sleeping Black to tell him in slurred tones:

"You should be proud, Son, eh. Proud. I am the first African to work on a NASA project. Back home I will be a big man. I na nnu, Obinna?"

And his Salvadoran mother, standing in the bedroom door, a dark silhouette against the hall light, shouting: "Let the boy sleep, oye, let him sleep!" Retreating she mumbled:

"NASA my foot, postdoc my ass, student with no money. What good is NASA with no money."

But Black's father, Frank, reached into the bed and picked Black up and sat him on his knee.

"Daddy, how come I have an Igbo name and you don't?"

"Sir," Frank said. "Call me sir. You're not a little boy anymore."

"But why?"

"Little boys shouldn't ask their fathers questions. America has spoilt everything," his father grumbled.

"Mira, leave the boy alone. America has been good to you," Black's mother shouted from the hall as she slammed into the bathroom. "Made you a big man."

"María, I am talking to my son. Man talk. If we were—"

"Yes, if we were back in your jungle you would beat me. Fuck you, pendejo."

Frank stood up, swaying a little. He wanted to lunge at the bathroom door and scream at María, but instead he smiled unsteadily at Black and led him by the hand out into the back garden. In the darkness beyond it lay the arroyo and the Los Angeles River. Black hadn't seen the river until he was older, but he knew it was there, because his father talked about it a lot. Complained about how the erosion was eating away at the land and how they would one day slide down the arroyo into the water and be carried off to the Pacific.

"Lose everything down an endless pit, down that pathetic excuse for a river," his father would mumble. But this night, as they stood in the back garden and Frank showed Black how to look through the telescope at the night sky, Black was especially excited. He had watched his father build that telescope.

The main tube of the telescope was an eight-foot-long piece of fiberglass that Frank had made especially just that summer, a few weeks after Black turned seven. That birthday had been different from the others. His father seemed to relax, to let out his breath all at once.

He talked while he worked, unpacking it onto the worktable he had built for it, the one they would use later for picnics, the table Black had lain on looking up at the sky after his father left and never came back.

"You see, it is important to have everything made by hand. In the old days astronomers built their own instruments," he said, using micro-calipers and an electric buffing cloth to smooth the fiberglass off just right, washing it in soapy water and drying it off at each stage. "Don't believe your mother when she talks about God, Son. God is a superstition. The truth is we make our own God, and this is mine: science. Something you can trust, something that doesn't need faith," he went on.

Black looked at him with a blank expression so Frank bent down and gave him a rag, showing him how to wash the telescope with him, how to get a good grip on the slippery tube, cautioning him to wash in one direction only, so that not even the micro-dust from the buffing could be dragged across it, scratching it. Black watched his father and remembered all the bath times Frank had missed because he was working late, or the times when he had been at home but wouldn't leave his science shows on television, complaining when Black cried as his mother scrubbed a little too hard, getting soap into his eyes. He watched and remembered, and when his father turned away, he picked up a stone and scratched a deep groove in the tube, knowing he would be spanked and barred from the work, but not caring.

Later, nursing a sore bottom, he watched as Frank tried to save the tube with putty and car filler, smiling at the tears in his father's eyes. His revenge against his father made the beating he got bearable. He hung around, barred from helping, and watched Frank finish the telescope without him. Watched him build a frame for it from carefully selected pipes and an arc-welding iron he rented from a hardware store.

"Close your eyes, Obinna," his father called as he lit the arc-welder, pulling the mask down over his face, his excitement making him forgive Black. But Black didn't close his eyes. He watched the metal melt into a liquid like hot butterscotch, feeling the sting of the sparks as their brilliance, like an exploding nova, burned.

Then the mirrors were laid, one up and one down.

"Finest craftsmanship. I should have ground them myself, but the Germans are so good I don't need to," he explained to Black. But Black had lost interest. He wanted ice cream and could hear the truck getting closer, but he knew his father wouldn't spring for it and his mother hated sweets. When Frank finished he didn't let Black anywhere near the telescope. He never would. The scratch, a never completely disguised scar, was like a wall between them.

But this night, standing hand in hand with his father in the backyard, promised to be different. Frank handed Black his beer bottle while he fussed with the telescope, swinging it around in tight circles over a particular spot of sky, looking for something that was a mystery, while Black shivered in the slight cold, feeling the beer bottle's chill. Finally Frank called to him.

"Obinna, bia, come and see."

Black walked over. It was a nice telescope with a small

eyepiece about three feet up its sleek black side, and Black had to stand on tiptoe to reach.

"See?"

Black felt his stomach fall away as he squinted through the telescope and saw an eye, all smoke and amber and blue fire staring back. Frank laughed when Black squealed.

"Is that God?"

"No, Son. That's the Cat's Eye Nebula."

"What's a nebula?"

Frank smiled and picked Black up, swinging him onto his shoulders.

"Always asking questions," his father said, smiling. "You're just like me, you know? That's what your name means. Obinna: his father's heart."

"You're silly, Daddy. I mean, sir," Black said.

Frank laughed and began to point out the stars in the night sky.

"Over there, in the shape of a lopsided house, is Cepheus, though the house is really a man upside down."

"Who, Daddy?"

"Cepheus was a king who sacrificed his daughter Andromeda to a sea serpent to save his people. But Perseus saved her and killed the serpent."

"I don't like Cepheus."

Frank smiled in the dark and squeezed Black's leg.

"I don't think Cepheus likes himself either. I always think he is upside down because he's hanging his head in shame."

Black clapped happily.

"That's right, Daddy," he said. "Just like me when I am naughty."

"Yes, just like that," his father said, fighting the urge to tell Black to call him sir. "And that one," he continued, "is the little dipper."

"Do the Igbo have names for stars?" Black asked.

The question took Frank by surprise and he hesitated a moment before replying.

"Of course. The little dipper is called the small drinking gourd. Over there is Draco, the dragon, which in Igbo is Ekeoku, the serpent of fire whose body is the endless darkness with the glowing jewel of fire on its head. If we ever meet that serpent the whole world ends."

"I'm scared, Daddy."

"Don't be, Son. I'm right here," his father said, tearing suddenly. He was glad Black was on his shoulders and couldn't see his face. There was an uneasy silence between them, and then a shooting star arced past.

"Quick, make a wish," Frank said.

Black closed his eyes tight and wished hard, his knees pressing into Frank's face from the effort. When he opened his eyes, he said:

"How come you know all the stars, Daddy? Are you a spaceman?"

"No, Son. But I would love to fly away in a spaceship. See the universe. One day, I'm going to do it. Build my own spaceship. Right here in this backyard. Just fly away."

"Just fly away, Daddy," Black repeated, giggling.

When María came out to call them inside, warning against the cold, her voice was soft. Like she had been sleeping. Black wished now, as he had then, that there were more nights like that. He was stroking the plastic patch around his neck and he turned it over and over. He wasn't sure why he wore it all the time, so close to his heart. Maybe it was an anchor to remind him that there had once been certainties in his life.

Echefulam.

Don't Forget Me.

The word unfurled on his tongue like an origami ball of paper opening into a flower with the wet of speech. The voice in his head was a breath on ice; faint, it resonated in him with all the timbre of a man's voice. His father's voice speaking as he left for a war that Black had just been born into. There were so many things he wanted to say to his father, but words were never his strength. At least not since the prayers his mother forced him to say before the Virgin, beating him when he resisted, when he got tired, beating him it seemed almost for the pleasure of doing it. But all that happened later. After his father didn't come back from Vietnam. After they lost the small house in Pasadena when the bank foreclosed on it. After they moved to East Los Angeles. After. After. After.

All he had now was this nameless and shapeless desire and the memory of strong hands, like his father's, strong hands and black and a face rough with beard and soft with tears, and lips full with the knowledge, whispering: Echefulam. And his mother crying in the corner, crying and hurting in a way that held all possibility. Was it true? Or did he just invent it all? Wasn't he too young to remember? But yes: there had been tears. Definitely: tears and strong hands and the rough of a beard.

Rubbing his stubble thoughtfully, Black was glad the voice wasn't a constant part of him. He heard it only when he reminisced about the past, about who he might have been. He returned to the present and the sprawling vista; he had an almost unimpeded view of downtown LA, parts of the 110 Freeway and the River. The city's planners had forgotten this part of the city; anywhere else and he would have needed planning permission for the spaceship, but not here.

He stood up, head sticking out of the skylight, and studied the city as he smoked. It was colder. He felt sure there would be rain. Between tokes his breath was faint on the near dark air. When he was ten, when he still lived in Pasadena with the River behind the house, there was a long cold spell and at dusk, mist, no stronger than a runner's pant on the air, would come, and with it the fireflies. When he stood really still in the middle of the back lawn, they alighted on his body. Arms spread, festooned with blinking insects, he imagined that he was an airplane, or a rock star, the deeper beauty of the gift eluding him.

flat.

The roof of The Ugly Store lit by the early morning sun and Black, supine in the shade of the spaceship. This was a near daily ritual for him: a mug of hot tea and a cigarette here on the roof before his morning workout. From up here, the city fell away to one side, the river, the other. Black loved Los Angeles; the expansiveness of it, like a sneeze still tickling at the back of his sinuses, able to become anything, or nothing. He loved that. The feeling that he could become the person he always wanted to be, even though nothing in his life pointed to it.

Finishing his tea, he placed his empty mug on the ledge carefully. Kicking at the pigeons roosting on the small green square of carpet he had hauled up here for his practice, he settled into a horse stance, hands in prayer pose in front of him, muscles rippling, veins waking slowly to crawl up and down his forearms like inquisitive worms. He took a deep breath and began the sequence of movements that made up his practice.

A mixture of kung-fu katas, yoga and tai chi, the movements were meant to give him a dancer's fluidity. But in these practice sessions he was anything but graceful. His near six-foot heavyset frame didn't make him clumsy because when he walked, he moved with the ease of an animal. Ease, however, wasn't grace.

Mercifully, it began to rain.

It was a painful sight: him leaping and cavorting, hissing and pointing open-palmed sabers into the air, eyes intense and glazed with pleasure and his body glistening from rain and sweat, and Gabriel, who appeared among the pigeons in his humanoid form, tut-tutted.

"Why?" he asked.

Black ignored him and continued moving awkwardly. The pigeons cooed sadly and looked away, embarrassed for him. Half an hour later, he made his way through the rooftop door, downstairs to his room. A couch pushed up against one wall and a bed against the other took up most of the room. Along the other wall were his old and heavy rolltop sewing machine and a worktable where he mixed paint and which held mounds of colored pigments in bowls. The only bare wall he used to hold canvases and it was splattered with paint. Next to it was the low cabinet that held the television, stereo system and the wig stand wearing the Mil Máscaras Luchador wrestling mask that Iggy had given him because she said it reminded her of him. He knew why. He had turned up on her doorstep one night, his face bleeding, his clothes torn. He didn't know why he had come to her, to The Ugly Store. Perhaps he came because everyone in the neighborhood talked about her generosity. Maybe it was something else: she wasn't a complete stranger to him. He had lived in the neighborhood since he settled down there at twenty, five years after he had run away to ride the trains across America. He'd seen Iggy many times as he went about his business, but he had never spoken to her or approached her until that night sixteen years before when he knocked on her door. She took him in without question and after cleaning his wound she gave him the back room on the condition that he begin to pay rent within the month. He never really knew what drove her to be the way she was, or why she had been so kind to him, but he knew she gave him the mask because he kept so much of himself hidden.

"Like me, true mystery," she'd said.

He looked away from the mask to where the acoustic guitar he had never learned to play leaned against the couch. Next to the guitar, in a neat row, were three headless mannequin torsos that he sometimes used as models for the occasional more formal portraits that brought in good rates.

A small fan hummed on the pattern-cutting table in the corner. It wasn't that hot, but Black always liked it cool. Next to it was a small case, a valise that looked like the ones Hollywood makeup artists toted around. It was half open and bottles and brushes peeked out. It had everything. Same as with the pros. In the business it was called the temporary face-lift kit.

Also on the desk, in piles on the floor around the room, crammed onto too-small cases, were books. In every imaginable binding and in every state—new, battered, hardbacks, paperbacks. Black loved books and he loved to read, but sometimes he loved books more than he loved to read. And sometimes, what he loved most about books was the space they left for him between the reading and the imagining. Sometimes he lived there more than anywhere else.

He toyed once or twice with the idea of opening an anti-quarian bookshop. He never did, because he imagined that in Los Angeles nobody would buy books. Perhaps, he joked, he could just sell carefully aged covers wrapped around suitably sized pieces of wood—or old videotapes.

Scattered around the worktable were several articles of women's clothing, collected at different times and places across the city: bikini tops and bottoms filched from Santa Monica Beach, sometimes from the women he initiated; G-strings and lacy bras from Charlie's; a tank top and one blue garter of unknown origin, but found in the bins around the fashion district. When he took them he told himself it was for art. Parts of women he wanted to incor-porate into paintings. He picked up the blue garter and toyed with it for a moment before putting it down.

Pulling the Luchador mask on, he sat at the workbench and stared at the large sprawl of rice paper on the wall for the Virgin cartoon that Bomboy's summons had inter-rupted. He approached it and with deft assured strokes, drew lines across the material in charcoal, neat straights and abrupt crosses. But instead of the Virgin, something else was forming or trying to form. A being both Virgin and not and closer to the profane than the sacred yet holding the two. The shape was elusive and though he rubbed out and resketched lines, it was unyielding. He paused. If he couldn't find her body in his body on the paper, perhaps he would find it in the space where the paper had been. It didn't make any real sense, but he knew that something had to give.

He picked up a pair of scissors and weighed the reassur-ance of its heavy sharpness for a moment before letting the metal beak bite into the paper. He smiled at the satisfying crunch. Something about the weight of scissors and its bite

filled him with lust. He hadn't had sex in a while. God, I
need to get over this obsession with Sweet Girl and find a
real girlfriend, he thought. But for now, he had to do
something. He looked at his watch: it was nearly one. If he
left now, he could still catch the lunch special at Brandy's.
If she still offered it, that is. He hadn't been there for so
long. He found her name in the classified section of the
LA Weekly years before. That first time she purred on the
phone in a voice that made him feel like a schoolboy, making him sweat so much he showered twice before going
round. He'd used his best cologne and stopped to buy her
flowers. He was surprised to see that she wasn't much older
than he was. He hadn't been able to get a hard-on, despite
the blowjob she gave him that lasted for thirty minutes.
And even though she'd charged him, she was kind and offered to share her crank with him, an offer he declined.
And then when she got high, she stood on the coffee table
in her modest living room and quoted Shakespeare at him:
whole sections from *Twelfth Night*. Viola was her favorite
character and as he watched her, he began to feel himself
getting aroused. From then on, until he stopped going to
her, she was Viola to him. That had been years ago. But he
felt he needed her now. He stopped just before the door
and lit a cigarette. Stepping out he took a deep breath and
blew it out with some smoke.

Los Angeles smelled like wet dog.

Getting off at Ninth and Santee he walked up to Los
Angeles Street and hanging a left, headed up to Sixth. On
the way he passed the usual homeless crowd shuffling
through the streets in the shadows of the skyscrapers. They
ignored him as they picked through the discarded offal of
the fashion district. He guessed he didn't look like he had

any spare change, or the propensity to spare it if he did. Prostitutes, mostly junkies pimped by the gangs that ran these streets, called softly to him from the shadows, careful to be ambiguous just in case he was working vice. He paused in front of the barbershop opposite Coles, under the sign that announced: NIGHT OWL BARBERSHOP, OPEN 24 HRS, which was of course a lie because in all the time he had been coming here, it had never been open. It was probably a prop left over from a movie shot here sometime in the past. This was a favorite location for gritty downtown shots and the walls in Coles were lined with autographed photos of Arnold Schwarzenegger and other stars, hanging out between takes, drinking and sampling the French dip sandwich that was Coles's other claim to fame.

He crossed the street, stepped over a fresh river of piss coming from a homeless drunk leaning against a bus-stop sign, and walking past Coles, went round the corner to a big metal door. It led to a hallway and an elevator that stopped at fashionable lofts on every floor. He buzzed Brandy.

"Yeah?" Her voice sounded bored.

Probably high, he thought.

"Hey, Brandy. It's Black."

The door clicked open.

He had never fucked Brandy twice in one visit. He never had the heart for it. Shame made it hard to get it up more than once. But an hour later, she came three times, while he wasn't relieved. Each time, visions of the Virgin would come as he thrust into Brandy and though they drove him wild, he could neither find relief nor stop the visions. Tired, he drank bottle after bottle of beer but noth-

ing helped. Even with the windows completely open, he
felt himself suffocating in the heat. Whether from the city
or himself, he couldn't tell. Still the Virgin's smile filled his
head, her eyes boring into him.

And.

Brandy was laughing, with pleasure or derision, he
couldn't tell at first. But her question made it clear.

"What's the matter? Did you take Viagra or something?"

"What?"

"Erections may last four hours or more?" she said, cracking up at her recitation of the television ad.

"Shut up!" he said, rubbing his dick. He was still turgid.
Inflamed.

She pushed him off of her and rolled him onto his back.
She straddled him and stuck her finger up his ass.

"Do you want me to fuck you? Is that what you want?"
she said.

"Bitch!" he said, pushing her off of him violently. She
fell onto the floor. He was on her in a second, fist raised.
The laughter died on her face, replaced with something
between fear and desire. He brought his knuckles down on
the wooden floorboard by her head, splintering it and cutting himself. He pulled her up and threw her back on the
bed muttering, "bitch," over and over under his breath.
With something like cruelty, he sweated between Brandy's
meaty legs, pounding himself to oblivion, but there was no
release. Exhausted, he stopped, crawling off of her to col-
lapse in a chair in the corner. With a contented smile, she
rolled over and was asleep in an instant.

He stared at Brandy, revulsion acrid in his mouth. He
pulled his clothes on, threw some money on the nightstand
and left. He walked for miles until he came to the main

train track that ran alongside the abandoned docks on the River. This was where Bomboy's illegal but very profitable Halal abattoir was.

Standing there, under the rusty dinosaur skeletons of disused cranes and the cramped hope of empty warehouses, he lit a cigarette, sucking on it greedily. Melancholy filled him like a wave, like a dream of the sea, which was more real than the sea. He decided that when he finished the cigarette he would throw himself into the River. Heaving from the effort, he climbed up a crane, the rust coming away in flakes of dry blood. At the top he paused to catch his breath. He was about to edge out to the rim when he saw Gabriel alight there. Without looking directly at him, Black stood there screaming in frustration, his voice drowned by the passing trains. Spent, he began the climb down.

God, he hated angels.

eight

There was something like a train.

It was the thing he couldn't name. But it was there, in rain, in silence, and in night. In the random minutiae of his daily life, it was there: like the warning sound of a raven's call, like the gathering of a storm. Like a child's nursery rhyme: *one, two, pick up my shoe, three, four, knock on the door.* The compulsive collection of omens that could transform the ordinary into the tarot; the neon cross on the Zion Call Church, the golden arches of the McDonald's, the plastic flowers in the window of Lolita's Bridal, the cake that was a pair of humongous pink breasts in the window of the panaderia, Pedro's taco stand with the plastic dinosaur on the top of it, and on and on. He stopped in front of Charlie's. After Brandy's, still turgid and desperate, there was nowhere else he could go. He had to see Sweet Girl and tonight he would get a lap dance, he thought, as he walked in.

He sat down. Sweet Girl sat beside him.

"I thought you were never coming back," she said, her voice a purr.

He shifted uncomfortably.

"Yeah?"

"Yeah. But I guess I was wrong."

"Can I buy you a drink?"

"Sure, honey. You maybe wanna buy something else?"

He nodded, licked his lips and pointed to the lap dance section. She laughed and pulled him along behind her, stopping briefly at the bar for drinks, then continuing on to the lap dance corner. Before straddling him, she shed all but her G-string. He stared hard, looking for—but not finding—any evidence of her penis. As she sat in his lap, she leaned forward and breathed:

"It's twenty dollars per song, baby."

And surprisingly the intrusion of money did nothing to erase the illusion that she was in love with him, that she desired him. He pushed up and dug into his pocket, fishing out a twenty. She smiled and folded the money carelessly into her clothes on the floor, almost as if it were an afterthought. Arms around his neck, she rubbed down, her ass working with the informed touch of a masseuse, searching for the hard of him. Soft, then down hard, then soft, twin cheeks clenching and releasing.

Black leaned back and relaxed into the curious touch of Sweet Girl's buttocks. They were almost like he imagined a man's buttocks would be. But that thought threatened a wave of something: lust or nausea, he couldn't tell which. Emptying his mind, he thrust his hips forward, trying to help, trying to feel something. But his dick was bent back, under him, still turgid, but trapped. His heartbeat was faster. Desire or fear? he wondered.

Sweet Girl paused, and Black felt both her ass cheeks locked in confused concentration. He guessed she was wondering why she couldn't feel his erection. She turned and faced him and he looked away, embarrassed. How could he explain that at thirty-six his penis was acting eighteen? Spontaneous erections lasting for so long he had to bind them to go about his day. He caught her looking at him from the corner of her eye, a tight smile on her face, and he wondered what she was thinking. She leaned forward, both knees on his thighs, breasts brushing his face, her breath teasing his ear:

"Is this good, baby?"

Black nodded. Smiled. Cupped her face lightly with both hands. He tried to kiss her, but she moved her head slightly, his lips landing on her neck where his tongue left a damp spot. She smiled, pulling all the way back.

"Feisty boy!"

He smiled and touched the side of her face, and she rubbed her cheek against his palm. He was looking deep into her eyes. Then his hands dropped to her lower back, resting like tired blackbirds on the ledge of her hips. Half crouching on his lap, knees spread, facing him, she rubbed her breasts against his face. The plastic pasties were hard against his freshly shaved chin. He breathed her in deeply, but all he could smell was the flowery scent of her body lotion. He was experienced enough to know the smell was common to all strippers, and thought it was probably something from Victoria's Secret. She pulled back to watch him as her pudenda, like the gentle pressure of an open palm, pushed into his crotch. Still, he eluded her. Then surprising them both, his tongue danced over her breasts, around the pasties. This was more touch than was allowed, but he hoped she liked it. Liked him. He hoped that she could sense his sincerity, sense that he was looking for more than what just her body could give.

Sweet Girl glanced around as though to make sure they were deep enough in shadow. Reaching down, between them, between their heat, she ran a hand down his pants.

In the background, Barry White crooned, "You turn my whole world around . . ."

Black shifted under her palm. He was trying to move his penis out from its cave, the shaft lying between balls stretching for comfort. Sweet Girl's hand slipped under the band of his pants and under the band of his boxer's and traced the full length of him.

And Barry: "Never have I met a girl like you . . ."

Black winced as Sweet Girl pushed against his balls. Excruciating, but he loved it too. Felt the rush of new blood, felt the rush of old memories.

Pain.

Kneeling on the shards of broken glass from the tumbler he knocked over in that long ago. Kneeling for the penance of his mother's devotion.

Pleasure.

Yes, my Jesus of the Heart of Flame, yes, I love you and renounce the world and my pleasure for sin, Black intoned in that long ago, all the while flogging the Bishop, so to speak.

Pain.

A finger held too long over the flame of a votive candle, while the other hand counted out the slope of the spell in the hard of wood, stroking, *Hail Mary full of grace.*

Pleasure.

His hands working himself in the dark when his mother had gone to bed. Stroking himself and seeing the Virgin in his mind's eye. Pearl-white plaster face. Stroking himself as he imagined her red lips whispering his name, her blue robe pulled up around her waist. Stroking himself as his other hand dug a bit of glass into his thigh. Stroking himself as he heard her whisper, yes, m'ijo, for pleasure, for pain, yes.

"Yes, baby, yes," Sweet Girl breathed into his ear, bringing him back. Her forefinger and middle finger, wet from her mouth, were rubbing faster and faster on the shaft of his penis, the shaft bent under him, the shaft bent away, into itself, like a vagina. Black was thrusting, thrusting, but he couldn't come. Frustrated, he pulled Sweet Girl's still wet fingers out. She looked him straight in the eye and sucked on them.

"Was that good?" she asked.

He swallowed. He didn't know how many songs had elapsed in the time she had spent with him. Reaching for his drink, he downed the whiskey in a gulp. Sweet Girl laughed and curled up in his lap, her face nuzzling his neck. He felt revulsion. He felt elation. He thought he might be in love.

"I don't usually do that," she said. "I'm a lesbian."

He nodded and reached for her drink. He sipped.

"Then why me?"

She sighed and stretched.

"I don't know. Maybe because you always look into my eyes."

He nodded. She ran a finger down the side of his face.

"Very few men see me," she said.

He nodded again. He wanted to get away. He turned his head and looked at the stage. A middle-aged dancer with glasses was building up a sweat but nobody was paying any attention. Sweet Girl pulled his face back.

"How come you aren't touching me?"

"I didn't know I could," he said. He didn't want to touch her. He wanted to get away.

"Touch me," she said, taking his hand and placing it on her stomach. He stared at it for a long time. She was lighter than him, and his hand, fingers splayed, looked like a dark crab on a beach. He moved it over her belly and felt his hair stand up. Sweet Girl purred under the stroke.

"Are you allowed to get so close to the clientele?" Black asked.

Sweet Girl sat up. She was smiling.

"I frighten you, don't I?"

"Why would you say that?"

She laughed, and taking a tube of lipstick from her bag, she wrote her number on the back of his hand. He pulled it away, looked at it.

"What's your number, baby?" she asked.

He was unable to lie. He told her, watching with fascination as she wrote it on the inside of her thigh. She was still laughing and it was mocking.

"I've got your number now," she said.

He pushed her off his lap, but not roughly. He got up.

"I have to go to the bathroom," he said.

"Sure, baby," she said, and laughed again.

There was a urinal against one wall, and a cubicle with a toilet in the corner. He didn't lock the main door as two people could easily use the bathroom. He slipped into the booth and bolted that door. He was about to flush when he heard a soft moan. Stepping on the rim of the bowl, he peered over the top of the cubicle.

A man was leaning into the urinal, one hand on the wall, fingers splayed, the other clearly working his penis. Black studied him: black sleeveless leather vest and pants, tattooed arms and a heavy silver Tibetan Vajra hanging around his neck from a black cord. His leather pants were bunched around his knees and he wore heavy motorcycle boots with significant heels. His long black hair was gathered in a ponytail, his beard was well groomed and he was heavily tanned.

As he masturbated, the man reached up and pulled his ponytail loose, shaking his hair around his head like a halo with a few practiced flicks, spreading it across his back like the sudden splaying of an exotic bird's tail. Moaning a little louder, he began running his other hand through his hair, his body swaying from side to side, hand sliding faster than a trombonist playing a hot blues. Black wondered if the man knew he had an audience and whether he was thinking about a man or a woman and why he couldn't wait to get home and what kind of passion and desire caused a person to masturbate in a strip bar toilet and why he didn't feel like this about Sweet Girl and why he was breathing heavily and why he had an erection and why he was unzipping and touching himself and why he was excited and whether this meant he was gay and then he came, hard and thick, the pressure causing him to slip and nearly lose his footing. He held the sticky mass in his hand, never taking his eyes off the man at the urinal. The man came with a sound that was a near shout, legs knocking against the tile wall. With a deep satisfied sigh, he rubbed the semen through his hair, then he zipped up his pants and turned away from the urinal. He stopped at the door, looked up at Black and smiled.

Waiting until the man was gone, Black left the stall and walked bowlegged, to keep his pants from falling off, over to the sink to wash the semen and Sweet Girl's number from his hands. He had no idea how long he had been in the toilet, and as he studied his face in the mirror he half expected to see it unraveling at the seams. He took a deep breath and when he pushed out of the toilet, he headed for the exit. Gabriel was a pigeon perched on the eave. He shat on Black as he left, then flew into the dark.

It was a good night to be an angel.

nine

Uncertain.

The flame flickered on the altar in the corner of the spaceship. Black knelt before the candle against which an icon of the Lady leaned drunkenly next to the little dog. A rosary dangled from his hand and his lips moved silently as he rolled each bead intently, squeezing the last drop of faith from it before moving on to the next. The shadow of his hand and the rosary on the wall was a fist-headed snake swallowing an endless string of prey. It was always the same. Whenever he went to see Sweet Girl, he came home and did penance. Penance to wash the pleasure from his soul, because in his mind, pleasure was a sin, but a sin he loved.

It was raining this Los Angeles night, washing across the Plexiglas skylight like hot tears, melting the light. His face, reflected in the skylight, was a water-smeared ink stain, the only feature standing out: his nose. Even in the smudged dark surface it looked big, reminding him of a nickname he used to have in elementary school—Electrolux. He paused halfway through a *Hail Mary* and stared hard at himself in the Plexiglas, but as the rain got heavier and the night darker, his reflection grew more unclear, just a shadow really. Not that it mattered, he thought. What he looked like. A man was more a sum of his character. The unspoken things that fill the blankness of a form reflected. Yet the things of character he was searching for in the window were too dark to show up here, long buried and forgotten. Dead things.

Like the fights between his parents that in his memories became one fight, remembered as clear as instant replay. Black was playing in the living room, on the rug, pushing a toy fire truck across the tight weave, pausing to stuff handfuls of Cheerios into his mouth. His mother was watching *I Love Lucy*, talking in her customary way to the television.

"If Desi Arnez is Cuban then I am not Catholic," she said, laughing out loud. "Lucy, now there's a real spitfire, a real Salvadoran, down to the red hair."

Black paused in his play and looked up at her. He was five in this memory and wearing a dress. He looked from his mother to the clock. It was eight p.m. and his father would be home soon, and Black was worried that his mother hadn't started dinner. It wasn't good.

"Can I have some ice cream, Mom?" he asked.

"Sure, m'ijo."

Black had just dug into the plate of vanilla ice cream with chocolate syrup when he heard the sound of keys at the door. Both he and his mother glanced up as Frank banged in, slamming the door. He walked past Black as though he wasn't there, nodded at María and went straight into the kitchen. Black and María could hear pots clattering, the refrigerator door opening and closing and then Frank came back in drinking from a bottle of beer.

"Too busy to cook?"

María ignored him. Black ate quickly, wishing he could get out without being seen.

"I mean anyone of your class should be happy to get a man like me. An engineer, scientist, in fact, a near genius," Frank said. "Why can't you leave that stupid sewing job and cook?"

"Genius? Lucky? If I am so lucky, puto, how come I am working at a factory where the owner gropes me with his oily Greek hands? When are you going to be a man, Frank, and provide for us?"

"So, no food then?"

María just kissed her teeth at him. Frank shrugged, walked over to Black, bent and took the plate of ice cream from him. He changed the channels, sat back down and began shoveling ice cream into his mouth. Black wanted to cry but knew better. Instead he looked to his mother. She smiled at him.

"Come, m'ijo," she said, putting out her arms. He ran into them and she carried him out of the room.

As they left, Frank muttered: "You are spoiling that child."

María ignored him and tucked Black in. He wanted her to read to him, but she took the book out of his hand and said: "How about I tell you a story, like my grandmother used to tell me?"

But while she talked, Black's mind wandered. He could tell from the tight set of her lip that she was mad at his father, but he was torn. He liked his father and lived for any attention he showed him. His father worked hard and

Black rarely saw him because he was usually in bed when his father got home. Yet no matter how hard Frank worked, there never seemed to be enough money. Whenever Black asked for anything, his father said: "Money doesn't grow on trees." Like that. And sometimes more harshly: "Don't be stupid."

At first his tone had been gentle and he would some- times rub Black's head when he said the former. But over time, his tone became more and more clipped and angry until most of the time he shouted at Black.

"Don't be stupid, money doesn't grow on trees."

And when Black didn't ask for anything, his father shouted still. When he forgot to pick up his toys and they got wet with dew on the front porch. When he acciden- tally broke a glass. Or tore a magazine. Always the same: Money doesn't grow on trees, don't be stupid! And the sharpness of that retort and the look in his father's eyes stung more than the smack that inevitably followed.

When his parents were sure he was sleeping, Black heard the fight that had been brewing for days, long before Frank walked in and ate his ice cream. He hated that his mother started it, yelling at Frank, calling him names. Even in his bedroom, in his mind's eye he could see her standing in front of him punctuating each insult with a fin- ger or a palm slap to her chest. At first Frank was quiet, and Black imagined him flinching at the roll call of his impo- tence. Then as María grew louder, Black got really afraid, wanting to call out to his mother, say no, stop, estúpido, he will, he will, but just then he heard the slap and imagined his mother collapsing on the floor, sobbing.

Now, in retrospect, Black wondered why he had looked forward to the rare moments when his father showed him any attention, attention he responded to with puppy-like eagerness that was almost embarrassing, and why with his mother, he was cool. He sought her out when he wanted comfort, but for the most part, he kept his distance from her. He couldn't pretend he didn't know why: he knew, maybe even then, as a little boy he had known why. He felt guilty, guilty that he couldn't stop his father from beating her, guilty that he hated her screaming at Frank because he thought she would drive him away, guilty that he was sometimes happy when his father hit her and she shut up, guilty that he was lulled to sleep by the sound of her crying almost as if it were rain.

On her deathbed, his mother had accused him of always siding with his father. He wished now that he'd had the words to say: It's not that I hated you, or that I loved him more, it's just that you were always there. So it was easy to put it all on you. What else could I do? How could I hate a man who never really existed for me?

Back in the present, Black blew smoke circles into the night, struggling to admit that his memories were a lie: that he changed toward his mother after his father left. He felt all the voices pressed tight against his brain with the pressure of a headache. Eight years old and kneeling on hard rice before an altar not unlike this one. Eight and the rice biting into his knees and sweat running down his face and his mother standing over him with a cane. Stroke after stroke on his back and he struggling to hold back the tears and her voice:

"Try harder, m'ijo, try harder to call the Lady."

And he.

"I am trying but she won't come."

"Why? Have you been touching yourself in the naughty place?"

"No, Mom."

"Liar!"

Whack.

"Please, Mom, please."

Whack.

"Do you see her?"

Whack.

"Mom?"

Whack.

"Do you see my Lady?"

Whack.

"Yes! Yes!"

"Where?"

"Over there, see how the wind is blowing the curtain?"

His mother looking to the window.

"Yes?"

"That's the Lady's robe brushing against it."

And his mother; falling to her knees.

"Madre, Santa Madre."

Then looking across at him, a deliciously cunning smile on her face: "You wouldn't lie to me, would you, m'ijo?"

Looking up through the skylight, Black snapped back to the present. He dropped the rosary beads on the floor and watched hovering planes winking like transient stars. He tried to think of them as fireflies hovering in the wet blackness, but knowing how big they were, his mind couldn't make the leap. Outside, the drape of night was pinned to the ground by the flat spread of city lights. There was magic here beyond the desire this city wove in the confusion of Art Deco, Hacienda, Lloyd-Wright and ugly sixties Modernist architecture. He ducked back inside, stopping by the photographs of Sweet Girl.

"The lights are pretty. They make everything look like Christmas," he said to her frozen face, and smiled.

Sitting on the floor, he opened up the makeup kit that he had lugged up and pulled out several tubes of lipstick, foundation, blusher, brushes, sponges, mascara and the white face paint with the touch of luminescence he had blended in. Laying them out on the polished wooden floor of the ship, he hummed a Madonna song under his breath.

Grunting to his feet, he walked over to where Iggy's wedding dress hung from a nail in the wall. It was still in the cleaner's cellophane. He had put it back in the cleaner's cellophane to store it, but he'd taken it out when he brought it home and adjusted the dress carefully to fit him. He had artfully sewn an extra hidden seam into the sides.

He tore a careful hole in the plastic and put two fingers through to feel the fabric. The lace was rough, like the leaves of the strawberries he drove out to Fresno to pick once. He'd had the dress for months, collecting it from the cleaners. Howie, the Vietnamese owner of D & L Cleaners, knew him, so it wasn't difficult.

"Iggy send you?" Howie asked.

"Yeah," Black said. "She wants to sell it."

"Is a shame to sell your wedding dress. Bad luck," Howie's Persian wife said from the back, and it was hard to understand her through the sound of steam and whirring machinery.

"Ignore her," Howie said. Turning to his wife he shouted in bad Farsi: "Tow man kharam!"

If Iggy ever wondered what happened to the dress, or if she knew, which she must, that he picked it up, she never asked. He had done it, he said to himself, because he needed it for the painting. But that wasn't completely true.

He had been collecting various women's clothing for a while, everything but dresses. He chose the wedding dress because the only dresses he could wear were wedding dresses. Ever since he had first used his mother's. Over the years he had used different ones but none of them felt right. Felt like his mother's. He couldn't use hers because that was what she was buried in. But Iggy's dress offered the same feeling. He knew that even before he wore or set out to acquire it. He watched the dress in the window of the cleaners for almost a week until he couldn't shake the haunting. Even then. A week before he plucked up the courage. It hung in the back of his closet all these months until tonight. He'd brought the dress up, along with a blonde wig and the makeup kit, because he wanted to wear it. The feeling was so overwhelming he just followed the impulse. Turning to the wig, he picked it up and brushed the cheap fake hair that snagged and pulled like a doll's. He put it down.

Still humming the Madonna tune, he returned to the makeup. Selecting a soft brush, he pulled powder across the roughness of his face. Pulled until his fingers told him that his face was as smooth as a silk stocking. Then he reached for the mascara. Carefully, because he was still afraid of the brush getting in his eye, he applied the thick black makeup. He couldn't judge how much was too much and only stopped when he felt the mascara pulling his eye-lashes together. The choice of lipstick took a long time. Ruby was too red, cherry too bright, pink too cheerleader-ish, blue too Goth, peach and caramel were invisible on him. Finally, he selected a purplish burgundy. He liked it. His lips looked like they had been bruised from too much kissing. Turning to the Plexiglas, he stared at himself. He was still too dark. Maybe the dress will change that, he thought.

He knew why he did this; dressed up in Iggy's old wedding dress, in any dress. He wasn't gay, he wasn't. He was also sure he wasn't a transvestite. That was Sweet Girl, not him. Black did it to feel safe. That was all, simple really when he thought about it. He did it to revive the magic of the white dress that had protected him from evil until he turned seven. Maybe if he'd continued to wear a dress his father would have come back and his mother wouldn't have died in that living room in Pasadena when they came to tell her that his father was MIA, presumed dead. Died to be replaced by the woman who'd hurt him until she died, seven years later.

Taking the dress down, he was careful removing the cellophane.

"Work your magic," he mumbled, like a spell into the stiff clean lace, saying a *Hail Mary* under his breath.

He dropped the dress over his head, sweating with effort to pull it down without tearing the lace. Even with the adjustment it was still tight. With a final grunt, he reached behind and zipped himself up. Fluffing the wig one last time, he pulled it on. With a dramatic flair, he turned back to the Plexiglas. He wasn't beautiful, but he was still stunned. He simply didn't recognize himself; at least not as Black. He began to cry. He struggled against the melting mascara. Pulling himself together, he realized that his face looked even darker against the white dress and blonde hair. He reached for the luminescent face paint. He would need to apply the mascara and lipstick again, he thought, as he rubbed the thick paint on, but that didn't matter. The result would be worth the effort.

And it was.

When he finished and looked up, he was aflame, as though he had become a thing divine. He was trembling so hard he needed a cigarette. Opening the skylight slowly, he scanned for Gabriel. No sign of him. Stuffing the pack of Marlboros and a lighter down his cleavage, he pulled himself out onto the roof of the spaceship. In the wedding dress it was no easy task and he almost tore it a couple of times. Finally he stood there under the moon, and though the rain had slowed to a slight drizzle, the air was still damp. Freedom at last, he thought, and lit his cigarette. A passing police chopper held him in its spotlight for a minute, then the spotlight cut off, replaced by a deeper darkness than before.

Half blinded as he hurried back into the spaceship, Black didn't see the people below on Cesar Chavez, kneeling in the middle of the street, staring in openmouthed wonder at the empty air where the apparition had been.

dawn.

A mongrel bird returned to a silent rooftop. A tired angel slept fitfully atop a spaceship, a once white wing hanging down the side, tipped with mud. In the barely darkness below, a lone police car fogged the street with a throaty exhaust. In clumps, like calla lilies waiting for the sun, white-garbed men hovered by the hardware store, not knowing, but believing that the day *would* bring work. The burrito van turned out its lights: McDonald's golden arches flickered on. Between this changing of guards, in the gloom of the bus shelter, a persistent cigarette.

Quiet happened.

We have the right to lie, but not about the heart of the matter.

—Antonin Artaud

rain.

Black could hear it drumming on the roof. He woke reluctantly and reaching for the remote control lying on the floor next to the bed, he flicked on the television. On every channel the same breaking story: brush fires were threatening the suburbs and there was a real fear it could spread to LA. As he yawned he wondered why the rain didn't seem to affect the fire that was consuming whole counties and showing no signs of abating. Probably not raining that far out, he reasoned. His thoughts were confirmed by the images on television: dry brown scrub, dry and on fire. Winter and the Santa Anas drove an evil wind through Southern California, fanning the flames.

As he watched the perfectly manicured reporter call in her story, he thought it odd she had an umbrella up even though there was no rain. Then he realized it *was* raining, live embers falling in a drizzle like slow-dying fireflies. Ash. Covering Los Angeles and the Home Counties with the disapproval of a Catholic penance. There was always a

fire in California, or a mud slide, or floods or an earth-
quake, and Black kept jumping channels, looking for something else, but the fire was on every station, each one playing
James Taylor, his nasal voice soft under the clipped tones
of the news anchors, as he sang: "I've seen fire and I've
seen rain," while silent images played: people staring with
a primordial fear as fire ate away at their homes.

Black stretched and got out of bed, walking over to the
stove. He cracked his knuckles as he set a saucepan of milk
on to heat. When it was hot, he emptied it into a cup with
a tea bag in the bottom. While it brewed, he thought how
simple things brought him such comfort: a cup of hot tea
on an overcast day, a street musician playing a plaintive
melody on a flute, or even better, a cello, or the sound of
rain chattering on concrete sidewalks. Carrying the mug
up to the roof, he climbed the ladder, with difficulty, to the
spaceship and sat in the open doorway, legs dangling over
the edge.

Falling away from him, houses spread down the hill like
an undecided rash, brown lawns corroding like iron left
out in the rain. The dust-heavy birds of paradise and the
odd tree in the odd yard looked hopeful. The heat hadn't
arrived to beat everything into clapboard and dirt heat
traps, but he knew it would. It was a fact of life here. It
sucked.

Los Angeles in the rain had a certain quality of light to
it, a cerulean more atmosphere than presence, unusual for
this town that bludgeoned you with everything. From
where he sat, even the cars on the snake of the 110 Freeway floated past, hydroplaning in a graceful, silent swan
dance. The red trail of their taillights marked every mean-
der of the slow river of black, like fairy lights on a distant

shore. This was the one time Los Angeles was honest, open and beautiful.

Wishing he didn't have to go out, he drank the last of the tea and snapped the bag out of the teacup onto the roof of The Ugly Store. It split and spread tea leaves in a rough heart shape. He stared at the pattern as it washed away in the rain, wondering if it was an omen. Gabriel fluttered down. Black saw him out of the corner of his eye and got up.

"Hey, Gabe," he said. He had taken to talking to Gabriel, though he still avoided looking at him. It was too frightening. "I was just leaving."

"Always running away, Black. Just like you did as a boy. You never had the patience to wait for your miracle."

"My mother's miracle, not mine. And why don't you go bother someone else?"

"You prayed for me."

"I didn't want you! My mother did!"

"And yet here I am."

"Fuck you!"

"Whatever." Gabriel sounded bored. "I see those misguided people are still down there," he cooed.

Black, thinking Gabriel had turned into a pigeon, looked at him. But Gabriel was still fifteen feet tall, and the hand dangling over his knee was easily the same size as Black's head. He exclaimed in alarm. Desperate for distraction, he looked down at the street. Even though it had been three weeks since the Virgin was spotted on the roof of the spaceship, the faithful returned every day. Some never left, setting up camp on the street. It was a little disconcerting at first as the makeshift shelters and tents began to spring up along the sidewalk, making the area look like skid row.

The local shop owners loved it as they were doing brisk business.

Black's attention was drawn to a dog so white it could have been a ghost dog, standing in a break in the crowd on the sidewalk, by a tree. Its head was cocked to one side and its dark eyes were fixed not on the crowd or the street before it, but up, on Black, making his breath catch in his throat, bringing back memories.

As a thirteen-year-old in East LA, he had stumbled on a dogfight in an abandoned warehouse where he was painting a mural after school. Peering through a hole in the wall, he hadn't seen much: a lot of men squatting around growling dogs that tore at each other, ripping flesh and fur. The smell was overpowering: the rust of blood and sweat from the cheering men, and something else he could never quite place. The sound they made held a peculiar joy: men cheering for the pain of something other than them, cheering from a place older than the shape it took now. When it was over and all the men had left, Black saw the dog that lost, not quite dead, but dying slowly in a pool of its own blood, whimpering. And Black remembered walking out to it, holding its warm body, feeling it growing cold. But it was the dog's eyes; the way they wouldn't let go of his gaze and the infinite sadness of them and something like gratitude. That—and the fact that several other dogs, wild dogs probably, gathered in yawning windows and doorways to watch as though witnessing Black witness the death. Or maybe they had gathered to eat the dying dog, he thought. He didn't know what to do, so he sang to the dying dog. He sang in the nonsensical sounds he had heard his father sing when he was drunk.

Leaving the spaceship, Black went back to his apartment,

showered and changed into his paint-stained overalls. He scratched his head, a little torn that morning, unable to decide what to work on. He didn't want to work and toyed with the idea of going to Echo Park, his local park. But with the rain Echo Park would be empty, the ground soggy, grass wet. It wasn't that he didn't like the park in the rain, he did. He loved to sit and read in the shade of a large umbrella, a large fifties style thermos of hot chai or coffee warming him. Taking a break he would put away the book, close the umbrella and take out an orange. Peeling it, the mist of citrus spicing the damp air, he would eat it slowly as the rain drenched him, alternating the bites of soft yellow flesh with a sip of the hot tea or coffee.

"You'll get pneumonia," Bomboy said to him when he found out. "You're not young anymore."

Black smiled and said, "It's like worship. You let the rain wash over you. It's like that."

"Stupid man," Bomboy mumbled.

But today, as he dressed, Black thought he should stay in and work. He could grind some dye for his murals. He mixed his own paint, from ground-up pigments and natural dyes like henna, sometimes adding a pinch of cooking spices to really bring out the color—curry or turmeric or saffron—all mixed into varying gum arabic bases whose secret compositions were so closely guarded, Black taught himself to forget them. At least that's what he told everyone. The truth was he couldn't remember them so he wrote them out, disguised as cooking recipes, and hid them in the pages of his Caribbean cookbook—the one least likely to be borrowed.

Each color was designed specifically for a particular part of a particular mural that he might be working on at the time, and each had a different chemical consistency and density so that he could apply the paint in layers that never bled or dried into each other. Like LA, he thought, a segregated city that still managed to work as a single canvas of color and voices. It was a trick he claimed to have learned by studying books on the old fresco painters of Renaissance Italy. It didn't matter if it was true or not. But he did it because this way, he could build up each mural from the skeleton, if it were a person, layering the musculature, flesh and skin and clothes on with different consistencies of paint. This allowed him to adjust mistakes from the inside out. Or if he was painting a mural of a landscape or a collage of LA images, he began with the prehistoric, built up through the Gabrieleño and Chumash, through the rancheros and missions, the former slaves and on until he got to the layer he was working on.

"Psychic history," he called it.

"A spell," Iggy called it.

They were in agreement.

He ran his fingers through a pile of ground henna, rubbing the coarse grains together contemplatively. The trouble was that he mixed paint for particular murals, and since he wasn't working on one, he couldn't really do that today. He rubbed his hand along his trouser leg smearing henna all over it. Perhaps he would return to working on the installation piece he had set up in The Ugly Store. Covering one whole wall in the café, it measured eleven feet high (the height of The Ugly Store) and thirty feet long (the length of the wall) and was composed entirely of jokes (racist and sexist ones preferably) that he had collected over the years from the walls of men's rooms in Los Angeles. That was the criteria. At first he had collected them himself but over time, as he had begun the installation, the community of The Ugly Store had started to collect them and pass them on to him. He was firm about their source, men's public toilets, but flexible about the cities they came from. The best part for him was when women gave him the jokes and graffiti they had snuck into men's toilets in restaurants and athletic clubs to jot down hurriedly. As Iggy's fame grew among the Hollywood and "it" crowd, Black began to get them from celebrities.

Paris Hilton gave him lines from the Hilton Hotel public restrooms across the globe, Aishwarya Rai from the men's toilets in Mumbai and Bombay, Penelope Cruz from Madrid (all in Spanish), Morgan Freeman from the toilets of river boats, Sharon Osborne gave him a juicy one from Buckingham Palace and just a few days ago, Julie Warner had given him one from the men's room in Spago's.

Running along the bottom of the installation was a border, six feet wide. Entered in like marginalia under the title *An Attempted Index of Self-censorship* was a list of all the places in the world the text had come from.

Everything he did was political, he liked to say, but this was the first one he thought was overtly and unmistakably so. The title had been difficult for him and he had played with American Soul, American Confessional and even The Birth of a Nation's Conscience. But none of them worked.

"What does it represent for you exactly?" Iggy asked.

"Well, I figured that racism and sexism had retreated from the overtly public to the private, you know, all the jokes and so forth that people only feel safe telling in the confessional space of toilets, but ones that still reveal the soul of this country to be racist and sexist, and I want to point to that heart of darkness."

"So why not just call it *Heart of Darkness*?" Iggy asked.

"Nah, too Conrad and too *Apocalypse Now*," he said.

"American Gothic II?"

He smiled.

"American Gothic: The Remix."

"The matrix?"

"No, I said 'remix.' "

Picking up a box with various colored markers, pieces of charcoal and pastel and oil pens, he decided to go downstairs and continue working. He opened the box to make sure that the moleskin journal with all the material was also in it, then turned and headed for the door. On his way out, he paused by the mannequins closest to the door. They freaked him out, made him think of ghost trains or crazy rides in amusement parks, so he took their heads off. That didn't make it any better, because now they terrified him. And yet he couldn't get rid of them. This mannequin was wearing Iggy's wedding dress and the blonde wig. For some reason it reminded him of Marilyn Monroe, and something else.

Once, but only once, when he was ten, dressing up in his mother's boa and red pumps, lips redder than those pumps, running through the living room, blowing kisses from pouted lips and yelling:

"When it's hot like this, I keep my undies in an icebox!"

Once though and no more, because his mother beat him so bad he bled from the cut above his left eye where the metal heel of the red pump had dug in. He did it to cheer her up, he told himself, later, as he put a Band-Aid on the wound above his eye. It was three years after his father left, a year since the army had delivered his medal and their apologies.

"I am sorry, Mrs. Anyanwu, but your husband is missing in action. At this time we can only presume he is dead."

But Black never believed, didn't dare believe his father was dead, holding on to the smallest shred of hope that he would return someday. His mother had taken the news of Frank's MIA status well at the time. She didn't cry, which surprised Black since she was such an emotional person. Instead she went really quiet and then began to pray. Obsessively. That day she began a rosary that never ended, calling for a miracle that never came. Black wouldn't have minded any of it if she hadn't conscripted him as the one with a purer heart. With time and the disappointment, she hardened and began to beat Black, blaming him for not delivering. He let go of the lacy dress he was rubbing between pinched fingers and opened the door, mentally wishing the memory away. He wasn't even sure it was real.

The Ugly Store was full. All the tables were taken and several people were standing around or sitting on the floor. All petitioners to see Iggy, no doubt, he thought. Ray-Ray was skittering about on his stilts doing his best to meet all the orders. Black thought he would wait until things quieted down before asking for a drink. He stepped over the CAUTION tape around his installation.

"Hey, mister," a little girl called. "I don't think you can do that!"

Black turned to her and smiled.

"It's okay, I'm the artist."

"I don't know," she said, arms folded.

Black sat on the floor in front of the installation and emptied the pens, paint-sticks and charcoal onto the floor like a shaman throwing divination bones. He spread them apart with quiet fingers, eyes never leaving the huge canvas, as he tried to get into the mood. The little girl came over and studied him. Black, already unaware of everyone in the room, opened up the black moleskin notebook and began to read.

"Say, is that the Bible, mister?" the girl asked.

He turned to her: "In a manner of speaking."

"We're here for the Lady," the girl said.

"The lady?" Black asked, clearly sounding confused because the little girl rolled her eyes in exasperation.

"Where have you been? The Lady, the Virgin."

Black shook his head slowly, still not catching on.

"On the roof!" the little girl said, pointing up.

"Oh!"

"Yes, my mummy says she will make Daddy better so we've been here for two days now."

"In here?" He didn't remember seeing anyone, and he and Iggy had been here the other night.

"No, silly, outside in a tent. We only came in here to eat and wash up."

Black took in the rest of the crowd: regular working folks dressed in their best clothes which were faded, if clean, from repeated washes, their faces shining from the same grease slicking their hair down and polishing their shoes. Earnest folk with wide-open faces and hands calloused from the hardness of their labors. He should have guessed. They weren't here for Iggy, these weren't the kind of people who paid a psychic for a tattoo and a reading; they were here for him. Well, not him exactly, but him as the Virgin. He should do something about it, he thought. Tell everyone the truth. There was no Virgin, it was him in a dress, a stolen dress, on the roof of the spaceship. He couldn't let them go on believing. Not when they were making their kids sleep outside in tents. But how?

"She's not real," Black said softly.

"Of course she's real. My mummy saw her, on the tree house."

"It's not a tree house, it's a spaceship," he corrected.

"That's not a spaceship, mister. It's fixed to a pole."

Black made a face at her. Her mother just happened to look up at that moment.

"Jacinta!" she called.

The little girl turned and ran toward her. Black was about to turn back to his work when he spotted Iggy coming toward him. She waved and he smiled at her.

"Hey!" she said, climbing over the yellow tape to join him on the floor, legs folded under her in a full lotus, arching her back as she did. He knew the metal loops were hurting her, so he reached across and rubbed her back gently through her top. She relaxed into his hand. "Oh, that's nice," she purred.

"Thank you," she said, when he pulled his hand away.

"You're welcome."

"I almost forgot, I have some lines for you."

He took the sheet of paper she handed him and read.

"'And the green freedom of a cockatoo/The holy hush of ancient sacrifice.' This is poetry, right?" he asked.

"Yeah," she replied. "Wallace Stevens. It's from *Sunday Morning*."

"All of these lines?"

She leaned over and pointed to, "In the darkness/they wrestle, two creatures crazed with loneliness."

"Those are from Valentin Iremonger."

"I like them but how do they fit here? Did you find them in a toilet?"

"Yeah, mine. Look, you need something to balance out the darkness, right?'

"Sure," he said, selecting two markers. He tore the sheet in half and passed it along with one of the pens to Iggy. "Join me?"

She took the paper and pen and smiled.

"Are you sure?"

He nodded.

"Anywhere?"

He nodded.

They worked silently, inserting the lines of poetry into the already crowded canvas. Black had rigged the wall with a pulley system. The contraption was simple. Two lengths of rope dangled down from a series of pulleys embedded in the ceiling. The rope ended in two wooden steps that looked like wooden bicycle pedals. Black could step onto them, and pull himself up to any point along the length or height of the canvas. He did it now, swinging up and across to insert lines from the poems in harder to reach places, while Iggy covered the lower sections, both working silently for an hour or so before taking a break. They both sat back on the floor to admire the work.

"What do you think?"

He took out a cigarette and lit it. The Ugly Store sometimes seemed like the only place left in California where he could smoke without offending anyone. He took a long drag and passed it to Iggy, blowing smoke as he spoke. He walked up to it and stared for a long time.

"I don't know. Nearly there."

AMERICAN GOTHIC—THE REMIX

What do you get when you cross a nigger and a spick? A lazy thief; WHAT DO YOU CALL THE USELESS SKIN AROUND THE VAGINA? A WOMAN. "And the green freedom of a cockatoo/... The holy hush of ancient sacrifice"——Wallace Stevens. What does FUBU stand for? Farmers used to buy us. Asians have small dicks, no fucky fucky long time. How do you blindfold a gook? Use dental floss. "Winding across wide water, without sound/ The day is like wide water, without sound"——Wallace Stevens. **A Mexican and a nigger are riding in a car, who's driving? A cop.** "Death is the mother of beauty, mystical/ Within whose burning bosom we devise"——Wallace Stevens. Only cockroaches and Nigerians will survive a nuclear holocaust. What does that say about cockroaches? What do 3 million abused women do wrong each year? They don't fuckin' listen. KKKK—Kill the Ku Klux Klan. I sit here flexin' trying to make another Texan. What do you call a man with his arm up a camel's ass? An Afghan mechanic. **What do you call a beautiful Moslem woman? Asif!** Fuck Conan O'Brien. Condoms are for Sissies. Jesus was a drunk. What do you call a black woman who had an abortion? A crime prevention officer. What do you call a plane load of black people heading to Africa? A good start. **'I've known rivers, mighty mighty rivers"—Langston Hughes. What do you call a bad driver? Asian. Catch a nigger by his toe, if he hollers, lynch the motherfucker.** Why aren't there any spics on startrek? Because they won't work in the future either. "Gazelle, I killed you/for your skin's exquisite/ touch, for how easy it is/ to be nailed to a board/ weathered raw as white/" —Yusef Komunyakaa. **If your wife and a lawyer were drowning and you had to choose, what would you do? Go to lunch or a movie? "In the darkness/they wrestle, two creatures crazed with loneliness" —Valentin Iremonger. What do you tell a woman with two black eyes? Nothing, she's been told twice already.** How do you hide money from a Mexican? Under a bar of soap. What's the difference between a pizza and a Jew? A pizza doesn't scream when you put it into the oven. Why does Stevie Wonder smile all the time? Because he doesn't know he's black. "The bud/stands for all things/ even for those things that don't flower" —Galway Kinnell. What is better than winning a medal at the special Olympics? Not being retarded. Hoodwink—what a member of the KKK does just before he lynches a nigger. Es una copa llena/ de agua/ el mundo —Pablo Neruda. Black . . .

An Attempted Index on Self-Censorship

Coles, 6ᵗʰ St. Corazon, Madrid. Spago's, Hollywood. Dutton's, brentwood. The getty. Lacma. Sunny's, leimert park. Lucy Florence. Psychobabble, n. Vermont. Goodluck club. Buckingham palace. Hilton, paris. Hilton, munich. Hilton, los angeles. Hilton, cairo. PHILLIPE'S, ALAMEDA. UNION STATION. CROCE'S, SAN DIEGO. LOS ANGELES SUPERIOR COURT. DOROTHY CHANDLER MUSIC pavilion. fifth street dicks; The world stage, leimert park. Ins building; Parker center, los angeles. Tottenham hale station, London. Internal revenue service, London. Ochel, cuba. Tony's, treasure beach, Jamaica. Elliot bay bookshop, seattle. Texaco building. World trade center, new york. Barnes and noble. Pharoah's tomb, Egypt. Oum kalsoum hotel, cairo. International library, Alexandria. Tia chucha's, los angeles. Pizza hut, Melrose. Japanese gardens, Huntington. Vroman's, Pasadena. Mobil station, Rakim tree. Ranger station, Rakim tree national park. Motel 6; The way station, palm springs. Coffee house. The performance loft, Redlands. Dinner cruiser, san diego. Center for race studies, new york. Museum of tolerance. Kali Koffee, Mumbai. Cut Leaf Café, Bombay. Taj Mahal. Taboo, delhi. Jazz bistro, lagos, Nigeria. Starbucks, Milan. Coliseum, rome. Samba-samba, rio de Janeiro. Exodus, Israel. Titanic café, Kabul. The rose, Seattle. Miyagi's, los angeles.

Iggy had joined him, standing next to him, head inclined, hand rubbing her shaved dome slowly.

"I like it."

"You don't think it is too dark?"

"Oh, it's dark. But that is a good thing."

"Yeah?"

"Yeah."

They stared at it for a long time without speaking.

"Coffee?"

They both looked up. It was Ray-Ray and he had two cups of coffee on a tray. Black reached for them.

"You know the rules," Ray-Ray said, pulling the tray back. Black smiled. It was an old game. Ray-Ray had been named after his mother's favorite writer, Raymond Chandler, and he loved to play quote games from Chandler's work. Black thought it was ironic that a black man should be named after Raymond Chandler, but he said nothing.

"'Shakespeare. He knew his liquor too.'"

"*Farewell, My Lovely*," Ray-Ray said, as though he were biting into soft nougat.

Black took a coffee and passed it to Iggy before he reached for his. As Ray-Ray left, Black muttered under his breath.

"Why can't he play a regular game like Monopoly? You can really destroy a person's soul if you own all the railways. Now that's a game."

"Like the Huntingtons."

Black didn't know what Iggy was talking about, but decided to pass.

"I'm going for more coffee," he said.

"Hey, Black," Ray-Ray said, as Black walked up to him.

"Hey, Ray-Ray."

"Coffee?"

"Double cappuccino but hold the foam."

"It ain't a cappuccino if it ain't got the foam," Ray-Ray said.

Black made a face. As Ray-Ray crossed over to the espresso machine on the edge of the bar, Black caught sight of the two-foot-high stilts he walked on. Being a dwarf, he needed them to reach the top of the bar. Black paid for the coffee and reached for the paper cup, but Ray-Ray pulled it back.

"'Freeze the mitts on the bar,'" Ray-Ray said.

"*Farewell, My Lovely*?"

"Damn, skippy," Ray-Ray said, releasing the cup.

Black saw June, Iggy's friend, walking through the store. She headed to Iggy and sat. Ray-Ray hurried over to her and came back to the bar to fetch her order. Black joined them. June was an artist. Black knew her well because she was a regular and had held several showings there. He loved June's work, prints with bold lines and startling colors. Something about them, maybe the grain, gave them soul. It moved him, made him realize how deep surfaces could be. His aesthetic was as wide open as his field of influences, although he drew the line, he once told June, at Shigeto Kubota's vagina paintings, which the artist did by attaching a paintbrush to her groin.

"Hey, Black," Iggy said. "Join us?"

"Sure. Hey, June," he said.

"Sit," Iggy said, rubbing her hand over her bald scalp. Black thought he saw more purple fuzz than usual. "June was just telling me about her new project. A map of Los Angeles without the religious place names."

Black paused, as Ray-Ray returned with drinks—coffee for June and some kind of tea for Iggy. Black took a sip from Iggy's cup and made a face. Wheat germ tea. Vile.

"Installation? Painting?"

"I haven't decided," June said.

"Doesn't matter, really, it won't be a map of Los Angeles, though," he said.

June laughed.

"But it would."

"The landscape won't change just because you alter the names."

"I know, but the psychic space will," she said.

"Exactly. So if it's not Los Angeles, then it's not *Los Angeles*, so to speak."

Black was pulling his overalls away from his stomach as he spoke. Iggy smiled. She knew he was conscious of his weight, and she wanted to reach out and rub her palm down his chest, say, stop, don't, you are beautiful. Instead she sipped her wheat germ tea.

"Oh, that's bullshit," June said. "That kind of mumbo jumbo is what keeps the superimposed perversion of religion in place." Her position on religion of any kind was well known to him. He once called her a Marxist idealist, but she demonstrated equal scorn for that.

"Black has a point," Iggy said.

"Pooey!" June said. "You two are no good together."

Black laughed. He couldn't figure out what these two white women had in common: an atheist artist and a Jewish fakir.

"When Parker plays 'Lover Man,' it's a different song from when Grover covers it. Same instrument, same notes, different song. Same landscape, same map, different town.

Not Los Angeles," he said. "This place is more than surface, June. It's about what it means to you."

"Which is?"

There was so much he wanted to say. Los Angeles for him wasn't Beverly Hills, or the movies, or Rodeo Drive. It wasn't the deception of movie studios that built sets with varying door sizes so that cowboys looked brawnier against the smaller doors and ladies daintier against the taller ones. It wasn't the Mulhollands and their water, nor the people everywhere with too perfect hair and smiles as fake as the teeth they framed. Nor was it San Marino and its pretend class, or even the Hollywood sign. It was in the angle of light caught in the trickle of the Los Angeles River as it curved under one of the beautiful old crumbling bridges of East LA. The way the painting of an angel wearing sandals and jeans, its once-white wings stained by exhaust soot and tag signs, smoking a cigarette on a support of the 10 East Freeway on Hoover, curved into flight if you took the corner of the on-ramp at speed. In the cacophony of colors and shapes in the huge piñata stores on Olympic, near Central; and the man pulling the purple wooden life-size donkey mounted on wheels down Cesar Chavez, wearing a nonchalant expression as though it was the most normal thing in the world; or the people who parted on each side of him as he made his way down the sidewalk, completely oblivious to the sight. In the occasional clip-clop of horses pulling a brilliant white bridal carriage that resisted the dust and dirt everywhere, and the line of cars following slowly in awe. It was in the solo of an unemployed saxophonist in Sunny's Café down at Leimert Park playing for tips.

Iggy reached over and rubbed the plastic pouch around

his neck. He smiled at her, leaning back. June felt uncomfortable in the face of this familiar intimacy. Iggy noticed.

"Did you know this is a photo of Black?" she said, indicating the fading photo in the plastic pouch.

June leaned forward and peered at it through the black leather-wrapped and zirconia-studded magnifying glass she wore around her neck.

"Really?" she said. "But you're wearing a dress."

Iggy laughed and Black smiled, a little embarrassed.

"Go on," Iggy said. "Tell her." To June she said: "This is fascinating."

Black hesitated. There was something about this female pressure that reminded him of his mother.

"Well?" June asked, tone impatient.

"My father told me that there is a curse on our family, that a malevolent spirit kills all the male children before they turn six. So all the boys are dressed as girls and sometimes even given girl's names until they turn seven. Then the dress comes off and we become boys again," he said.

"Sort of a second birth," Iggy said.

"Fascinating," June said. "So your father explained this to you as a child? Didn't he go away when you just turned seven?"

Black nodded.

"To Vietnam," Iggy said.

"He never came back," Black said, in a voice that sounded like a pebble dropping into a well.

"So how did you find out?"

"This letter. It came with the photo. After he died in Vietnam," Black said, flipping the plastic pouch over, showing the letter. "Of course I didn't read it until I was fifteen. Until after my mother died."

"That's why he wears it like a talisman," Iggy explained.

"Yes, I can see that," June said. "How do you feel about that?" she asked Black.

"About being a girl for a while? Confused, I guess. I'm not sure. Look, I can't get into this," he said.

They were silent for a while, but when June went to the bathroom, Iggy brought up the rent. It was two months overdue.

"I'll give it to you soon," he said.

"When?"

"Soon."

Iggy nodded and arched her back. It cracked with an explosive sound, the metal loops on her back jangling melodically.

"Oh, that was killing me," she said.

twelve

esus is my Homeboy.

Black, sitting on the concrete lip of the River, saw the T-shirt first before he saw Bomboy Dickens. The shirt was tight, outlining Bomboy's body, and Black fought the urge to run to him and pull the fabric away.

"Black. How now?" Bomboy asked as he walked over.

"I'm fine," Black replied. He really wasn't up for polite conversation with Bomboy. It was mid-afternoon and hot. He had just returned to the crane where he'd tried to kill himself the other day, and was still a little out of breath from climbing it. There was something about the view of the wall of Bomboy's warehouse-abattoir that had made an impression that day, but he'd been so busy evading Gabriel he hadn't paid enough attention. He still couldn't tell what it was, but it would come. That was part of the process for his art: waiting.

"Taking a break from work?" Bomboy asked him. "I saw you up there," he added, pointing to the crane. "Nice view?"

Black nodded, taking in Bomboy's blood-spattered orange T-shirt. Bomboy understood meat. And knives. Black had seen him work. Seen him talk tenderly to the beef and sheep cadavers as he carved them into choice cuts. Tell his coworkers how the muscles were connected to each other, and how the tendons held everything in place like the cables of the Golden Gate Bridge, which he saw once on a trip. And Black knew enough to know that if Bomboy wanted, he could carve cadavers all day and not get a spot of blood on him. Blood was a choice he made.

"So," Bomboy said.

"Are you alright, 'mano?"

Bomboy nodded. Then:

"You know Pedro is a mean mothafucker."

Black nodded. He not only didn't know who Pedro was, he also didn't care.

"You know Pedro, right? With the taco stand?"

Black shook his head.

"Well, the other day I was buying a burrito from him, and as he chopped the meat he looked at me and said, 'Is this how you guys killed each other back in that jungle?' Imagine the cheek of that, eh? I mean I couldn't eat it after that, but I still had to pay. That mothafucker."

Black nodded. He wondered how someone like Bomboy, who owned a successful, if illegal, business, had the time for these petty quarrels.

"So what are you mad about? The insult or paying for the food?" he asked.

"Paying for the food was paying for the insult," Bomboy said. Black stared at him. If Iggy thought his head was a frightening place, he thought, then Bomboy's must be the third circle of hell.

"You need help."

"Exactly! So, how do you think I should revenge?"

"I don't know. Why don't you let it go?"

"You think?"

"Yeah."

Black lit a Marlboro and passed the pack to Bomboy.

"So you know what happened to me yesterday?"

Black didn't know and didn't really care.

"I saw this army recruiter at the mall," Bomboy said.

"Uh-huh."

"Fox Hills Mall to be exact, precise and accurate," Bomboy added, as though it were important.

"Is this story going anywhere? Or should I just save us some time and say, 'Forgive that mothafucker too'?"

"Black! Your words are wounding."

"Yeah? Fuck you, hijo dela chingada."

"Black!"

"What? Do I look like Oprah? Tell me the story or shut the fuck up already."

Bomboy laughed, and then grew serious.

"Anyway, this army recruiter said if I signed up for the war in Iraq I could become an American citizen."

"No shit," Black said, stepping on his cigarette butt. "Is that who they're sending now?"

"I guess."

"So what happens if you don't survive?"

"I will."

Black nodded and lit another Marlboro.

"This army guy said they could use men like me. Men who knew how to handle themselves, get the job done."

"Men who could get the job done?"

"You know my background."

"But how did he know?"

"I told him."

"Seems to me like you've already made up your mind."

Black looked out across the River. The rain had swelled it, and it ran fast down the concrete channel, dragging the burnt-out skeleton of a car with it.

"Do you miss it?" Black asked. He was picking at the calluses on his palms, staring at each strip of skin intensely before dropping it into the river.

"You know the last time I got those?" Black shook his head. "In Kigali," Bomboy pressed on. "Defending myself."

"Look," Black began in an attempt to head off the conversation.

"The Hutu Army captured me and some other orphans hiding behind the church. They said we had to fight the Tutsi. We were afraid to refuse because we'd seen them killing people. Plenty people like this," Bomboy said, mimicking the hacking action of a machete with his open palm. Black flinched. "They gave us cutlasses and marched us many days to reach the Tutsi Army. A week passed and we didn't see any sign of the army so the Hutu soldiers, our people, took us to a Tutsi refugee camp, only women and children. They told us to kill them, or if we couldn't, to cut them well well."

Tears were gathering in Bomboy's eyes and Black fixed his gaze on an inflatable doll floating past them on the river. The doll was deflating fast, and the open "O" of the mouth on its crumpled face seemed even more surprised. Black shuddered as he realized that Bomboy's tears bothered him more than the details of his story.

"I cut. I was afraid so I cut. Hands. Legs. Heads. Chests.

I couldn't look. I just wanted to finish. I cut and cut until my hand blistered, until my knife was dull. Human bodies are hard to cut with a dull knife; cause many blisters."

"Easy, man," Black said, casually placing a hand on Bomboy's back. Bomboy seemed to be done talking. He looked embarrassed. Black didn't know what to say, so he looked at the murals along the length of the concrete dip opposite. They were all his work, crawling along like modern hieroglyphics or a Minoan script. To the left, on the 4th Street Bridge, traffic, at a standstill, shook the old supports, flaking white paint into the water. A kid on a skateboard stopped on the lip of the culvert opposite them. He seemed lost in thought, but finding whatever he was looking for, he shot down the side into the water. It looked dangerous. The current was fast, but the water was, as usual, shallow in this part of the River. Black didn't understand why the kid was doing it, but guessed the danger was the thrill. The water curved in a spray on either side as the kid came up the other lip, almost to where they sat, before sliding back again.

Black lit another Marlboro and passed one to Bomboy. They sat smoking silently, brows furrowed in thought. Unbidden, images of Black's mother stole upon him. Iggy was right; this was one ghost he definitely attended. He liked it, he thought. No point denying it. No, not liked, savored, and the taste in his mouth was regret like the mud cakes he made playing alone in the backyard of their house on Fourth and Soto. Mud cakes a ten-year-old boy shouldn't have been making. He and his mother had moved here when they lost the house in Pasadena. He was the only biracial kid for blocks and it set him apart. Everyone could tell he wasn't quite one thing or the other, and yet since his father wasn't around no one could tell what he might be. Kids were cruel and didn't cut him any breaks. And his mother, yelling at him, calling him her sin, her mud in the mouth from God. And so he had eaten those mud cakes. Tasted every morsel, every grain of their shame, hoarded every bite in his mouth until the saliva dissolved it all, but yet his body held on to that memory.

But still he felt the need to punish himself more. Blaming himself for the disappearing woman that was his mother. Dying of something they wouldn't have a name for until much later, but not dying gracefully. Instead filling the house with hate, each corner pulling in the acridity and holding it in the spiderwebs. His mother was intent on re-membering this hate, or at least on making sure Black would remember this hate, so she passed it on. First by changing his name to Black, to the emptiness of this inter-nal night she felt. Then she added to it with every look, with every late-night cry or moan, with every stench of death, decay and bodily failure, with every hateful word that she uttered, until even her hacking breath, as it suf-fered on, became a curse to fill even the sunniest East LA afternoon with the despair of night.

"You know, m'ijo," she used to say, always said, from when he was eight. "You are my punishment from God. Do you know why? Because I got pregnant before I mar-ried your father. Against my family's wishes, I dated that moreno. And now I have to live with you. You are my liv-ing sin, m'ijo. Pray, pray that God forgives you."

"But I didn't do anything!"

"Neither did Judas, really. But still he hanged himself. Now pray to our Lady, mira, pray for forgiveness. *Hail Mary, full of grace, the lord is with you . . .*"

He was fifteen when his mother died, and he left home to escape going into the foster care system. That memory was always at the edge of his mind, like a shadow that he would come upon. Things had been clearer then, he liked to think, but he knew they weren't. He was just younger, younger and like a newly hatched gull, unaware of the sea's hunger. But still, he remembered it as the only glorious time in his life: five years of riding freight trains across the country, leaving nothing behind except the occasional painting on the side of a boxcar, looking forward to the sharpness of a new town's smell and the chance to work and fill his belly before the next train. From fifteen until he was twenty that had been his life. Until he came back to Los Angeles that night, and a little drunk, he had gone for a walk by the River and ended up under the bridge. That night put an end to his wandering, but it also brought him to Iggy and The Ugly Store. He cleared his throat. He knew Iggy said he was still searching, she said that, but he felt like he had stopped searching the day he got off that train.

Black shuddered at the memories. He had to exorcize this ghost, he knew that, otherwise he would never find out who or what he was. Maybe if he gave it a clearer form? But deep down, he knew the form was tied to him, his mother, the Virgin and Sweet Girl. A loud bang from somewhere across the river brought him back to the present. He scanned the path opposite looking for what had caused the sound, but saw nothing.

"Say, Bomboy, you know that project I'm working on?" he asked, turning to Bomboy.

"The one that makes you look like a Japanese horror movie?"

"Yes," Black said. The joke sucked the first time. But that was Bomboy. "That one."

"What about it?"

"Well, I need a canvas and I think the side of your warehouse would be perfect."

"The whole side?"

"Yes."

"But it's fifty feet high at least."

"I know."

"I don't know . . ."

"It's not like you own the lease or anything. I'm only asking as a courtesy."

"I know. But I'm here illegally, you know? I don't want to attract attention."

Black pointed to the gutter Bomboy had laid from the warehouse to the lip of the culvert. Blood ran in a steady stream down it into the River.

"If that didn't get you noticed, I don't think one more mural in a city full of them will."

"I suppose."

"Thank you."

"Will you pay me?"

"Yeah, güey, with this." Black held up a fist. Bomboy laughed.

"A fifty-foot-high Virgin. A little obvious even for you, no?" he said.

"That's the thing. When I began to work on the cartoon, she turned into something else. Someone else."

"Who?"

"The perfect woman."

Bomboy shrugged. "You lost me. Isn't that what the Virgin is?"

"No, this woman is different. Something else."

"Well, I am off to work," Bomboy said, standing up and turning back to the warehouse. "Knock yourself out," he added, gesturing to the wall.

Getting stiffly to his feet, Black headed back to his van, which was parked under the bridge at Fourth. God, I'm getting old, he thought. The climb up the crane had taken its toll. He returned pushing an old shopping cart full of paint cans and plastic drums and brushes with his right hand. A ladder rattling under the cart made it hard to steer one-handed. Bomboy watched him with interest.

"See you later," he said, heading back to the abattoir.

Black turned back to the wall. He would need to prep it of course. He sat down in front of it and smoked a couple of cigarettes. No hurry. White, Black thought. He needed to cover the wall with at least two coats of white paint. Only then could he sketch out the figure. He wanted to start as soon as possible because the image was burning a hole in his mind.

Wrapping a tool belt and a length of orange synthetic rope around his waist, he propped a ladder up against the wall and climbed to the last rung. Then he drove a metal pin into the wall, stepped on it and levered up, driving another pin into the flaky concrete. He climbed the wall slowly and once at the top, he rigged up a couple of pulleys and then lowered himself.

Mixing up a batch of paint, he used the complex system of ropes and pulleys to cover the whole wall. He was aware of being watched: the homeless pushing down the river, carts rattling; kids from the school across the culvert; people in cars speeding by on the 4th Street Bridge. But he didn't pause and by the time the sun was low, the wall was white, a fifty-foot-high white canvas. With an excited chuckle, he packed up and wheeled the cart two-handed back to his truck. Behind him, a plane flew in front of the sun, throwing the shadow of its wings across the wall: a dark cross on white.

i

ggy was playing with Jesus.

Black, just entering The Ugly Store, watched with interest as she attempted to attach a clay penis to the anatomically incorrect doll. Jesus looked resigned to the indignity.

The table in front of her held a laptop and a few dolls. A Barbie. A pre-retirement Ken. A G.I. Joe and the more aggressive-looking British Action Man. They were all naked, clay penises hardening in the slow heat, including Barbie. Each doll was lying next to a selection of female clothing. Looking up when he came into the room, Iggy smiled.

"Hey, Black! What's up?"

"Nothing. Still playing with dolls I see."

"I never got to as a child, so this is my time."

"But a penis on Jesus?"

"He had one. And since he was probably black, it should be a big one, no?"

Black shrugged. He peered around the café checking to see if Ray-Ray was in sight. He wanted a drink. No sign of him. He pulled a chair out from the table and sat opposite Iggy, picked up the Barbie and tested the penis with the tip of his finger. It was hard. Like him. He shifted in the chair, trying to ease the pressure.

"You like?" Iggy asked.

"Just what every child needs. A transsexual Barbie," he said.

"Here, help me dress her."

Black picked up a small sequined miniskirt between clumsy fingers. It didn't look like it would fit. Not with the penis anyway. Putting the skirt down, he picked up a pair of silver plastic boots. Those would fit. He tugged them on and stood the doll up. Silver boots and a hard penis.

"Mattel will be pleased," he said.

Iggy laughed. While she waited for Jesus' penis to dry, she took the Barbie from him and dressed it, along with the other dolls. Lining them up she laughed out loud.

"Santa Monica Boulevard, here we come," she said.

Black smiled. The smile became a full-bodied laugh as she dressed the now hard-penis Jesus in a purple miniskirt, a black tank top and red knee-length boots.

"Gives *Jesus Christ Superstar* a new spin," he said, between guffaws. "Playing with Jesus dolls seems dangerous," Black continued, looking around as though expecting a thunderbolt. Iggy laughed. Collecting herself, she called:

"Hey, Ray-Ray, two chais over here."

"Coming up."

"So, Black," she said, turning back to Black. "What's wrong?"

"How do you mean?"

"You seem distracted. What's up?"

"Nothing," he said. "Actually, that's not true. I just began working on a new mural."

She nodded. She knew only too well how he got when he was working, or about to begin a new project. She could sense it, read the signs: the return to the mural in the café; the disappearance of her dress; the odd moments earlier when she'd passed him in the hallway, moments too small to mention, but in which she could have sworn he was wearing makeup. Iggy had felt a strong pull to Black when he first arrived: a silly, blushing schoolgirl kind of attraction. It had persisted for years, then died down to a dull glow, but at moments like this, when he was in flight as an artist, she felt the familiar stirrings. However, sixteen years of living under the same roof had brought it home to her that they were better as friends. She couldn't handle his mood swings—elated one moment, euphoric even, then angry and suicidal the next. Talking about going over the side of a bridge. Of course he never did, and even that chain lost its yank after a while.

He had come home one rainy night, bleeding from a cut to his face, babbling about the dogs. He claimed he couldn't remember much about what led to him carving up his face, but said it had been to stop himself from going over the bridge that night. She never totally understood him, he was by far the most complicated man she had known. It would be clearer if she could read him, but he always resisted. Said the idea of needles was too scary. Still, maybe it was time to try again.

"How's it going?" she asked, meaning the mural.

"Really well. Actually, that's kind of premature since I've only just prepped the wall today. But this one is different, Iggy."

"Yeah?"

"Yeah. It's a woman."

"Almost all of your figurative paintings are women."

"Really? Well, this time it's different. The image just hit me."

"Really? I thought you'd been working up to this painting?"

"Started that way, as the Virgin, as Mary. But now, well, this is different."

"It just came to you?"

"Whole. Not in parts that I had to put together like a jigsaw puzzle, but whole. That's the first time. She is great."

"She?" Iggy couldn't keep the jealous tone out of her voice, but Black was oblivious to it. "Does she have a name?"

"Fatima."

"That's the first time you've named a painting."

"Yeah? I was thinking of my mother."

"I thought her name was María."

"Yes. But I was thinking about the way you say I attend to my ghosts and I thought if I confronted this one, I could finally move on, you know?"

"So the mural is of María?"

"No. It's about release from María, about something inside me, I don't know what."

"I know I've said this before, but your mother messed you up bad, you know that?"

Black nodded.

"I know, I know." He paused, then continued. "On the one hand I couldn't wait for her to die, and yet on the other, I dreaded the moment that was coming."

"I'm sorry."

He shrugged.

"It's funny. My father died before I really knew him. I mean, I have memories of him, but I can't be sure they aren't things that I made up. So much of who I am, could be, is tied up in the ghosts of my parents. It seems like I turned a corner one day and ended up in an alternate life, an alternate city, and you're right, I have to do something to find my way back."

Iggy held his hand, squeezed it, then ran her palm tenderly down the side of his face.

"Well, it sounds to me, Black, like you're lost in the forest and need a trail of bread crumbs," she said.

"What do you suggest?"

She made a buzzing noise while running her finger over the back of his hand. He'd never noticed them before, but he saw that her fingers looked more like a man's than his did.

"A reading?" she said.

"A tattoo?"

"Yes."

"No way," he said.

"Are you sure?"

He nodded.

"Come on, Black. You've seen me work."

"That's right, you crazy white witch. I have seen, and it looks painful."

"So what's a little pain between friends?"

"No."

"I'll use the henna. No pain."

"No."

"Fine, Mr. No. You seem in such a negative mood for someone working on a new painting."

He laughed.

"No."

"Sounds better with a laugh," she said, relenting. "But a girl never likes to hear no. Well, then can I share an idea with you?"

He nodded.

"Promise to be positive?" she said, reaching for his Marlboro, wanting to distract him.

He nodded again.

Just then Ray-Ray set two big steaming mugs of chai before them, and Black asked: "How's it going, Ray-Ray?"

"I feel old, 'like a fly with one wing,'" Ray-Ray said, with a shrug. Smiling at Iggy, he turned and returned to the bar. When he was gone, Black said:

"Why does he keep doing that?"

"What?"

"Quoting from *Farewell, My Lovely*?"

"Raymond Chandler was his mother's favorite writer."

Black scratched his nose. It didn't explain anything.

"But *why* does he do it?"

"I don't know. Because he's Ray-Ray."

"Tells me nothing," Black mumbled under his breath.

"What was that?"

"Nothing."

"Aren't you going to ask me about my idea?"

"I was just going to. Jesus!"

She laughed.

"So what is your idea?" Black said with mock seriousness.

"Live music."

"Where? Here?"

"Yeah, it would be a good way to keep things going here at night."

"This place keeps going till nearly midnight every night as it is. What you need are stronger sleeping pills."

"I know," she said. "But I want it to go all night."

"I don't know, Iggy."

"I've already spoken to a few people, bards, you know. Anyway, this guy I saw in Leimert Park the other evening and really liked, said he and his band would do a late gig here for gate takings only. And tips."

"Who?"

"Damian Thrace."

Black knew Damian and loved his band: Rakim on sax and flute, Taylor Ryan on bass, Raul on piano, Jo-Jo on drums and Walter Henry on percussion. The idea sounded good but he wasn't sure if people around here would pay to come and see jazz, and late. Most of them began work at four a.m., and he said so.

"Not everyone around here is an illegal and has to work at ungodly hours. Have some faith in your community."

He just shrugged. Iggy studied him for a minute, marveling at his ability to be so self-involved. Part of her wanted to slap him, the other part wanted to help him, be near him, part of him. They were quiet for a while until she spoke.

"Remember my goodoo dolls? I told you about them," she said, leaning forward, seeking common ground.

He shook his head.

"Men," she muttered. "I was working on the catalog copy earlier. Read it over, let me know what you think," she continued, pushing the laptop across to him. He popped the lid and waited for it to boot up. It was on standby and so didn't take long at all. He read quickly.

The Original Goodoo®™ Doll: directions for use. For good luck hang your goodoo over a doorway or place on your desk or table to bring you good luck all day and ward off any evil spirits. Write your wish on a piece of paper. Fold or roll the paper and using a string attach the wish to the goodoo's arm. Tie the wish to the goodoo's left arm for attraction wishes (love, peace, money, happy home, etc.), tie the wish to the goodoo's right arm to release or let go (past loves, old resentments, etc.). Bury the goodoo doll. The black eyes of the goodoo guard against evil spirits. If your goodoo has different colored eyes, you are in luck! Your goodoo has a unique and special gift! One blue eye—brings clarity and intuition. One yellow eye—brings happiness and laughter. One red eye—brings love and beauty. Two nonblack eyes—Expect the unexpected!

The Original Shithead®™ Doll: directions for use. This doll has only one function. Its head is made of compacted manure and its body of clay. It comes in an attractive coffin-shaped presentation box. Send it to a hated boss, a rival or a lover that has jilted you. Set on fire.

Goodoos®™ are made from all natural ingredients and will not harm the earth. After 3 to 6 months the goodoo power will wane.

Goodoo®™ types: Long Dong Goodoo (for virility and potency, this goodoo has a substantial third leg), Royal Goodoo, Original Goodoo, Love Goodoo, Blank Faced Goodoo (master goodoo), among several others.

He snapped the lid of the laptop closed and laughed. The sound was unfettered, his first moment of release that day. It startled him. Iggy smiled in relief.

"You like?"

"I love it. The shithead doll's my kind of doll."

"Yeah? I can't get it off the ground, though. I'm broke."

"Do they work?"

"Of course they work. What kind of question is that?" He shrugged.

"I'm sure you'll find a way," he said.

She looked at him quizzically, collecting foam from the surface of the chai with a finger. Transferring the foam to her mouth, she sucked on her finger for a while.

"You know, Black, sometimes I can't read you," she said.

"Good," he said.

"Hey," Ray-Ray called across, "hey, I have a business idea too."

Iggy shook her head. Privacy was impossible in this place, she thought.

"Yeah, I want to set up a web business called dwarves-for-hire or rent-a-dwarf or something," Ray-Ray continued.

"Shut up, Ray-Ray!" Black yelled. "We're talking here. Jesus, fucking cabrón."

"What? Dwarves are people too!"

"Shut up, Ray-Ray!" Iggy snapped. She looked away and then glanced back at Black, who was playing with the transvestite Jesus.

"I don't mean to get into your business," she said to him, "but have you figured out the deal with Gabriel?"

"I don't want to talk about it."

"That's such bullshit, Black," Iggy said. "You can ignore it, but it won't be wished away."

"What won't?"

"This thing that you are."

"Which is what exactly?"

She shrugged again.

"This thing that I am," Black said, rolling each word around in his mouth as though it were the pit of a succulent cherry he was reluctant to let go of in case he missed a shred of sweet flesh. And the way he let each word roll, Iggy expected him to come back with sarcastic wit. But he didn't. He asked her: "When were you married, Iggy?"

"Married?"

"Yes."

"I was almost married. Look, Black, what is this? A pathetic way to divert the conversation?"

"No, I want to know. What do you mean, almost? What happened?"

"All this time you've known me and now you ask. Why?"

He shook his head, not wanting to say, "Because I wear your wedding dress sometimes," saying instead, "I wasn't curious before."

"My fiancé, Raul, he . . . left me at the altar."

Black stared at her. From the tremolo in her voice he could tell this was hard for her and part of him wanted to comfort her. Hold her and tell her it would all be fine. But he wanted to know. It seemed important since he was wearing her wedding dress now, even if she didn't know. But as he had been thinking, the pregnant pause, the silence between them, had grown heavier. He knew she wanted something from him, some prompt, but he wasn't sure what.

"I'm sorry to hear that, Iggy," he offered, trying to sound like the doctors on daytime soaps.

"I don't want your pity." But she didn't sound angry, just matter-of-fact. That bothered him, always had, the way she could say something difficult without rancor, but just because it needed to be said. The truth was, he didn't pity her, he was more curious than anything, and he said so. She smiled. This she could deal with.

"It's alright," she said. "God, men are such fuckheads anyway." And there was humor in her tone.

He lit a cigarette, took a drag and passed it to her. As she took a drag, he asked: "How old are you, Iggy?" He figured since she was talking, he might as well ask all the questions he'd always wanted to. When he first arrived at The Ugly Store, he'd been attracted to her, and he had declared his love for her. Black was drawn to overly dramatic gestures, and the first time he declared his love for her was by building the spaceship and offering it to her as a gift. Wisely she had declined, saying:

"Seems this is too much a part of your soul. I think this spaceship is for you. Anyway, I'm too old for you."

The second time he had been drunk, and from a table-top in the store's café he proposed to her. Both times she'd deflected him, saying she was too old for him. Now he wondered what might have happened if he'd persisted. Would he still be obsessed with Sweet Girl? He felt Iggy watching him, searching his face as though trying to read the motives behind his questions.

"Old enough to be offended by your asking," she said finally.

He laughed, startling her. There was a contained wild-
ness to her that he loved. Maybe that was it. Perhaps he
had never been in love with her, but in love with the tem-
pest of her. She was a woman in the way he had seen only
in women like Cesaria Evora—earthed lightning. The pull
from Iggy was powerful but frightening, the way the pull
to his mother had been. He knew that in his mother all
that fire had turned to perversion, and Iggy held none of
that, but still, the fear was deep and irrational. Is that why
I'm drawn to Sweet Girl? he thought. Sweet Girl was alive
and powerful, but in that soothing way water can be. It was
all so confusing.

"How old were you when Raul left you?" he asked,
changing tack.

"Twenty-five."

"Is that why you came here?"

"Look, let's not talk about it anymore. Origins aren't
important, what happened, who did what to whom, that
whole postmortem crap. Matter of fact, even the change
away from it isn't important. What's important is commit-
ting to the new life, whatever it is. Some things you just
put in the ground and leave alone."

That phrase about origins not being important echoed in
his brain like a Ping-Pong ball ricocheting off the insides of
his skull. The fact of the matter was that he was obsessed
with origins, and he believed that in his case, origins held
the key to self-discovery. It seemed, though, that those with
a clear sense of the past, of identity, were always so eager to
bury it and move on, to reinvent themselves. What a luxury,
he thought, what a thing, to choose your own obsession, to
choose your own suffering. Him, he was trying to reinvent
an origin to bury so he could finally come into this thing he

wanted to be, and he knew that if he didn't find it soon, it would destroy him, burn him up. But he was unable to find the words to say what he wanted, unsure even what he was feeling or why he felt he needed to fill it with words.

"Iggy," Black said, and Iggy looked at him with eyebrows raised, but he shook his head. They sat there in a comfortable silence until Ray-Ray turned the frother back on and Black stirred.

"Want me to lock up?" Ray-Ray called from across the room.

"No, I got it," Iggy said.

"Can I get a salary advance?" he asked.

"Why? Are you going to buy more drugs? That shit, what's it called? Wet? I don't want the karma, Ray-Ray."

"How you goin' ask a grown-ass man how he's gonna spend his money?"

"Ray-Ray! Those drugs are going to kill you."

"How do you know? Did you do a reading for him?" Black asked.

"I don't need a reading to tell, Black. Look at him."

"It's his choice."

"You're right," she said. "Anyway, perhaps death will be a welcome release for him."

"Should we talk about this here? He's just across the room, he might hear."

"I've told him to his face already," Iggy said.

"Just now?"

"No. Calmly, before. It's the cold truth."

"Do you tell all your clients that kind of cold truth?"

"He's not a client, he's my friend."

"Damn, you're cold," Black said.

Ray-Ray had been addicted to some kind of drug or the other since he was about ten. Black knew he used to huff gas, then urinal cakes, and last time he heard, Ray-Ray had been doing crank. It wasn't that Black approved, but he didn't think it was his place to lecture Ray-Ray.

"Iggy?" Black said. Iggy relented.

"Okay. Take a hundred from the register," she said. "A *hundred*, Ray-Ray," she added as the machine pinged open.

When Ray-Ray left, they smoked some more Marlboros in the gathering gloom of the store, not looking at each other. Now that the espresso machine had fallen silent, now that the store was dark and full of the creaking of wood and metal relaxing, the sounds of the faithful just outside filtered in. Their shadows filled the windows and the sound of prayer was a low but steady hum, broken only by the occasional scream as the Holy Spirit anointed someone. There was an odd comfort to it, and they both hid in it. Finally, Iggy turned to Black.

"Those Virgin sightings are something, aren't they?" she asked.

"There's been more than one?"

"Yep. She's been appearing all over town. Seems strange to me," she said.

"Yeah?" He didn't sound interested. "You'd think people would care more about the fires."

"I suppose," she agreed.

"Do you think there's any truth to it?" he asked distractedly. He was sipping on his tea, scanning the street beyond the window, watching the faithful in their vigil.

"Who knows?"

"I have to go," he said, getting up.

It was raining again when he climbed into the space-ship, and a strong wind caused it to sway dangerously. Wrapping himself in the scratchy lace of the wedding dress, he thought:

I'll fix those loose screws in the morning.

turgid.

But not from the usual early morning rush of blood. He sat up and stared at his crotch, wondering if nature meant this as a way to remind early man not to leave the cave without his spear. He stretched, but it only exacerbated his discomfort. Why couldn't he get off? He was sore from his own efforts and the skin was beginning to tear. Shit. What he wouldn't give to be a woman right now.

He skipped his ritual of tea at dawn in the spaceship, choosing to go down to his room and get straight to work mixing up paint for the mural. It was easier to be naked anyway. For the next couple of hours, he wore nothing except a bag of frozen peas tied around his penis with his robe's belt. As he passed the mirror, he thought he looked ridiculous. He pulled off the bag of peas and stared at himself, remembering this from his childhood: standing in front of a mirror bending his penis back between his legs to make what he called a man pussy, the spreading swell of his balls resembling labia. As he did it now, he remembered his marvel at the smoothness. How much it looked like a vagina. If he were still distended by the time he left, he would have to do that. In the meantime, he reattached the bag of peas, flinching at the cold.

Not red.

The color Black was cooking up. A shade, the variation too subtle to be named, perceived only by his discerning eye. The only time he used store-bought paint was to white-wash; all other times, he made his own.

"Like Leonardo," he would tell everyone.

This batch was for the new mural. He'd sketched out a cartoon for it on a ten-foot-wide sheet of rice paper and was considering trying it on a small segment of the river wall before transferring it to Bomboy's warehouse.

Black yawned and stretched. He hadn't slept well. Dreams of Iggy's wedding dress chasing him through a desert kept it fitful and restless. The desert floor was lit-tered with the skeletons of sea horses, and the tiny bones cut his feet. That was when he realized that he was naked in the dream, and that the wedding dress was holding a meat cleaver. He decided to make some coffee, spooning too much into the machine. It would be bitter but it would wake him up. He set it on and returned to work on the paint. Surrounded by the warm smell of percolating cof-fee, the sharpness of turpentine and the gummy sweetness of the dyes, he drew different imaginary studies of Fatima. Unlike his usual murals, this time he knew there would be no layers below Fatima, other than those of her own body. This was freedom.

This was love.

Finishing with the mixture, he left it on the worktable to air. All his paints needed time to air, for the mixture to breathe. Even though he knew it was probably a purely scientific process, he liked to think it was mystical. He showered quickly, wincing as the water and soap stung the raw flesh around his penis, where his efforts at release had abraded the skin. It was still erect, but not as full and hard as when he woke up. Nonetheless, he had to wear a couple pairs of boxers, stuffing his penis back, bending it up to his ass. It was uncomfortable, like he was riding a half cucumber, though he thought half a cucumber was a slight exaggeration. Dressed, finally, he grabbed his keys, closed the door and headed downstairs. He wanted to go to Ravi's. Pick up some more dye. There was almost no traffic, which in LA was spooky, but it did mean that he made good time to Ravi's. He parked right under the pink and orange sign that said simply: RAVI'S.

The smell of burning frankincense greeted him as he stepped into the store. It was small, and shelves running along the walls and in the middle of the floor cramped it even further. It seemed like the store sold everything. There were jars of pickles and chutneys made of every fruit and vegetable from innocent cucumber to lush mango, from mild to hot. Tins of beans, sardines and tomatoes hassled loose packets of curry, turmeric and chilies in every shade of green, red and yellow. Manioc roots and potatoes lounged next to onions and coconuts wearing brown husky shells in cardboard boxes on the floor beneath the shelves. There were magazines displaying women whose veils covered more than their scanty dresses did. Newspapers in scripts that curved away in mystery like road signs to nirvana, videotapes of Bollywood films, music tapes, Korans, malas and other prayer beads scattered through the shop. Next to the till and the

statue of Ganesh, in an open cardboard crate, fresh naan
breathed.

As he searched for the kegs of pigment and powdered
dye, he kept shaking one leg, like a dog, to ease the pressure in his pants. He wasn't sure what set off his erection
again, the smell of incense or the seductive eyes of the
women on the Bollywood video covers. Shit, he thought,
how do drag queens cope?

He bought an ounce of powdered saffron for twenty
dollars, and some pigments in blue, ochre, green and a
color that looked like amber, listening while Ravi warned
him against putting too much water into the mix. It was
the same every time. At least since the time that Ravi, confusing him for Indian, asked: "Where are you from? I'm
from Kerala."

"I'm not Indian, man," Black said. "At least not your
kind of Indian."

He got the feeling Ravi didn't believe him. He figured
the constant formality was his way of letting Black know.

"Just a pinch, no more—otherwise it'll be unusable,
yaar?"

"Sure." God, my dick hurts, Black thought.

"And for every cup of water, you need about one spoon
of gum arabic or a cup of egg whites, although milk and
honey will work too, yaar?"

"Sure," Black said, thinking, Am I mixing paint or making tea? God, he wanted to whip out his dick and beat Ravi
to death. Maybe then I'll get off, he thought, as he left,
the frustration like grit in his eye. He rubbed at it, the
memory of the man masturbating in the bathroom returning. Back at Bomboy's warehouse Black mixed up a
solution in a plastic drum at the base of the wall, the black

paint for the skeleton. He dipped a metal pail into the drum, half filling it.

On the floor, at the base of the wall, spread out like a picnic blanket, was the new cartoon of Fatima. Black lit a cigarette and sat there on the ground, metal pail beside him, staring alternately at the wall and then the cartoon. When it seemed like he had turned to stone, like he would never move again, he stubbed out the cigarette resolutely, grabbed the pail with his left hand and with his right swung himself up onto the wall.

He hung on the vast white expanse of wall like a bug on a windscreen, hands moving fast, like a blur. One holding, one painting, alternating. Bomboy came out to watch him, blood dripping from the cleaver he held. Across the river, at the school, teachers and students pressed their faces against the chain-link fence, entranced by the spectacle.

A fifty-foot-high skeleton in black emerged in a very short time. Black rappelled down from the wall every so often to fill up the metal pail from the drum. Finally he was done. He stood back from the wall and lit another cigarette.

Though the skeleton was huge, it was delicate. In the gathering dusk, it seemed almost frail. Like the giant Brontosaurus skeleton in the Natural History Museum on Exposition. Like a sneeze could knock it all over. Black smiled happily, gathered his tools together and headed back for his van. It was parked on the lip of the bridge.

fifteen

There was an altar.

Black could see it from the bridge. It wasn't an altar in the grand sense. It wouldn't inspire the slaughter of a bull to Mithras, or the ripping out of young virgins' hearts. It wouldn't even make it in the side chapel of a Catholic church. Nor was it a cairn, that purposeful collection of stones the faithful leave on mountains. This altar was ordinary and commonplace.

Black was curious. He had never seen an altar outside a church in East LA. Sure, there were bathtub Mary's in people's backyards, with the white and blue plaster Virgin garlanded in garish Christmas lights, and even the odd cluster of candles and flowers at scenes of shootings or car accidents, but never this deliberate concentration for its own sake. This was new to him. He decided to take a closer look.

As he made his way down to where the bridge met the road, he wondered if the altar marked one of the Virgin sightings. It certainly fit the pattern that Iggy explained to him. Maybe there was something to the rumors, though he couldn't quite imagine what the Virgin would do in East LA. It wasn't that there weren't enough devout followers; she probably had her largest constituency in Los Angeles right here. It was just that every time he tried to visualize her, he saw one of the plaster statues from his Catholic childhood in a church that wore a blue robe marked by poverty and bullet holes from drive-bys. There were fingers and even part of her nose missing where the plaster had been chipped from age and careless handling, leaving the rusting chicken wire frame exposed. That Virgin hadn't inspired rapturous devotion, at least not in him. What he felt for her was a mild compassion, like the vague dismay he felt when he heard that his uncle William, whom he'd never met, had died.

On his ninth birthday he'd received the call: in mass on Sunday. Already tired from two hours of praying at home before church. Two hours of kneeling on sharp pebbles, sackcloth under his nightshirt chafing with an infernal itch that he wasn't allowed to scratch. Two hours of saying *Ave María*'s trying not to count them off as he progressed down the rosary because if he seemed too pleased that it was coming to an end, his mother would add an extra chaplet. Calling, calling, calling: but still no Virgin and no sign of an angel, just a fly buzzing annoyingly around his head, resting on his forehead to drink from his beads of sweat. Two hours of having hot wax from the fast melting candles dripped onto his skin, his arms, stomach and sometimes even his penis. Acts of contrition, his mother explained gently.

He was tired from the sermon that had been going for nearly as long as his morning torture, it seemed; tired of this charismatic movement and the small fiery-eyed priest who was pounding on the pulpit, screaming, "To the Blood of Jesus! The Power of God! The Savior of the Heart!"; this priest calling for a miracle, for the "Holy Ghost to rain down Fire!; to show the unbelievers!; to rout Baal from the hearts of the congregation in Jesus' Name!"

At that exact moment, as the priest was thundering from the altar, clear as a bell, Black heard the Virgin call to him. Not just any Virgin though. Not the Fatima Virgin, or the Lourdes Virgin, but this white-faced, red-lipped crumbling plaster Virgin of indeterminate pedigree. A general Virgin, all Virgins as it were, for the price of one.

She asked him to free her. Demanded. Ordered. Compelled. He didn't believe it at first, thinking his mother's dream to see the Virgin was making him see a live one in a plaster statute. But the voice was real enough, as was his plan to free her.

His mother was on her knees, eyes closed, pounding out the act of contrition on her chest, oblivious to the world when he snuck away. Stopping in front of the statue, Black lifted one of the votive candles and placed it behind her, by the old parchment dry robes she wore and snuck back to his place next to his mother. The flame caught just as the priest was yelling at Jesus to come to his aid and show the congregation a sign, "to come like Yahweh to Elijah," in a voice all fire.

So.

She became the Virgin of Flames.

Perhaps it had been a miracle.

Black turned off the road and doubled back under the bridge. The area was mostly full of warehouses and abandoned train tracks, bounded on one side by the river. He walked to the water and stood on the concrete lip of the culvert. Built in the thirties by the U.S. Army Corps of Engineers to control the floods, the river fought its concrete prison, changing course every few decades. Even now, looking down, he noted the slight curve and sway in the culvert wall, as though the river were an overfed python turning sluggishly to digest its prey. From above, it looked like one straight concrete line, but up close, it was possible to see the slight variations. This River was alive, this River was here before anyone knew this was a River, before anyone saw it and said, River. And its personality shaped this city. *Was* this city.

Black turned his attention back to the altar. The front yard of the disused factory was haunted by dust and the acrid smell of piss. Black stood by the gate, which was listing on its side, hesitant. He approached the rusting metal drum that was the center of the altar. On the top, in the dust that sheathed it, was the clear imprint of two feet, and he wondered if the Virgin left footprints. Someone had spray painted the side of the rusting metal drum: *Ave María*. The drum was attended by a couple of candles in tall glass sheaths wearing images of the Virgin and Jesus of the Sacred Heart. They had burned down to a puddle. A bouquet of flowers was wilting in the heat.

Pulling up a small wooden crate, he sat down in front of the altar. He didn't know why, or what he was doing. He just sat. It was hot out, even in the gathering dusk. He began sweating. A slight unease settled over him. But he sat. And on, and on. And then he realized he had been here before. Years before. There wasn't an altar then, but he had been here. The memory that came flooding back was so vivid, so real.

"What the fuck!?"

Black spun round straight into the mouth of a gun barrel. There were many ways to describe the moment. He would find all of them later. Catalog them, classify them, analyze them, name them. Terror, fear, life flashing before his eyes, certainty, tunnel vision: all of these and more. But right then, all he could think was how cold the metal felt on his nose as he turned into it. How cold on such a hot day. He knew then that death wasn't just a metaphor. And there was another thought. How much he had loved bananas as a boy. Part of him studied the face of his aggressor, searching perhaps for any sign of leniency, of compassion. There was none. Then the two parts came back together with the suction of a vacuum cleaner and suddenly he felt himself rushing down a dark tunnel. Then he was back by the altar, feeling the persistent, insistent pressure of the gun barrel.

"Please," he said. It was barely a sound.

The gun was held by an overweight young man with a shaved head. From the baggy shirt over a white T-shirt, baggy jeans, Timberland boots and the tattoos on his arms and the bandana around his neck, Black guessed he was a gangbanger. His eyes were obscured by dark glasses.

"Shut the fuck up, puto!" Bandana said.

That he hadn't been shot yet was a good sign, a reassuring one. Black knew that if the young man meant to kill him, he would be dead already. And yet in many ways this situation was just as dangerous. He had clearly stumbled into some gang territory or on to some drug site, but if the worry were about business, he would have been executed already. This was more a pissing contest, or as Iggy would say: "Willy waving." He had to be careful, though.

"Please," he said, tone as quiet as possible. "I'm sorry."

"Don't nobody care about that, cuño," Bandana said, slapping Black across the face with the flat of the gun barrel. Black grunted as he felt the metal cut his lip.

"Take off your belt," Bandana said.

Black's trousers, liberated from their belt, fell to the ground. Bandana smiled.

"Take out your dick," he said.

Black hesitated. Bandana picked up the discarded belt and whipped Black across the face, the heavy buckle drawing blood.

"Your dick, puto, now!"

Black pulled his dick through the gap in his Y-fronts. He had a partial erection.

"Please," he said.

Bandana kicked him and he fell over, curling up into a fetal position, coughing.

"Get up."

Black struggled to his knees. He was looking straight at the young man, but the only detail that stood out vividly was the bandana. He started to sob as Bandana loosened his belt and pulled his fully erect dick out. He waved Black closer with the gun barrel. Still on his knees, Black shuffled over.

"Closer," Bandana said.

Black shuffled forward.

"Closer."

Black could smell the musk from Bandana's dick.

"You know what to do, cabrón," Bandana said.

When Black opened his mouth to receive Bandana, he heard the priest in his imagination: body of Christ. Amen, he said aloud.

"I knew you was a fag," Bandana said, thrusting into Black's mouth.

Mushrooms, Black thought in spite of himself. It tastes like mushrooms. And also the red ants he would burn with matches as a child, their acrid scent furring the roof of his mouth like guilt. And he wanted to gag, and he wanted more. Like the wood of the cross his mother would force into his mouth to make him have visions, Black could feel Bandana hardening in his mouth. It felt like home, and he lost himself until the sting of the gun on his cheek.

"Watch your teeth, mothafucker."

He pulled away. Stared at the wet hardness swaying before him. Bandana smiled.

"You like that, eh?" he said, pushing Black down roughly, onto his back on the concrete floor. A piece of glass from a broken bottle dug into his back and he relaxed into the pain, protecting himself from the stab of Bandana. He didn't feel him going in, just the cool run of tears down his face and the abrasive rub on the inside, a burning, which felt right. He was going to hell anyway. Bandana was sweating over him, pushing, straining with a desperation near tears. Then Black's left hand, with no help from him, began to stroke Bandana's hair. And Bandana was coming in spasms that seemed to shake the very foundations of the bridge. He lay slumped over Black for a few minutes, then pushing the snout of the gun into the ground he pushed off and up. He straightened his clothes. Looking down at Black, who was still naked, he smiled.

"Don't thank me."

And he was gone. In this memory, Black lay in the dark, on the floor for hours. Around his head, a fly buzzed with the insistence of a guardian angel. The angel spoke.

"Relax," he said.

"If any of your limbs should offend, cut if off and throw it away. It is better to enter life crippled . . ." something else said. Something inside him.

"Than to have both hands and feet and be cast into eternal damnation. Matthew," Black said. And he made his way up, to the top of the bridge. Climbing the balustrade that hung over the River, Black hung there for a long time.

"Jump," the thing inside him said.

"Rest," Gabriel said.

"Die," the thing inside him said.

"Live," Gabriel buzzed.

Black swiped at the fly that was Gabriel. He put his hand in his pocket, felt the knife. A limited edition original Spirit of the Navajo knife by the Franklin Mint. He folded the blade out. It was thin and perhaps two inches long; no more. On one side in English was the word: *Freedom*. On the other, in Navajo: *A-zeh-ha-ge-yah*. Which really meant escape, but Black didn't know that.

"Forget," Gabriel said.

But Black tottered on the edge of the bridge, unbalanced. To pull himself back, he pressed the blade hard against his face and felt the blood, like tears run down. The pain pulled him back, gave him back his name.

"I am Black," he said. "I am Black!"

He climbed back over the side of the balustrade, pulling himself with both arms, and stood leaning over the bridge.

"I am Black," he said.

But still he tottered, able to fall over into the void at any moment. Then he felt a soft, but rough, wetness on his palm. He looked down. A black-and-white mongrel was licking his palm, whimpering softly. Black bent to the dog.

Bent and fell back onto the concrete of the bridge, and the dog was licking his face.

"I am Black," he said to the dog.

"But not your heart," Gabriel buzzed.

That buzzing pulled Black back to the present, to Gabriel, as a fly, buzzing around his head. Black shuddered. He had gone for years without having to face the memory of that night. He let out a high-pitched scream that followed him as he stumbled up Cesar Chavez, past the fortress of the County Prison with its arrow slit windows and past Union Station. By the Pueblo on the corner of Alameda he ran into a crowd surrounding a maríachi troupe. The crowd was large and covered the sidewalk, spilling into the street. He hated maríachi music. Pushing through the crowd, his eye caught a young girl standing off to the edge of the crowd. There was nothing special about her except her eyes, which burned like two coals, and the space her aura made in the crowd around her. He stopped to stare at her, suddenly oblivious of the crowd and the people jostling him. Something made him want to save her. No, he wanted her to save him. He opened his mouth, but nothing came out.

She stared straight back at him.

n

o crow dies alone.

That's what Gabriel told Black when he asked him why he wouldn't leave him alone.

"The others don't help. They just gather to watch. To sing it along the dark path."

Black was sitting on the rail overlooking the 101 North. Gabriel could tell Black wanted to jump, and he couldn't care less, but this was his job: to make a perfunctory attempt at saving humanity from itself. He was perched on the rail next to Black, wearing his pigeon disguise. Anyway, deep down Gabriel knew Black wouldn't jump. If he was going to, he would have by now. All these years of carrying the darkness like a perverted torch. All these years and still searching. He sighed, thinking humans always did things the hard way.

"Some comfort," Black said. The metal rail was cold and hard against his still turgid dick. Every time he shifted, he winced because he pinched his balls.

"What do you want from me? I'm a fucking pigeon."

"That's another thing. Why do you appear as a pigeon to me?"

"Only sometimes, though, right? I mean that's the caveat. Only sometimes."

"Still, it's doubtful Mohammed or Mary would have taken you so seriously if you'd appeared to them as a pigeon."

Gabriel shrugged. At least Black thought he shrugged, but he couldn't be sure. He was a pigeon.

"To each his own hallucination," he said.

"Oh, watch it there, buddy! That's blasphemy."

Gabriel cooed. Black lit a cigarette. The night sky was a navy blue sheet with the freeway for a seam.

"Do you want to see what I showed the old prophets?" Gabriel asked, after a while.

Black shrugged.

"Sure."

"Follow me then," Gabriel said, his words nearly lost in the flutter of wings. In the distance, the moon trembled on the lip of the Hollywood sign.

angels Walk.

Black and Gabriel on a quest unfolding like a rosary. And these were the stops. The beads unfolding in sweat-grained piety. These were the stops, not the steps, the careful measure of each, the small steps in which it was done and undone, the subtle movements that made and unmade a life, like the constant seismic tremors of this land, this city. No, these were the major stops; the steps were a different measure. Each stop was a mystery: The Ronald Reagan Building. Biddy Mason Park. Bradbury Building. Victor Clothing Company. Million Dollar Theatre. Grand Central Market. Angels Flight. Hotel Inter-Continental, Los Angeles. Museum of Contemporary Art. Watercourt at California Plaza. Wells Fargo Center. Wells Fargo History Museum. ARCO Center. Ketchum YMCA. Westin Bonaventure Hotel. Bunker Hill Steps. Library Tower. One Bunker Hill. The Gas Company Tower. Regal Biltmore Hotel. Pershing Square. Jewelry District. Oviatt Building. Pacific Center. Los Angeles Public Library and

Maguire Gardens. Macy's Plaza. Fine Arts Building. Home
Savings of America Tower. Seventh Street Metro Center.
Citicorp Plaza. Seventh Market Place. Visitor Information
Center. Union Station/Gateway Transit Center. Olvera
Street. All the stops, when connected, traced the outline of
a plump bird on a branch. A dove? Or vermin? Say, a pi-
geon?

Stop.

The Joyful Mysteries.

Step. In the Alley on Santee, plump Armenian matrons
sorted through clothes they only dreamed about fitting
into. Pausing in a cosmetics store, they passed around a
small mirror, and tubes of lipstick they would not buy.
Tired, they went to the Starbucks and sucked on ice-cold
caramel frappuccinos. Step. A dog. Alone. Bit down on a
flea. Shook itself. Trotted off. Nothing more. Step. A man
with no teeth called notes through gummy lips on an
imaginary bass that his fingers plucked in the air, forgotten
by the world, forgotten and forgetting everyone and everything but the music and the full-bellied curvaceous belle
he had maybe plucked once. Step. A girl outside the public
library on Fifth, in the garden of water and concrete, bent
over a book spread like an eagle's span, discovered wonder.
Step. That trout was plentiful in streams an hour from the
city. Step. That sometimes the clouds were near enough to
touch. Step. The simple pleasure of a hummingbird flying
round and round the light on a porch. Step. The way an
old Victorian house in green wood leaned against a fence
barely holding back a strip mall. And the trees on this
street, thick and shady, said that once somebody had loved
this place, paid attention, and in that moment, even here,
there was hope for the eternal. Step. A Winchells donut

shop where women sat and nursed cups of coffee and where men, pretending they were long lost friends or family, bought the fourteen-doughnut Winchell's dozen and picked up these prostitutes. Sweets for my sweet. Sugar for my honey. Step. Lavender jacaranda blossoms like mauve gossamer falling. Step. And step, the boundless joy of a cold Coca-Cola on a hot day, or the freedom of children playing in a park, and all of it, every bit, weaving into a tapestry of promise.

Stop.

The Luminous Mysteries.

Step. That the light here was rumored to be the same light everywhere: a Hanoi sunset seen from the prow of a canoe casting fishing nets into a vast ocean; sunrise over a stubbly hill in eastern Nigeria and rays that shredded the clouds in a crown of fire; the mid-afternoon Coppertone on an old wall bringing back a rare yet sunny New England autumn; harsh noon sunlight on Broadway's traffic melting tarmac to New York licorice, and a lazy Santa Monica evening where a day weary sun sighed into an ocean that could be off the coast of Kenya. Step. That men came here with all the greed for gold but stayed for the honey of rich earth, oranges and sun. Step. That brilliant and hungry fires lit up night skies. Step. That the taste of fruit here was the taste you had always imagined. Step. That architecture here was no more than child's play and time was the sea washing it away. Step. The earnestness of the Staples Center's searchlights raking the endless night for a Clippers victory. Step. The twin searchlights of the Spearmint Rhino Gentlemen's Club pulling men off the 10 like sirens singing ancient ships to wreck. Step. That the endless stretches of freeways were new rivers carrying this city's angst out to sea, their names echoing with the vibrational power of old Hebrew: 405 North, 110 South, 101 North, 405 South, 110 North, 5 South, 5 North, 60 East, 710 South, 60 West, 605 West, 710 North, 605 East; like the longitude and latitude of a treasure map, and that Angelenos scurried around looking for their dream of themselves. Step. And another step, all light, all miasma, all luminescent freeway signage paint, no more than car headlights cutting faintly through an early morning mist wrapping the spires of downtown in mystery like Avalon.

Stop.

The Sorrowful Mysteries.

Step. A meat-faced policeman fished deep inside a prostitute for the drugs they both knew were not there. And she, face like the old stone wall behind her, dirty, tired and adorned with graffiti-like makeup, blew smoke into the night. Blew shame. Step. A stain on the sidewalk on Main, under a tree, by the closed metal shutters of another failed mercantile dream. This stain was like any other here and yet unlike any other. This stain was not gum, or spilt alcohol, or feces spread by a homeless beggar too far gone to the other side of the river to know, to care. This stain was where a nameless Black boy shot a nameless Brown girl even as she smiled at him, even as he closed his eyes in terror and squeezed his fear out in metal. This stain was a medal. Step. A discarded shoe, lying on its side, heel grouting the crack in the sidewalk. Lost perhaps as someone ran for a bus. Or from the police. Or from a mugger. And did he make it? And was it a he because it was a workman's boot? And how much of personality can truly be shaped by the feet? Step. And there was a woman known sometimes as Epiphany Love, sometimes as Sweet Black, who stared at him from behind eyes that had tired of tearing. The crescent scar on her nose was more like a question mark, one that was still forming the question. But it was the casual strength of her hands and the way they hung limp at her sides, yet coiled like mambas. And he knew these hands had wrung more than clothes on a washday. Step. A young man lounged with his compás, smoking weed, laughing loud and grabbing crotch in the swagger that was all the power of the young and yet his eyes said: Please, I just want to go home, please. Step. Mildred, the bard of Union Station, crooned a song of fractured syllables in a language too old to have formed yet, held tender between lips like the cooling of lava on the edge of a lake, bitten off by teeth broken by life, while placing flowers curbside for a dead man, or woman or child that no one wanted to remember. Step. The guard outside the INS building on Los Angeles Street hassled fellow Chicano immigrants waiting in line. They said nothing, looking instead with eyes riddled with questions and questions and the guard's eyes said, We don't go there. We don't. Step. The Mexican woman who owned the bench in front of the Dorothy Chandler Pavilion knew that this land was hers and her mother's before her. She crocheted, a way to grind down the white man's clock, stitching and unstitching a scarf she would never wind around all the land that was hers and her mother's and her mother before that. Step. A man in a pink fluffy bunny suit on a hot Los Angeles afternoon handed out leaflets for the new fried chicken restaurant behind him, a slow-burning cigarette dangling from one pink paw, fed intermittently through the gap in the pink neck to his mouth. Step. Face like old leather, eyes cold and dark as a window in the night, the young Sierra Leonean, not much older than a boy, sat at the bus stop waiting. To go from one job to another. Waiting. For the new life promised here to begin. Waiting. To forget the blood. Waiting. He studiously licked a pencil and underlined his dreams in a torn Jackie Collins novel. Step. This woman, hair falling in lush ringlets of dark, smelling of oil and lost dreams, trod cautiously to the cheaper jewelry stores around Broadway and Seventh. She picked through these streets on heels not meant for the cracked and broken sidewalk. She sucked on mints and wished for a distant sun where her language rang out with the cadence of fire from an affluent house on the Caspian Sea. And even here, she despised the poor. And yet what everyone held in common was a unique poverty. Step. Found here in the trash can by Temple, a woman's severed head. Step. And here, a woman who had never been to prison, but was born Catholic, born guilty, so like a snail, she carried the burden of her penance with her everywhere she went. Night was her biggest fear because then the faces of the children she killed, her children, three of them, before losing her courage, came to her. What a terrible thing; to lose courage in the face of this act. It wasn't their anger she feared, but the fact that each small crying face in her nightmares forgave her. Step. A torn flyer desperately clung to a parking meter on Santa Fe begging for information. Telling the world that the search for the missing María was forty-two days old. Two days longer than Christ's fast in the desert. Step. And step. And step. Each one driving the nail of grief deeper, the rivet of sorrow.

Stop.

The Glorious Mysteries.

Step. Sometimes rain, but not especially. Step. And light

and light and light. Step. Sometimes it was too bright to see. Step. And step. And step. And nothing, or maybe everything.

Stop.

Black, standing on an outcrop of concrete on Bunker Hill, looked down. And Gabriel beside him, like the devil, offered it all. It was evening and a gentle wind was playing through the streets. Below, in bright lights, there it was. The jewel.

El Pueblo de Nuestra Señora La Reina de Los Angeles del Río de Porciúncula.

Soledad.

Para.

IDOLATRY

What is divinity if it can come
Only in silent shadows and in dreams?

—Wallace Stevens

eighteen

Oscillating.

Swathes of light cut by the spaceship on its slim pole high above The Ugly Store swinging in the wind like a lantern on the prow of a ship. Rain threatened in slow-paced drops that were blown lazily into a slant by the wind and felt like cool pebbles against the skin. In these moments of wind and rain, Los Angeles revealed its kinship, he thought. What was otherwise a large garbage pile left to compost in the heat pulled its sleeves back and demonstrated the trick of its becoming; a city constantly digesting its past and recycling itself into something new. The red glow against black storm clouds wasn't the sun being slowly consumed by the heavens, he realized, but the reluctance of the brush fires to give up their gluttony.

It had taken Black a while to walk the distance from Olvera Street where he left Gabriel, to the corner of Mission and The Ugly Store but he only paid little attention to the buildings lining the Cesar Chavez that looked out of place in Los Angeles. Two-, sometimes three-story brick buildings that leaned on rusty metal fire escapes that would have been more at home in New York, and he could understand why this street, built up by migrant Jews from the East in the early twenties, used to be called Brooklyn Street.

He passed Lolita's Bridal, and the clothing store next to it with a four-foot-wide by ten-foot-long sign that said STETSONS in bold white letters that sold everything but Stetsons. The crooked windows of the Zapata Shoe Store, which did sell Stetsons, but in white only, made it look like it was leaning up against STETSONS like a tipsy date. The 99 Cents store further down sold the best ice-cream cones in East LA. On the opposite side of the street was a panaderia displaying cakes in various shapes from generous breasts in pink frosting to masked Zapatista rebels. Next to that, a Pupasena wrapped round the corner and in bright orange graffiti on its wall was the message: *Jesus Saves*. Another tag artist had added, in a bright blue, the phrase, *At Washington Mutual*. Right beside it, before the corner, a KFC hustled the LUCY Laundromat, which pushed up against a check-cashing establishment, which did its best business on Mother's Day, the local euphemism for the Mondays, every fortnight, when the mothers on welfare cashed their checks.

Turning at Soto, he made his way back toward Mission and The Ugly Store. Hanging a left on Mission, he walked past all the auto scrap yards, past the twenty-foot-high statue of a lumberjack looming out of the darkness that reminded him of Paul Bunyan. He soon came up to the old Mission. Once the center of civilized Los Angeles with the Spanish garrison to one side and the Pueblo across the river at Alameda, it was now no more than a glorified tourist attraction that attracted almost no tourists. It had long since lost out to Six Flags fun parks and Universal Studio's theme park. It looked sad, not in the way of a rejected wallflower, but more in the commonplace shame of a community center. A place kept open by a grudging love.

He stared at the statues of long forgotten Mexican generals and the early rancheros, and wondered if their ghosts still haunted the area, caught between the Mission and the grassy roundabout where they stood, hemmed in by traffic.

Suddenly exhausted, Black sat on a bench in the shadow of a statue. Staring at the traffic streaming past, he tried to grab hold of the thought flapping about in his head like a piece of torn cloth caught on a barbed-wire fence. But it was moving too fast. With a grunt he got up.

the slight drizzle was ash.

Black guessed the brush fires outside of Los Angeles were still burning. A homeless woman turned a circle in the middle of the street, face to the sky, open as a child. In one hand she was holding an umbrella. The other was palm up, to catch the fall. Her face was a ghostly white from all the ash she must have wiped across it as though it was precious water, or the blessing of rain. Black stood watching her for a few minutes. Smiling, he got into his van and drove home.

The Ugly Store was dark. Black paused outside. The faithful were still camped there on the sidewalk, waiting for the Virgin to appear. He almost wanted to give her to them. He was fascinated by their devotion. One of them, an old woman in a wheelchair, smiled at him. She had no teeth. He smiled back.

"Why do you wait for a miracle that may be a lie?" he asked her. "This Virgin, if it is the Virgin, may not be able to heal you."

"I didn't come here for the Virgin to heal me," she said. "Besides," she added, "all miracles are lies."

"Then why are you waiting?"

"For my heart to open," she said.

When he turned away from her, she was still laughing. From the corner of his eye he thought he saw Gabriel sitting at one of the tables leaning up against the shop's façade. But it was nothing. Just a shadow. To the left, a small whirlwind picked up some garbage and spun it around. Across the street, the taco stand was doing a brisk business. Black could see Bomboy arguing with the owner, whom he guessed was Pedro. Calling him a mothafucker, no doubt, he thought, trying to read the slogan on Bomboy's shirt in the orange glow of streetlights that made everything seem like a dream. TWO WONGS CAN'T MAKE A WHITE, it said just below the corporate logo.

He opened the door and stepped in, trying not to look at the moa towering above him. Maybe that's why we are such an ignorant species, he thought, because all humans do is turn away from their fear.

Iggy was behind the bar making drinks. The hiss of steamed milk was a familiar and reassuring sound. She looked up as he came in and smiled at him.

"Black," she said, and it held all the comfort he wanted to hear. "Where have you been?"

"Out."

"I'm making tea. Do you want some?"

"Yes," he said, then after a pause, adding, "please."

He walked over to her and slid onto a bar stool.

"What's up?" he asked.

She glanced up at him. Her hair was growing out, about three inches of her natural blonde hair with purple tips.

He hadn't noticed it before, even though it must have been that way for a while. Her different colored eyes searched his face. It was a disconcerting feeling, as though she could read into all his hidden secrets. He thought it might be a good idea to empty his mind, so he focused on deciding which of her eyes he liked best, the purple or the green one. He was wondering why she never dyed her hair green when she said:

"How is Black?"

"Fine," he said, not showing surprise at her use of the third person.

"Talkative as ever."

"I'm tired."

"Strippers wear you out?" she asked, putting a steaming cup of tea in front of him.

"I object to that," he said.

"I notice you don't deny it, though."

"But I still object. Okay, so I did go to Charlie's earlier, but I've been working on Fatima too," he said.

"Oh," Iggy said. "And she didn't mind that you were wearing the musk of another woman?"

"Jeez, Iggy, relax. How do you know I went to Charlie's anyway?"

"Psychic, remember?"

He took a sip of tea. It was too hot.

"Thanks," he said. "For the tea," he added. Sometimes around her, he found himself wanting to be exact, to be precise. On his best behavior even.

"Sure. By the way, have you seen Bomboy?"

"Yeah. He's outside fighting with Pedro."

"He was in here earlier looking for you."

"Thanks," he said, and then as she turned to go he asked: "How did you know about Charlie's, really?"

She smiled. "I was up in the spaceship today," she said.

"Why?" he asked.

"You gave it to me, didn't you? It's mine."

"I know it is," he said. "But you've never really been up before."

"I went to see what all the fuss was about," she said.

He nodded. "You mean with Gabriel?"

"And with the Virgin."

"And?"

"I saw the pinboard with the photos."

"Yeah, I was playing around with the idea of the Virgin for a while. Maybe that's how Fatima came to me," he said, dropping his eyes.

"And Sweet Girl?"

"How do you know her name?"

"It is written under the photos. Black, should I be worried?"

He shivered at her tone. The implication in it was like a snake slithering over stones. He would never harm Sweet Girl. He wouldn't. Iggy was looking at him, eyebrows raised, so he shook his head. She let out her breath.

"I found something else."

"What?"

"My wedding dress."

She sat down next to him and though she was holding her own cup of tea, she blew on his and leaned over to drink from it. He was holding the cup and he tipped it for her. She slurped some onto his hand. It burned but he didn't flinch, glad for the distraction. Iggy put her fingertip to the wet patch and smeared it around.

"And I found the makeup," she said, after what seemed like an eternity. He took a gulp of tea, surprised to find it was still hot enough to burn.

"You did?" he asked, in a voice that sounded like he had a mouthful of pebbles.

"You know, Black, I'm not one to judge. I mean, how can I, right?" she said, indicating The Ugly Store with a sweep of her palm.

"But?"

"I don't know. I mean I don't understand what's up with you, but it seems like you're coming apart at the seams. What is it? Do you want to be a woman?"

He looked into his cup.

"Black?"

"Why would you think that, Iggy?" he asked. "That I would want to be a woman."

"I don't know why you would want it. But you have an obsession with a transvestite or transsexual stripper whose photos are plastered all over your spaceship, then I find my wedding dress and a makeup kit. What am I supposed to think?"

He shrugged.

"How do you know Sweet Girl is transsexual?"

Iggy laughed. Black nodded.

"I'm sorry, I forgot you're psychic."

"No, it's not that. Have you seen the wrists on her? There are things that no amount of hormones can disguise."

"I see," he said. He wanted to laugh, but he was confused. He was partly angry because he felt that she had violated his privacy, and he was also disappointed because he expected that she of all people would understand what he was going through. Would accept him.

"Black," Iggy said, voice soft, the familiar Iggy. "What is going on?"

He shook his head and drank some more tea. Outside the faithful were getting restless, several falling into the ecstasy of tongues as they called out in vain to the Virgin.

"I don't know."

"I'm sorry if I sounded off a moment ago. I was just surprised."

He nodded. "It's okay." Then: "Do you think there is another explanation for it?"

"Well, yes. Perhaps you are just going through a tough time and returning to the familiar safety of your childhood."

"You think so?" He sounded hopeful. Even though he'd considered it himself, it was comforting to hear it echoed back at him.

"Yeah. I mean, how could you forget something like that?"

He wanted to leave, felt the old panic at this particular discomfort rise. But he had pried the lid off the box that first night. Now he had to look inside. He rubbed the plastic pouch with the photo and letter for a pensive moment, then he took it off and put it on the bar top between them like the passkey to some secret government research lab.

"Alright. Black, do you remember when I told you about Raul?"

"Your fiancé? Yes."

"I wasn't being entirely honest with you. I was never engaged to anyone called Raul. Truth is, I've never even dated a person called Raul."

Black was puzzled. "Where are you going with this?"

Iggy sighed.

"I bought that dress about five years ago. I bought it because I realized I was getting old and I was afraid to end up all alone. I bought it and pretended to myself for two whole years that I was getting married. I went on diets, I tried on the dress every night, alone in my office, I planned a whole fucking wedding: seating plans, menus—smoked duck and foie gras, which is weird because I hate duck."

"Why?"

"Too oily, I think."

"Iggy!"

"Sorry. I guess I needed to be needed, you know? At first I told myself, of course you're loveable, of course you are desirable and, goddamn it, even though I am a strong and powerful woman, I wanted, I needed to be desired. To be seen as a woman and not some kind of freak always attending to others. But it was all a lie . . ."

"But you are . . ."

She waved him into silence.

"Shut up and let me talk. It was a lie, at least the way I had done it, it was. It wasn't even a kind of sympathetic magic. It was just foolish desperation. So I put the dress away and went back to living my life. But this time it was easier because I had lived out my desperation, acted it out as it were. Now I know what I want, what I need, and it does include love and desire and companionship, but I am happier. See? I gave the dress to Howie last year to clean and sell it."

"So, is this about paying for the dress?" he asked tentatively.

"Fuck, Black! Even you can't be that stupid. For once pay attention. Jesus! I figured out why I needed that dress and then I didn't need it anymore, so I passed it on. You have to know why you need that dress, Black, so you can either pass it on or keep it, and for you, to know is to remember!"

"The thing is, Iggy, I don't remember," he said, his voice so low she had to lean in to hear him.

"What?"

"I don't remember."

"But you have that thing," Iggy said, pointing to the plastic pouch.

"I don't remember any of it, Iggy. The truth is I knew nothing about any of it until just before my mother died and I found this letter with the photo in it," he said, pulling the letter out.

She picked up the plastic pouch and stared at the photo that was still firmly ensconced in it. She turned it over and read the scrawled inscription: *Little Black Angel*.

"Did your dad write that?"

Black shook his head.

"I don't know, but I know the handwriting doesn't match what's in the letter. And that's supposed to have come from him."

"Your mother?"

"She said she didn't write it."

Iggy played with the letter, spinning it round by flicking on its edges with her finger.

"You can read it," he said finally.

She was as careful as she could be, given her excitement and haste. She unfolded it and read:

Dear Son,

If you receive this letter then it means that I am not coming home. I am sorry also to be blunt but if this war has taught me anything it's taught me not to waste time. You probably won't understand this until later, but it is important regardless. I know that I told you to believe only in the rational, in science. As a scientist it was important for me to give you that, Son, so you wouldn't be held back by superstition, but after what I have seen here in two years, I urge you to find something to believe in that brings you comfort and when you find it to hold on to it with both hands. I won't tell you about the death here, the blood, the endless mud of it and an enemy none of us can see, or the mosquitoes and the heat that covers everything with hopelessness. Instead I will confess one truth and one lie to you.

The truth is that I love you more than you can possibly imagine and the enclosed photo, which I have carried with me as a talisman against harm, is of you at two in a dress. I figured carrying it in my breast pocket near my heart was as good as praying. I want you to have it as I have you in my heart.

The lie is that I only believed in science. In fact, I have always believed in forces other than science. The reason you are wearing a dress is because our family has a curse, an evil spirit that kills all male offspring before they are six. So we have always hidden our sons, dressing them like girls until their seventh birthday. Forgive me for this lie, Son, but know that I did it out of love for you. Grow strong and make our name proud.

Your loving father,

Frank

"Your father was a scientist?" she asked.

Black shrugged. He still didn't feel closer to either of his parents or any real truth about himself. What he did feel was closer to this ambiguity he was becoming; and all of it was tied into dresses and makeup, and it was a lie: he did remember, and he wanted to tell her about the time when he first wore a dress consciously. It was just before his mother died, when he was still taking care of her.

They had only just found out what was wrong with her. It wasn't like they had medical insurance or anything, and since his mother became ill they really only had Frank's army pension. But Frank's best friend in 'Nam, Eric, was a doctor now at the Veteran's Hospital on Wilshire, and Black finally overcame his anger at Eric (he felt that his father's best friend should have come round more, cared more) to go and find him. Eric came round to the house on Soto and took María away, his eyes sad, sadder even when he returned her after running tests.

"You should have called earlier," he said to Black. "If we'd found the tumor in time. These kind of brain tumors are genetic," he explained. "But if we had found it sooner."

"Can't you do *anything*?"

Eric shook his head. "No, son. No. Now it's just a matter of time. The medicine I prescribed for her you can come by and pick up for free at the hospital, but it's mostly just for pain. I'll send a nurse round from time to time."

Black knew the nurse would never come round. This was East LA.

"Did the doctor explain?" Black asked his mother after the doctor left.

"Yes, m'ijo. I am paying for my sins," she mumbled.

"No, I'm paying for your sins," he said, realizing that he might soon have to do everything for her.

But this day he had just fed her, a chore he hated because she spat the food everywhere, her eyes defiant, letting him know she was no baby, that this was a willful hate. Finally, in anger he pushed the plate of mushy rice into her face and left her sickroom, retreating to the living room. It was a hot day and he took off his shirt and lay on the couch. It was covered in plastic to protect the fabric and in the heat he began to sweat, his body sticking to it. At first it irritated him and then it slowly began to drive him crazy, and he swore that as soon as she died he would rip off that plastic and bury her in it, like her own personal freezer bag. But then something else began to happen to him as he lay there. He began to feel his body. Really feel it for the first time. Even then, at fourteen, he was already five foot eleven and two hundred plus pounds. He felt the soft fall of his body and the sticky plastic. Felt the sweat crawl down his back like curious fingers and smelled his animal smell. He took off his pants and lay there, feeling all of himself. Not sexually, but sensually, as body, as heat, as alive. Then he thought of his teacher, Mrs. Bovay, three hundred pounds and her voice all softness and kindness like her flesh and her hug that pulled him close into the smell of sweat and talc, all sweet like a baby and something else; the faint scent of pecan or nutmeg from the pies she baked for the class. She was everything his mother wasn't.

And then he thought of his mother's wedding dress and went into her room, still naked, ignoring her hate and her bile, and pulled the dress on, tearing a deep gash in the side. He went back to the couch and lay there, pretending to be her, to be dead, to be lying in state, and all the while, the gash let in a cooling breeze. But he didn't tell Iggy any of it, instead Black blew on his tea.

"I don't know. I don't remember," he said.

Iggy nodded.

"Do you have any cigarettes?" she asked.

He passed the pack. She lit one and took a long, deep drag, her brow furrowed from the effort and from the thoughts he imagined were racing across the screen of her mind. As she let the smoke out, she seemed to be smiling.

"What?"

"I was just thinking about the dress and the makeup in the spaceship and I realize what that means. You are the Virgin. You're the fraud these people have gathered to see," Iggy said.

He wanted to say, Well, duh, took you long enough. Instead he looked away and nodded.

"Oh, Black. That's wrong on so many levels."

"I know. I've been thinking of a way to tell them," he said, indicating the loud faithful outside with a nod of his head.

"You can't. Not now. You can't just snatch this away from them."

"So what do I do?"

Iggy opened her mouth to speak but was interrupted by Bomboy banging loudly into The Ugly Store.

"Black, I came to see you," Bomboy said, sitting at one of the stools and putting an alarm clock on the bar in front of him. Black set his cup of tea down.

"Iggy, can I get a beer?" Bomboy said.

Iggy shot him a look.

"Please," he added.

She got up, went round the bar and fetched him a beer. Meanwhile, Black was watching her movements, the easy sway of her full thighs, while pretending to be studying the alarm clock. It was very ornate, with gold painted fleur-de-lis on it. There was also what looked like a banner with a message in Arabic inscribed at the bottom. Bomboy was studying Black.

"It says: there is only one God and his name is Allah," Bomboy said, pointing to the scroll.

Black nodded.

"But you're not Muslim," Iggy pointed out.

"I know," Bomboy said, "but this is business."

"Business?" Black asked.

Iggy took the money Bomboy passed to her for the beer.

"Well, guys, I think I am turning in. Black, lock up when Bomboy leaves," she said.

"Wait, Iggy," Bomboy said. "I want your opinion."

"Fine," Iggy said, sitting down. "But make it quick." She was sick of the way men always came to her for validation, but never gave her even the most basic respect.

"Listen," Bomboy said, and pushed a button on the clock. The call to prayer filled the room in a high-pitched tinny whine, somewhere between chant and lament. Black listened to it for a few minutes then pushed the button, returning the room to silence.

"You see?"

Both Iggy and Black shook their heads.

"This is an alarm clock that wakes you to the sound of the call to prayer," Bomboy said.

"Well, technically it's not the call since it is recorded," Iggy said.

"Yes, but I am planning to take these back home and sell them. I get a good discount for bulk purchase."

"But I thought your people were Christians?" Iggy asked.

"Yes, but the Tutsi are Muslims."

"But aren't they . . ."

"Yes, but it is peace time now."

"Ah," Iggy said, with a slight shudder. "I wouldn't buy one, but then I'm not a Tutsi Muslim with bad taste. What can I say?"

"Black?"

"I'm going to bed," Black said, getting up.

"I guess that means you have to go, Bomboy. Drive careful and be sure not to run over any of the faithful," Iggy said.

"Bloody Americans," Bomboy threw over his shoulder as he left.

twenty

The room was dark when Black woke. It seemed like in the distance, bells were ringing, but he couldn't be sure as he slipped in and out of sleep. He lay back in bed. He was so tired. So tired. But the telephone was ringing. He reached for it.

"Black?"

"Shit," he swore under his breath. It was Sweet Girl. He wished he hadn't given her his number after the lap dance. "Yes?" No point lying. She knew it was him.

"Black," she said again. And he heard all the loss and longing in her voice. It was unbearable. He didn't know what to say so he hung up. He got up and washed his face.

Fatima was calling.

goog**le.**

It hardly seemed like a word, much less an explanation. But it was. That's how Sweet Girl found him, she told Black.

"I googled your telephone number," she said. "And your address popped up just like that. I didn't think you'd mind. I figured if you didn't want to be found you'd have an unlisted number."

He stood in the doorway looking at her. It was late at night and he was still half asleep.

"I was worried," she said. "When you hung up. I was worried so I came."

"Why?"

"To make sure that you are okay."

She had been crying. He could tell because her mascara had run and she hadn't bothered to clean it. Her face was swollen too, puffy, but not from crying, he didn't think, but more from drugs, or something like that. Maybe drink.

"Aren't you going to let me in?"

"Sorry," he mumbled, stepping back from the door. She hesitated on the threshold for a moment. "Come," he said. "Come in."

She walked in and he realized that she was wearing a raincoat and it was wet. She undid the belt and took it off. Turning to hang it over the hook by the door she paused. There was a wedding dress hanging there, and behind it, a tuxedo. She turned to look at him, catching him mid-yawn.

"Long story," he said, following her gaze and taking in the clothes hanging behind the door. He took her coat and headed into the bathroom, where he draped it over the shower rail. When he came back, she was standing by his worktable, staring at the mounds of pigment.

"What are these?"

"What I make paint with."

"You make your own colors?"

"Well, technically paint has no color of its own," he said. "It's just a way to block all other parts of the light spectrum and reflect the one you want. I am finicky about my work, so I don't rely on the paint alone for the color. There is the light, which depends on location, the base material I am painting on among other variables."

"Stop," she said. "You're making my head hurt."

He laughed and walked over to the kitchenette and came back with a half empty bottle of vodka from the freezer. All his alcohol was stolen from the bar downstairs. He held out a glass and Sweet Girl took it. He poured. She tossed it back in one gulp. He poured again. She sipped slowly this time as he poured one for himself.

"So what's up?" he asked. "You look like you've been crying."

"I haven't."

"But your eyes are so sad. I mean, what have you seen?"

"I am a Mexican transsexual. The question is what haven't I seen."

He nodded and drank, refilling both their glasses.

"Are you trying to get me drunk?" Sweet Girl asked.

"Something is different about you," he said, putting down his glass and walking over to where she stood by the workbench. He pulled out a stool. "Here, sit."

"What?" she asked, sitting and pulling him down onto the one next to her. He put out a hand to steady himself and it landed in the bowl of lapis, sending a blue cloud up.

"I'm sorry," she said, finishing the rest of her drink. But he waved her apology away.

"I know what's different," he said. "Your accent is more American now. In the club you sound more Mexican, more like Salma Hayek."

She shrugged.

"In the club people pay to see exotica, so I give it to them. I'm no less Mexican now."

He nodded, distracted by her perfume. He leaned into her and inhaled deeply.

"What is that scent?"

"Charlie," she said. "Remember it? By Revlon."

"That's the smell of my childhood," he said. "I haven't smelled that since the early eighties."

"My little joke," she said, laughing, her eyes lighting up for the first time.

"But . . ."

"Tell me about this," she said, indicating all the mounds of pigment with a delicate hand.

"These pigments are what I make my paints from. It's that simple; pigments and a glue to bind them, in my case,

I use gum arabic," Black said, rolling a couple of the large, clear crystals of gum arabic between his palms. He set them down next to the bowl of powdered lapis lazuli. Taking Sweet Girl's hand, he buried it in it, making her run her fingers through it.

"It's easy to make paint," he said. "First you choose your pigment, say lapis lazuli, or virgin blue . . ."

"Why virgin blue?"

"Because in the old days it was used to paint the blue robes of the Virgin Mary. It is the most expensive, most beautiful of all blues. An artist can always use azurite, which is almost the same color as the best lapis, but it can't be ground as fine. There's also smalt, which comes from ground cobalt glass . . ."

"I get it, lapis is your favorite. What's this?" Sweet Girl asked, grabbing a handful of red pigment like a baker about to toss flour to roll dough.

"This is cinnabar, a mineral red, sometimes called vermilion. I had a hell of a time with my last batch of vermilion because it kept turning black for no apparent reason. This is carmine, made from an insect native to Mexico. These here are red ochre, yellow ochre and purple ochre, which are just clays," he said, rubbing the coarser grains between his fingertips. She did the same thing, and then laughed.

"It's just colored sand," she said.

"Yes," he said, licking the ochre from his fingertips.

"Oh, oh, green."

"Yes. The green is malachite, which is best coarse. This is terre verte made from moss and other substances. I use it mostly for underpainting flesh. This yellow is orpiment, but I enhance it with saffron or turmeric or sometimes curry. I get all my black from bones, here. Want to feel it? No? Don't worry I'm not a serial killer, I just buy ready-made bone black."

"And for white?"

"For white I use white lead. In the old days it was made by suspending plates of lead above vinegar or urine and scraping off the resulting corrosion. Now you can just buy it," he said, placing clumps of pigment on a slab of por-phyry. He wet it a little with the vodka. She arched her eyebrows and he smiled.

"Makes the paint shinier," he said. He stood behind her, handed her a muller, which was just a smooth stone, and placed her hands on it. He placed his over hers, his fingers tracing patterns on the back of her hands.

"I found this stone in the sea off Big Sur. It just called to me. I use it to grind the pigment," he said; voice no more than a breath over the hair on her neck, making her break out in goose bumps.

"See? Next, we add a crystal of gum arabic to bind it. See?"

"Yes, it's like making Kool-Aid," she said.

Sweet Girl was smiling at the strange colored paste coming together on the stone. The color was like nothing she had seen outside of nature, like maybe the bottle blue of a fly or like the blue-tinged skin of fish. Black picked up a saucer and scraped some of the paste onto it.

"It's basically ready," he said. "Would you like to paint something?"

"Yes," Sweet Girl said. She dipped a finger into the mix-ture, turned around and painted him on the face. He laughed and ran, and she picked up the saucer of paint and chased him around the room, both of them giggling harder than drunken teenagers. Exhausted they collapsed into bed, passing back and forth the bottle of vodka that one of them had retrieved as they circled the room. Finally it was empty, and they lay there staring at each other for a long time. Then Black leaned over and kissed Sweet Girl hard on the mouth. They lay lip-locked, fighting for air and loving every moment. Then Sweet Girl pulled away and kissed him lower and lower and lower. And as Black felt Sweet Girl take all of him into her moist mouth, he saw Gabriel watching from the fire escape. Fucking angel, he thought, then, Oh, God.

Oh, God.

twenty-two

Purple flame.

Against the white wall, the bougainvillea was an alien. Like much of the flora of this city, it came from some- where else: palm trees from the Canary Islands, eucalyptus from Australia, bougainvillea from Brazil, birds of para- dise from South Africa. Nearly everything now native to Los Angeles came from somewhere else. That was perhaps its beauty, Black thought. That it never tired of reinvent- ing itself, producing as many shades and nuances of being as a bougainvillea: pink, magenta, purple, red, orange, white and yellow.

This city wasn't a city. And if it was, it was a hidden city. There were several cities within it, and you had to yield to it, before it revealed any of its magic to you. It was a slow realization, but walking down Soto one hot dusty day, the smog layering the city in a mid-afternoon shimmer, he thought, I love this city. Los Angeles was a rambling maze that didn't apologize for what it was. Instead it forced you to find the city within you. In that way it was a grown-up city. This was a silence that tourists and other outsiders would never know. This was not a postcard of Los Angeles, a city of joyful shallowness. And even in this city with no blizzards and a fiberglass mastodon pretending to drown in a tar pit, truth could be found on misty mornings.

He was sipping a cup of coffee, looking out of his window. He was still tired. He wasn't getting enough sleep and it was affecting him. At least he hoped it was the lack of sleep. Sweet Girl had left sometime in the night, leaving only the faintest hint of her perfume and a few blue lapis lazuli crumbs on the sheet. Black reached down and touched his crotch. He wasn't hard. The pressure he felt was the ghost of Sweet Girl's lips. Her mouth. His mouth. Whatever, he didn't want to think about it. Must have been the vodka, he told himself, I must have been drunk because my head is pounding from this hangover.

Everything sounded louder than usual: the ants crawling along the window ledge, dragging a crystal of sugar; a cockroach, out of sight in a crack, rubbing its antennae together; a bird landing on the roof of the spaceship, high up and invisible from here; a weed whacker buzzing away in the distance.

When he finally slept last night, after tossing uneasily for a while, Sweet Girl snoring softly beside him, his dreams had been of blood. Of being stuck in the River and of blood in a flash flood washing him away and then, sailing toward him on an upturned wooden box, was the Virgin except when she got closer and reached out her hand, he saw it was Sweet Girl and then just as she was pulling him to safety, she turned into his mother and drowned him.

He turned away from the window, and through the

steam rising from his coffee cup watched the television: the news was on. The volume was low, but the image was of a large southland hill burning. The brush fires were relentless this year.

Although he wouldn't entirely admit it, he was disappointed with Sweet Girl. Having watched her from a distance for so long, having glorified and celebrated her, last night wasn't the meeting he envisioned. He realized now, turning back to his window and the shanty of East LA, that she had become emblematic of his unspoken, even unknown, desire. Thinking about the image board in the spaceship he knew that she was linked to his obsession with the Virgin, but he wasn't sure how. Maybe the Virgin was the light in him and Sweet Girl the darkness, the icon of the virgin of the damned. He chuckled at this thought.

Something else bothered him.

Her easy attraction to him, her reversal of the obsession. Perhaps it was karma, the stalkee becoming the stalker, but he knew that wasn't it. It wasn't even that she had been watching him all the time he was watching her, but that she seemed more able to lose herself in the moment of their consummation than he was. He wanted to be the one to do that. To melt into the desire of the moment while she resisted and that tug, that tension of the chase, would have been more delicious than the merging itself. He wondered if that was a thing only a woman could do. He was listless, not wanting to work today. Just before he left, he saw Gabriel's wing droop over his window, filtering the sun in slats.

Like a Venetian.

twenty-three

Not always.

But often enough, the spaceship on the roof took Black's breath away. In this misty and moon-silver night it really did look extraterrestrial. He'd been working on the mural of Fatima for most of the day and into the early evening with only the moon and the orange and lemon light of a few desperate streetlights. Working quickly, he'd finished her musculature. Another day and night and he might have the whole picture, but only if he could maintain this pace. Maybe he would slow down, take a few days off. He needed to earn some cash to pay Iggy's rent. He sat in the van, idling in front of The Ugly Store, and didn't feel like going in, so he parked on the corner of Cesar Chavez and Mission, climbed onto the roof of his van and took in the panoramic views of East and Downtown Los Angeles. At night, like it was now, the lights made it look more beautiful than it actually was, leading to its nickname, Malibu el Barrio.

In the distance a dog barked. Frank Sinatra was singing too loudly in someone's living room, the sound spilling out into the street. "Gray skies are gonna clear up, put on a happy face."

The blur of Ray-Ray's reflective jacket was bright orange as he rode up on his bicycle; a child's bicycle. Black took in the sticker on the rear wheel cover of the bicycle: SAFETY FIRST.

"What's up, Black?"

"Nothing," Black replied.

"Pass me the beer, huevón," Ray-Ray said.

Black tried to pass the can down, but it was fruitless. Laughing, he jumped down and handed Ray-Ray the can of beer.

"Hey, fuck you," Ray-Ray said, taking the can.

"Where are you off to?" Black asked him.

"Nowhere in particular. Just trying to get some exercise. Small man like me can have it rough in a gym."

"Exercise?"

"What, mothafucker? I don't look healthy to you?"

"No, cabrón. You look like shit."

"Yeah? Well, fuck you," Ray-Ray said, passing the can of beer back. Black took a swig.

"Wanna ride?"

"Where are we going?" Ray-Ray asked.

"Wherever the road leads, man. Stow your bike in back and get in, amigo."

Ray-Ray stowed his bike and opened the door and got in. It took a while. They drove in silence. Swinging a left, then a right and another left, Black pulled up by the River. To the left, falling away in a valley below the culvert level was a train yard. Cargo cars sat rusting in the moonlight, silent as grave markers. To their right, they could make out the 4th Street Bridge. A girl was leaning over the ledge.

She could have been an angel.

Even the gun in her hand didn't negate that possibility. Didn't angels smite for God's love? But it was her hair more than anything that decided it for Black. The way it blew back from her face in the cold night. Nothing more.

From this distance, the gun going off sounded more like a firecracker. The angel wasn't alone. An all-female host surrounded her. They were laughing loudly. The shots were interrupted when the host of helpers hurled a dark shape off the bridge. Whatever it was seemed silent and inanimate. Soon after, the shots began again.

"Shit! Those bitches!" Black said.

Ray-Ray, not understanding Black's urgency, was slightly afraid because he knew Black was heading for the bridge.

"Where are we going?"

"Don't you see what's going on?"

"The shooting? Shouldn't we call the police?"

"What do they care if dogs are shot?"

For a moment, Ray-Ray was confused. He thought Black was making a racial reference, but something in the way he said it made Ray-Ray realize that he was really talking about dogs.

"People come here to throw away dogs they don't want or can't afford to feed. They just drive up and throw their dogs off. The poor creatures die slowly, blood and brains splattered everywhere."

"Shit," Ray-Ray said.

"Damn right. Then the gangs come along and use the dog corpses for target practice."

By now they were on the bridge and heading toward the group.

"Fact that they haven't shot at us means they only have the one gun," Black said. The shooting had stopped and Black guessed the girls had run out of ammunition. As he watched them leave in a squeal of tires, he knew he was right. Black parked on the bridge. Before he got out, he reached into the glove compartment and took out a clump of sage, which he shoved into his back pocket. Then he made his way down to the concrete bed of the River, followed with great difficulty by Ray-Ray. There were about ten dogs lying around. Dead or dying. Many of them had their legs and mouths taped, perhaps to ensure a heavy landing, or perhaps to keep their whines from haunting their killers. Black stood in the middle of the circle and began to cry. Then, raising his arms to the moon that was low and full in the sky, he wailed, like a dog. He reached into his pocket and pulled out the sage. Struggling against the wind, he lit it and walking amongst the dead animals, he smudged them in the smoke. Ray-Ray stood outside the rough circle, watching. He needed a hit of something. Shit. He shivered.

Black stopped beside an animal. Bones stuck out of its fur and its legs still jerked. Black whispered into its ear and it looked at him as if it understood, as though it was forgiving him. Then with a quick twist, he dispatched it. He turned to Ray-Ray.

"Hey, 'mano, can you get me my hat and some blankets from the bus? I think I'm going to be here for a while and I don't want to catch a cold."

Nodding, Ray-Ray did as he was asked. With his short legs, it took longer than it should have, and when he came back he saw that Black had moved the dead animals into a tight circle and that he had placed the smudge stick on the riverbed in the middle. Wrapping the blankets Ray-Ray gave him around himself, he set his hat on his head, and sank to the floor.

Ray-Ray stood there, unsure what to do.

"Hey, Ray-Ray," Black said, voice soft.

"Yeah?"

"There's a joint in the glove compartment of the van. Good shit. Why don't you have a hit, güey. This will take a while."

Relieved, Ray-Ray returned to the van. He lit up, sat back and blew smoke out the window at Black, who was sitting among the dead and dying dogs, hands stroking their blood-soaked fur.

Black sang to them, the rhythm carrying their spirits across the other mythical River. The joint was working and Ray-Ray felt himself slipping away. He took one last look at the scene. It was an eerie sight.

Black, a dark huddled mass in shapeless old blankets, an eagle feather rising out of the top of his battered black felt hat, a mound of sage burning beside him, the dogs lying still, silent, like corpses, at least one with its big head in his lap, and in the background, the gentle throb of the city, and Black's voice rising like something old and long forgotten, breaking through the resistance of night in a formless sound that was all sand.

The chant as familiar as skin.

twenty-four

Noctilucent.

That was the word that came to Black as he looked at the still-burning streetlights wearing halos in the early mist. All of the dogs had passed over, and he had done right by each one. Ray-Ray left at some point during the night, but Black hadn't noticed. He was tired, though, tired of everything, of this weight that was pressing down on him and yet remained invisible, like a succubus. He knew he was a little crazy, even he couldn't pretend that away anymore, not even to himself. But what afflicted him or why remained a mystery.

He needed to paint. He needed Fatima. That mystery was the only thing that could save him now. That mystery was his only hope. The way her body, a woman's body, fell into light. The way desire wasn't about the vagina, but about the lips. About disappearing into the warm, moist-ness of another.

He stopped on the bridge and looked at the figure rising up the wall in the early light like a vision of a goddess.

How to get to her? The base of the wall was in the back of Bomboy's warehouse and the only way to it was through the warehouse, or from the River. I could always climb down the side of the bridge, Black thought, and make my way along the culvert lip. It would be hard work with paint, but he could do it. Going back to his van, he took a length of rope, wound it across his body in a cross. Then he tied several paint cans to each end. He tied another length of rope around the cross, firmly strapping the paint cans to his body. Selecting the same length of orange rope he had been using to rappel up and down the wall, he climbed over the side of the bridge. As he hovered there, the artist in him marveled at the intricate and ornate ways the concrete had been worked. Worked for love, for art, in pride, and almost nobody saw this anymore, nobody that mattered anyway, and yet even for being invisible, this particular beauty was part of what lit this city. Every silent moment was part of the big noise.

Finally he was down and making his way along the lip of the culvert, watching the ripple and flow of the water. He was careful not to fall in as the recent rains had raised the water level several feet and he knew the currents under its dark surface could reach forty to fifty miles an hour. Making it to the back of Bomboy's warehouse, he unloaded himself and went to smoke by the River. Legs dangling over the edge, he was halfway through his fifth to last Marlboro, night getting lighter, when he noticed that in the drainpipe opposite, a young man's head and arms were caught in the locked grill, the rest of his body disappearing into the pipe. He looked like he was half swallowed by a snake. He was clearly dead. A lizard person, Black thought. Stupid teenagers who raced each other supine on skateboards through subterranean flood drains and sewers that were linked to the River. He threw his cigarette away and returned to Fatima.

He began to paint.

Sunflowers.

So many it seemed Fatima would disappear in the forest of green stalks and large yellow faces. Each petal turned up to catch the most sun, each petal like a pane opening onto a brilliant light. The flowers crowded around the figure of the woman. She was still pink and red gristle and in some places, black bone, like the cadavers Bomboy loved. Split open like the heart of a pomegranate.

Then the blackbirds.

Thirteen, to be precise, filled the field of yellow flowers, black dots in the brilliance, auguring. And still Black painted. The only details on the birds were their eyes, which were alive, like coals in a fire smoldering in the back of a cave.

Then.

With broad sweeps of his brush—in this case, a household mop—he covered the brightness with whitewash. Covered it up until there was nothing but Fatima in a sea of white. Still: the flowers shone through. Still: the blackbirds sang. Still.

When he was done, he hung from the ropes, swinging like an effigy of a lynching while he smoked a cigarette and looked out onto the river. This River held the truth, he thought. What it was, though, he would only know when he reached it. And he would.

Yes.

This River was distant, yet never far.

Morning.

As the first clutch of cars began to gather in a jam on the bridge, Black finished the painting. He lowered himself and stepped back, lighting his last Marlboro, thinking, none of it belongs to us, none of it is ours until we finish.

After.

All of it.

After the sun has lit the way.

After the night has passed into a dream.

After our fear is no longer the thing.

Rising fifty feet, on the side of the abattoir wall, in a head to toe yashmak, was the figure of a Muslim woman. Only her eyes and hands were visible. In one she was strangling a dove. The other was wrapped around something that, though still largely unformed, was meant to be an AK-47. The image was stunning and more than a little disturbing. The sheer scale of it would terrify onlookers, in the way Black knew they imagined an angel must tower over everything. But he wasn't swayed by that, couldn't be, for to live there, in the viewer's fear, was to be like a blind man staring at a sunset, able to see only what was already inside of him. But for him, the true terror was her eyes. Black. Unrelenting.

Behind him, Black heard the whistle of a train, like some omen. He turned to it. There was only the train.

And the riddle of tracks.

twenty-five

Straight.

The line dropping from the sky was the side of a high-rise. It fell, not slowly like a leaf on a lazy wind, but directly, like a determined note of music. It fell straight down until it hit the arc of the overturned bowl of an umbrella, hesitated for the briefest moment, then rolled like the deep belly laugh of a bass down to hover at the tip of one spoke. Trembling there for a while, it made the leap of faith to the street where it was lost in the cracked lines of sidewalk, spreading out into the day like sound pushed around a drum's skin by a pair of brushes. Iggy turned and walked away, the fleshy jiggle of her ass slowly beginning the downward spiral of her day.

Siren.

Hardly the sweet song of Greek mythology, she thought, ducking behind the near life-size piñata of George Bush leaning against the entrance to the store on Olympic. There was the sound of approaching emergency vehicles and Iggy ducked into the shop. From the safety of

George's wide back, she watched the bedlam pass: two police cars cockroaching through the underbelly of the city.

Black's derision at their haste came back to her. "Oh, they gotta get to the doughnut shop before it closes," he would say, and laugh. At her, perhaps, she thought. Black's derision always seemed able to take on multiple targets.

Emerging from the store, Iggy hesitated for only a minute before buying the George Bush piñata. Once she paid for it, she wasn't sure why she had bought it. Did it remind her of an oversized doll, a fetish of some sort, an oracular object like the effigy of Kings which the Roma destroyed in ritual to remind themselves to be humble? As she looked down at the piñata in her hands she realized she needed to see Black. Or perhaps it was Fatima she really wanted to see. None of his earlier figurative work had particularly moved her, or intrigued her as much as this idea of Fatima. She wasn't sure why, but felt like it was tied into her discoveries in the spaceship. At the very least she and Black could have a great time beating George senseless, she thought. Just like politics, she thought, hefting the big paper doll over her shoulder and making her way up Central to Fourth Street and the bridge under which Black, like a self-respecting troll, was sitting, cooking up the magic of his murals and threatening the people passing above with his art. Just like love.

Nobody paid any attention to Iggy as she walked up the street, except a homeless man on the corner of Fifth and Central. The man asked for some money for food, and when Iggy shrugged him off, the man reached for the paper doll. He punched a hole neatly through George's leg, hoping to pull out a handful of cheap sweets, but came up with air. Iggy cursed under her breath and kept walking.

She paused by the picture window of a mannequin store. Several male figures stood backing the street, hands crossed over naked buttocks. In the corner a female mannequin faced out, wearing leather bondage clothes and holding a leather cat-o'-nine. Next to it was a small shop selling Christian literature and a cart selling mouthwatering hot dogs and burritos. Her face looked back at her from the window. She smiled but her eyes remained dark. Turning away from the window and her eyes, she bought two burritos and continued up the street.

Making a left on Fourth, Iggy headed east. In no time she was by the bridge near Bomboy's abattoir. She crossed it to the opposite side because she wanted to get a clear view of Black's mural. Turning around halfway across, she stopped short. Fatima filled the sky. Iggy suppressed a shudder and a sob at the same time. God, she's beautiful, and how I hate that fucker, she thought at the same time. Why couldn't she fill someone's sky this way? For the first time in a very long time she felt alone.

Sighing, Iggy headed back the way she had come, for the abattoir and Black. In a few minutes, having come in the main gate and walking past the warehouse, she could see him sitting on the culvert lip, smoking.

"Hey, Black," Iggy said, approaching Black and then sitting beside him.

"Hey, Iggy," Black said. He was surprised. She never came to his work sites. He wondered what was up. "Check out the wall," he added.

"I saw," Iggy said.

"I told you. This one is different."

"Yes, you did," Iggy said quietly.

"Hey, guys," Bomboy called.

Black turned. Iggy cursed under her breath.

Bomboy ambled over with a lopsided smile on his face. Iggy couldn't tell if it was relief at being able to take a break from work or whether he was just high from the blunt he was smoking.

"Not working this morning? And who's your new friend?" Black asked Iggy, indicating the piñata.

Before she could reply, Bomboy was there.

"Can somebody get a hello?" Bomboy asked, amiably, offering the blunt to Black.

"Hello, somebody," Iggy said, with a forced smile.

Bomboy sat down next to Iggy and Black. He reached into his pocket and produced an assortment of accoutrement: paper, weed, resin, tobacco and matches. He began to roll a joint expertly with one hand, while the other shielded the wind.

"What's up?" he asked.

Iggy shrugged. Black silently puffed on the blunt he was given. Bomboy finished packing the paper, rolled it over with one hand, while the other quickly packed his paraphernalia and stash away. He licked the joint once, sealed it, passed it to Iggy and struck a match. The sulfurous flare bit into Iggy as she took a deep drag on the joint and passed it back to Bomboy, who offered it to Black. He shook his head and Bomboy smiled and took a deep drag, letting out the smoke in stages.

They sat in silence for a while as the smoke fogged around them. Iggy didn't smoke much, but Bomboy and Black were passing the joint back and forth and eventually they both began to giggle. Drug heads, Iggy thought, looking away at the River. She reached into her bag and passed Black one of the burritos she bought from the roach coach on the corner, nearly knocking George over with the vehemence of the move. She hated that phrase, *roach coach*, but she used it. Black accepted the burrito, tore it in two and passed one half to Bomboy. They ate silently for a while.

"Why a Muslim woman?" Iggy asked. "Is this some clichéd statement about 9/11?"

"You know I don't do that shit."

"Then why?"

Black shrugged. "I don't know."

"Personally," Bomboy began, interrupting. "Personally, I don't like that she is a Muslim."

"Why?" Iggy asked. "Weren't you going to sell alarm clocks with the call to prayer in Rwanda?"

"You are just obstinate and obfuscating. Don't you know that was strictly business?"

"So why don't you like Muslims?" Iggy pressed.

"I don't think you want to open that door," Black cautioned.

"No, she asked. Let me answer," Bomboy said.

"No, Bomboy. I've heard enough about Rwanda and your bullshit," Black insisted. Iggy knew Black thought he was being gallant and protecting her from whatever gory details Bomboy was going to share with her, but she knew it had little to do with her really and everything to do with his ego. In the end, with men, it was always about them.

"I appreciate you trying to spare me, Black, but I think I can handle it."

"Yeah?"

"Yeah," she said. "I had this client, obviously I cannot tell you her name, a middle school teacher in Wisconsin. It was around the time when the worst atrocities were happening in Rwanda and she'd just been fired for her unorthodox approach to teaching current affairs."

"Unorthodox? Wisconsin?" Black interrupted.

"Why don't you just listen? Anyway, she told her students about the war and about the killings and got no reaction. Next day she brought in an assortment of dolls and knives for each student."

"Is this something from Oprah?" Bomboy asked.

"Picking up a doll," Iggy continued as if he hadn't spoken, "she hacked its arms off, explaining matter-of-factly that this was happening right now in Rwanda to children like them. The class flinched and some of them looked like they were about to cry. 'Do it,' she told them, 'hack the dolls to pieces.'"

"That's just creepy," Black said.

Iggy nodded. "I guess. But she was confident that she could tap into their latent goodness and that they would realize the gravitas of the situation."

"And?" Bomboy asked, leaning forward.

When Iggy spoke again, it was eerie. Something changed in her voice, her tone and her eyes. It was almost as if she was channeling her former client, as though the woman was actually there, speaking through Iggy.

"They paused, knives poised high," Iggy said. "Then they hacked at various parts of the dolls, timid at first, giggling nervously. Then they grew bolder, hacking and laughing until in a frenzy they butchered all the dolls like mad elves in a deranged Santa's workshop. The teacher said she was frozen, appalled. She was broken, and if they hadn't fired her, she would have left anyway."

Both Bomboy and Black were staring at Iggy openmouthed.

"Did it really happen?" Black asked.

"Yes."

"What does she do now? This client?"

"She's a cop," Iggy said, then laughed at the look of horror on Black's face.

"Why do you always act so shocked, Black?" Bomboy asked, also noting the expression on Black's face.

"He's sensitive," Iggy said.

"Sensitive? You know he is an African, we don't have time for that shit," Bomboy said.

"How is that African, and how is it that I am African?" Black asked.

"Your father was African, and so therefore, you are African. Simple logistics."

"Logic," Iggy said.

"That's what I mean. You know what I mean."

"What do you think, Black?" Iggy asked.

"He can think what he wants, truth is truth," Bomboy said smugly.

"I don't know," Black said.

"You're getting repetitive."

"Sorry."

Even as he said it, a part of Black watched with an amused stare, wondering why he wouldn't say the things he was thinking to Iggy or Bomboy. He hated the part of himself that ran away from confrontation. It was the same part that was constantly trying to reassure white people that he wasn't out to mug them, wasn't the criminal they expected he would be, should be. It was ridiculous, but he couldn't rid himself of these tics. Like waving his ATM card around while waiting to use the machine, to reassure those in line before and behind him. Everything slowed down when he did it. The feeling was like tugging on a pair of wet jeans that were two sizes too small with cold, numb fingers.

"Okay," Iggy said, changing tack. "Who do you feel you are?"

"I don't know, I feel confused."

"So you are searching. Searching is good."

"Is it? My father was searching for something, but I have no idea what. I have often thought about him and the way he would talk about flying away on a spaceship, getting lost in the stars. I thought he was an artist at heart, or at least a scientist like Einstein: a dreamer. I thought that was why I have the same existential melancholy, that's why I followed this River from the Pasadena arroyo where I was born to here."

"Oh, Black, such big words," Iggy said, smiling. "And now?" she asked.

"And now I'm not sure. I think that I have idealized my father's discontent. Maybe it was something as simple as racism, maybe he couldn't find fulfillment in his job, or with my mother."

"Those are not simple concerns," Iggy said.

"I know. But they lack the romance and magic I want. I've always felt like Parsifal or some other Knight of the Round Table on an eternal quest, a never-ending search," Black said, voice wistful.

"There is no search about it. Black is African, end of matter," Bomboy said.

"I think Black is talking about something a little more complicated."

"Like what?"

"Should I?" Iggy asked Black.

Black shook his head. "No, I will." Taking a deep breath, he turned to Bomboy. "I have been wearing a dress, pretending to be the Virgin."

"What do you mean? How many times?"

"Many. Including that night on the spaceship that started all this palaver."

Bomboy threw his head back and laughed hard. Iggy and Black were surprised by his reaction.

"Black, you are very funny. What's the scam here? How are we going to cash in on it? Merchandising? Selling miraculous souvenirs to the crowd outside? No? An exclusive for *Entertainment Tonight*?"

"There is no cashing it in," Black said quietly. "This isn't a scam."

"Come on now. If you are pretending to be the Virgin it has to be a scam. Don't tell me you are doing this for real."

"It's not a scam or for real, it was an accident."

"I see."

"Good, because I don't," Iggy said.

"That's because like a true American you are looking for the cause of this. Maybe something happened to him as a child—"

"But it did. He was dressed as a girl."

Black hung his head. It was no longer his life.

"So?" Bomboy said. "I was naked and eating shit off the floor as a child. I'm not a dog now, am I? You people. Sometimes a thing is just what it is, a thing. In Rwanda when we see lightning killing people we don't ask why, we just stay out of thunderstorms. That's how come we have survived so long."

"More's the pity," Iggy said.

Black laughed and then grew serious.

"I wish I knew myself," he said.

"That there is the key, my friend. To know yourself. The story of your life, well, it's just a story, you tell it and tell it and then you believe it. It's not the same as your life, though. We are all the same in this, we find a story we can live with and just get on with it. In your case, you are most likely a homosexual," Bomboy said. "When you have seen what I've seen you know these things. You shut off all this bleeding heart bullshit. You shut down and ginger up, there is life to live."

"Fuck you, hijo dela chingada!"

Bomboy shrugged. "Homo! You know I'm right. The risk is that suffering too much shuts you down. I think you're shut down."

"No, Bomboy," Iggy said, shaking her head. "For Black, shutting down is not the risk. That's obvious. Joy, joy, that's the risk."

"Homo!" Bomboy repeated.

"It's not that easy. What if he's wearing the dress as a way of getting back to a moment of safety when he could discover his parents and therefore himself?"

"That's just the problem," Black said. "I don't know if I wear that dress because I am looking for my father, myself, because I want to be a woman or simply because Sweet Girl is a lesbian."

"Sweet Girl? What has that person to do with this?" Bomboy asked.

"You know Sweet Girl?" Iggy asked.

Bomboy nodded.

"She's his girlfriend," Iggy said.

"Girlfriend or boyfriend?" Bomboy asked.

"Black?" Iggy said.

Black laughed uncomfortably and kicked George Bush. "When are we going to smash up this puto?" he asked.

Iggy looked at him for a moment. He looked away. But in that brief exchange something had shifted in him, and they both knew it. Bomboy grabbed the piñata and hopped down into the culvert and splashed through the water to where a piece of rusted iron jutted out of the concrete. Bomboy hung George by his neck, and watched him turn in the wind, his inane smile never slipping. Black joined him. As the two men watched the swinging effigy, they remembered their shame, and the centuries of shame that they had inherited because of who they were, and even more, the shame of dancing to that shame, of fanning that shame, of falling short because of that shame, of becoming that shame. And the effigy swung in a hypnotic turn that was winding up to something. A release perhaps, or at least a temporary stay of the waters that threatened wet darkness. This was sacrifice.

Iggy hesitated for a moment, then waded into the water herself. The current near the edge wasn't too strong, but the water came up to her knees, although she was only a couple of inches shorter than Black. Bomboy had been rooting around and handed each of them a piece of wood or metal, as he found it. They stood, unsure at first, watching the paper doll dance giddy as a kite. Black noted that although Iggy was sensuously fleshy all over, her arms, probably from having to hold them in awkward positions for tattooing, were well defined. When the first blow landed, it wasn't the soft tear of paper, but the crunching of bone and the fragility of ripping skin. The second blow tore a gash in the stomach, releasing a flutter of paper like offal. And then the blows came hard and fast and too many to separate into moments. There was just the beating. Blow by blow by blow the way rain cannot be broken into drops but is a sheet draped against the sky. When they were spent, George was nothing more than a wire frame with a shred of paper caught here and there. A tattered edge of a smile fluttered from the bent wire of the doll's mouth. Iggy saluted. Bomboy and Black laughed and sank into the water. But they felt empty. The piñata had yielded nothing. Iggy had forgotten to fill it up with sweets.

twenty-six

Cemeteries.

Iggy thought, like guilt, are not for the dead, but the living. Sometimes, but only for the lucky few, they are a way to remember love. She usually avoided cemeteries because she believed in the malevolence of ghosts. The dead always come back; she knew this. She also knew they never come back correct.

But having left Black and Bomboy at the River with Fatima and the remains of George Bush, she felt the urge to get home as quickly as possible, and the cemetery offered a shortcut. Anyhow, this cemetery, especially in the day, seemed peaceful, welcoming. She whistled as she walked up the path, admiring the old headstones, imagining the lives now masked by the crumbling granite. In the distance a film crew was setting up and from the demon-costumed-actors she figured it was an episode of *Buffy the Vampire Slayer*.

As she rounded an old tree, she saw a funeral party beside a grave. They were dressed in white. She guessed they were Chinese. She stared hard at them, trying to determine if they were for real or whether they were part of the *Buffy* shoot. She couldn't spot any cameras or lights, and as she approached, she decided the Buddhist monk in brown and red robes chanting sutras wasn't part of the shoot. She paused for a few moments before a grave marker. It was blank except for a figure spray painted on it. It was well done, depicting a woman who could have been Mediterranean, although her features seemed more Northern European. Wrapped around her waist, its head and neck dangling down between her legs like a grotesque appendage, was a python. Arched over her head was a banner that said: *Mami-Wata*, and in the corner were Black's signature and a date. It was two years old. She didn't know what to make of it but decided to ask him when she saw him. Turning away, she continued to the low wall bordering the street. Ignoring the tagger signs, she jumped over it. The Ugly Store was right across the street.

When she got inside, she was surprised to see a gaggle of the faithful who had been camped outside in the café. They were surrounding something or someone who was on the ground, but Iggy couldn't make out who it was.

"What's going on here?" she asked, striding forward.

"The little man fell," a woman said.

Pushing her way through the crowd, Iggy gasped when she saw Ray-Ray lying on the floor. He seemed unconscious, and her first thought was, He is dead from an overdose. She bent down and picked his large head up, laying it gently in her lap. She stroked his face with one hand, while the other sought his pulse. It was there, but it was faint.

"Call 911!" she shouted at someone in the crowd.

"Someone did already," another woman said.

"Here," a third one said, pressing a washcloth wrapped around ice into Iggy's hand. She must have got it from the bar. Iggy pressed it to Ray-Ray's face. Slowly his eyes opened.

"Iggy," he croaked.

"You bastard!" Iggy sobbed. "You bastard, I thought you were dead."

Ray-Ray smiled.

The paramedics never came.

Black let himself into The Ugly Store. He couldn't see anyone so he called out.

"In here," Iggy replied from her office.

"What's up with the dwarf?" Black asked Iggy, pointing to where Ray-Ray lay on the divan in the corner of her office, holding his stomach and groaning loudly. Needles stuck out of the side of his face as though he was slowly morphing into a porcupine.

"Hey, Black. He's trying to detox. We had a scare today. He passed out and I thought he was dead."

"So you thought you'd finish him off with the needles," Black said and laughed. It sounded hollow.

"The needles are there to help," Iggy replied, punching him in the arm. Ray-Ray had been in and out of detox many times over the years. Black wondered what Ray-Ray was on now. As though reading his mind, Iggy said:

"Wet."

"What?"

"He's addicted to wet."

"What's that?"

"Joints soaked in formaldehyde, you know, embalming fluid. It gives a good, cheap high, but it's dangerous because it atrophies your internal organs until it preserves you perfectly. Then one day your lungs stiffen up and you die. Or get stuck, as they say."

Black looked around the room. Ray-Ray groaned and Black's attention returned to him. Seeing him wheezing on the divan, Black decided Ray-Ray didn't really look like a porcupine; more like Pinhead from *Hell Raiser*.

"What's that smell?" he asked Iggy.

Iggy sniffed.

"Formaldehyde. It's leaking out of his pores. Let's talk outside, in the café," Iggy said, leading Black out of her office.

The café was empty. Iggy had closed the shop after the incident. Black glanced at his watch. It was mid-afternoon, her busiest time. The espresso machine was still humming. Iggy walked behind it and began to make herself a cup of coffee. As the steam hissed in the metal jug full of milk, Black sat opposite her. From the corner of his eye he saw someone had spray painted a bright blue burning heart in the middle of his mural. It hadn't been there before and he wondered how the tagger had done it without being seen. He peered closer and decided he liked it. He noticed the goodoo dolls that Iggy had put in an old vending machine, the kind that let you slide a plastic door back to get your item. TEN DOLLARS A DOLL PER DOLL, a sign said. Not bad he thought.

"They selling?" he asked.

"Pretty well."

"Funny this."

"What is?"

"You, an ascetic who pollutes her body with coffee."

She smiled.

"And to think I was about to offer you one," she said.

"I'm sorry. Yes, please."

She filled two mugs with hot coffee and steamed milk, passing one across to him. Coming out from behind the bar, she walked over to a table, putting a chair down before sitting.

"So I meant to ask you, I saw a painting you did of a woman on a gravestone. You wrote Mami-Wata on it, what is that, who is she?" she asked.

"Lots of questions," Black said. "What were you doing in the cemetery? I thought that place gave you the creeps."

"Some cemeteries, not that one. Anyway, answer the question."

"Mami-Wata is an Igbo sea and river goddess."

"Such authority in your voice, Black, but how do you know? You never even knew your father, let alone had access to your culture."

"I read about it, Iggy. Jeez, for someone who has so much of her own bullshit you sure do give everyone else a lot of crap. God!"

"Why did you paint it?"

"I don't know. I read about it, she seemed cool. She's a new goddess, early nineteenth century. I think some guy was walking on the beach one morning and saw a masthead of a mermaid washed up, probably from a slaver sunk by the Royal Navy and took it as a sign from the sea to start a cult."

"Why does she have a snake draped down her front like that?"

"Don't know. The book didn't say, but I think it might be a fertility symbol."

"You think?"

He suddenly caught on to her thinking, but didn't see how the painting of Mami-Wata had anything to do with what he was going through just then.

"No, it can't be. That thing is almost two years old."

"Black, do you know what your murals remind me of?"

"No, what?"

"On Angel Island, after the main Chinese record building in San Francisco burned down, they would hold new immigrants for years sometimes before letting them come on to the mainland. In the buildings there, those people carved exquisite characters in the walls. Later they were found to be poems about home. Here they were, caught between the home they left and the one they had yet to make, and they carved marks for home in the shadows of those walls."

"So?"

"So don't you get it? When people are desperate they make these marks, these ways of inscribing themselves on the world in a tangible way to make sense or to make real the things that are too frightening to contain in any other way."

"Is that what your tattoos are?" And though he said it like a question, he meant to mock her.

"In some ways, yes. My clients come to me when they feel they have no place else to turn and I use the tattoos to anchor them, to hold them here while I read their lives. But it still doesn't change the fact that you are desperate and have been for some time," she said.

"The only thing I am desperate about is the rent, Iggy," he said. "And a way to get out of this town."

"This town or this situation? This becoming?"

She had put her hand on his, one finger pointing out as though subtly leading the way.

"Is there a difference?"

"Maybe not, but you do have to face it."

"I'm trying to, Iggy. I wish I was better equipped!" His tone was sharper than he meant it to be.

"In LA we are always becoming, and any idea of a solid past, as an anchor, is soon lost here. And I mean *any*, that's why there is no common mythology here, that's why people come here, to get lost or to be discovered, makes no difference. It's the same coin. Other cities, like New York, have an overwhelming myth, and there is no you, as it were, without this—shall we say—New York state of mind. But here, there is none of that bullshit, there is just you and what you see and imagine this place and your life in it to be, moment by moment. If you can't change, if you don't embrace it, you destroy yourself. The only landscape in this city is in your mind. It's very Zen," she said.

"Your theory has one flaw," he said.

"What?"

"I didn't come here. I am from here."

"I know, Black, and that's what's so tragic about it. The first change is always the hardest, but for most of us, that change is the move out here. For you it is worse because you have nothing to fight against, nothing to let go of, and so how do you become this if you can't let go of that, see? That's why there are no visible native Angelenos. Do you understand, Black?" she said, her finger on the back of his hand moving a little, tracing an imaginary tattoo, even after she'd finished speaking. "Ambivalence is the heart of this town. Not *in spite of*, but *because of*."

He shook his head, pulling his hand back. "No. The answer for me lies here," he said, showing her the photo around his neck. "In my childhood."

"Black, love, don't you know childhood, at least the way most of us remember it, is a violence we do to ourselves? How come you aren't looking at the journey you made from there to here? There is no core to anything, Black. It's like an onion; if you just keep peeling away, you will disappear. There is only the you you're becoming or have become. You're going about this all wrong, Black. It's everything, not one thing. Everything and then the cracks in between; especially the cracks in between!"

"What am I going to do, Iggy?"

"Well, Ray-Ray's sick and I need a barista. Wanna job? I hear you owe a lot of rent."

"Yes, but could I start tomorrow? I have some errands to take care of."

"Always avoiding things, aren't you, Black?"

"Shit, Iggy, you sound like Gabriel."

"Sure, whatever," she said. "It won't harm us to close for one day. I need the rest anyway."

"Thanks, Iggy," Black said, checking his watch. "I'd better go. See you tomorrow?"

"Sure," she said, as she watched him head for the back door. Just before he disappeared behind the Anubis statue she called after him. "Black? Sweet Girl called for you. I left her number on your door."

His reply was muffled.

fluttering.

In the draught coming in from the window at the end of the corridor was the yellow Post-it stuck to the door with Sweet Girl's number. He reached up and peeled it off. Shutting the door firmly behind him, he went over to the stove in the corner and was about to turn on a burner for some tea, but he reconsidered. He needed something stronger. Opening a cabinet in the small kitchenette, he took out a bottle of Jack Daniels that was about a fifth gone. Not bothering with a glass, he took a swig directly from the bottle. The red dye on his hands came off on the bottle and for a moment he was puzzled, thinking perhaps he'd cut himself. Realizing it was just paint, he washed his hands in the sink.

He paced the room. By the door he noticed that he had gotten some red dye on Iggy's wedding dress. Swearing under his breath, he took it down and carried it into the bathroom. Running water in the bath, he laid the dress reverentially, as though it were alive. Squeezing some scented body wash into the water, he tried washing out the red dye, relaxing as the warm smell of soap filled the bathroom. Having no luck, he rinsed it, hung it out to dry over the shower curtain and returned to the living room and the pacing, stopping occasionally to breathe deeply from his cupped hands.

He should call Sweet Girl. Why was he delaying? What was he afraid of? He sat. He knew what he was afraid of. He was afraid that he would be disappointed. He already was. A little. Somehow the distant adoration of her was more rewarding than this intimacy. He put on the television. The fires were still burning and everything was covered in a layer of ash. It was falling as hard as rain in cities closer to the fires. In Los Angeles, the newscaster said, it was still only a drizzle. Then she made a joke about hoping it didn't rain, otherwise there would be black rain. Black watched her intently, studying the manufactured normality of her. Sexy in the way teachers were, but prim and proper enough to make it seem wrong: a delicious mix. He lit a cigarette and studied her more closely, trying to memorize things about her. With a sigh, he returned to thoughts of Sweet Girl. He should call. He picked up the phone and dialed quickly before he could change his mind.

"Hello?"

"Hey there."

"Black?"

"Yes."

"What kind of name is that for someone, eh? Negro," Sweet Girl said and laughed.

"You love mocking me, don't you?" Black said. His voice was strained.

"Oh, come now, don't be so sensitive," Sweet Girl purred.

Pause.

"So Iggy tells me you called."

"Iggy? Oh, you mean Barbara," Sweet Girl said. "Why do you call her Iggy?"

"Because she is. So what's up?"

"Nothing."

"But you called."

Sweet Girl was silent for a while and Black wanted to kick himself. Why was he being so aggressive?

"I just wanted to talk to you," she said finally. "Don't you want to talk to me?"

"Yeah, of course."

"So, how's your day been?"

"Oh, so-so."

"What did you do?"

"I beat the hell out of George Bush."

"What?"

"I'm sorry. You had to be there."

"Clearly."

Another long silence.

"You're not very good at this, are you?"

Black chuckled.

"I guess not."

"I won't keep you."

"Okay."

Pause.

"Why don't you come by the club later."

"Tonight?"

"Yes."

"Okay."

"I could leave early. We could go get some dinner."

"Okay."

"Or I could come meet you somewhere."

Pause.

"Black?"

"Yeah?"

"You know the deal, right?"

He wanted to say, Sure I know the deal. You don't really fraternize with the clientele. This is just a bit of fun. You are a lesbian. I know the deal. Instead he said:

"Yeah."

"Good. Black?"

"Yes?"

"I like you."

Pause.

"I'll see you tonight," he said, hanging up. He took another swig of whiskey, changed the channel to some reality show where people were getting plastic surgery and settled down for a mindless afternoon, but not before throwing a bunch of clothing lying on the workbench over the phone to muffle it. It didn't have a volume button and he didn't want to be disturbed. He must have dozed off.

There was a knock on the door. Black sat up. It was late. There was another knock. It wasn't hard, but soft. There was silence, then the sound of feathers dragging down a wall. Getting up, careful so that the couch springs wouldn't squeak, he walked to the door and peered out of the peephole. Gabriel walked down the hallway and turned at the bottom to head up the stairs that led to the roof.

"Fuck!" Black said. "Fuck! Fuck! Fuck!"

This was really freaking him out. He was being stalked by an angel. Then his phone was ringing. He walked over

to the worktable and moved some articles of clothing looking for the phone. He finally found it under a pair of Iggy's
white panties that he had stolen from the laundry room.
He held them up to his nose and inhaled before answering.

"Hey, baby."

It was Sweet Girl. He felt trapped as he agreed to meet
her the next night for dinner. Yes, he knew where the
Palms restaurant was on Hollywood, he said. Who didn't?
It was home to Thai Elvis. As he hung up, he was glad Iggy
wore regular cotton panties not G-strings.

G-strings reminded him of Sweet Girl.

twenty-eight

Kitsch with conviction.

That, for Black, summed up the Palms Thai restaurant: deer in crispy mint leaves, wild boar in spicy coconut sauce, deep fried frog's legs in chili and a Thai Elvis impersonator. Iggy, who called it the Thai-light zone, had brought him years ago. Now here he was again, this time with Sweet Girl. As they were shown to their table, Black felt compassion for the small Thai Elvis impersonator. As convincing as he sounded, as much as he was giving to his performance, nobody was paying attention. In fact the harder he sang, the louder the conversation grew, to drown him out. He came to the end of "Jailhouse Rock" and received a polite smattering of applause. Black felt a real kinship with him.

They sat. A waitress dropped off menus.

"So?" Sweet Girl said.

"So what?"

"Do you like it? Have you been before?"

"Yeah, I've been here."

"I guess I'll have to find something else to make my first with you," Sweet Girl said.

He shrugged. Then the waitress was asking what they wanted to drink.

"A beer for me," Black said.

"Me too," Sweet Girl said.

The drinks came with the inquiry as to whether they were ready to order. Black looked at Sweet Girl.

"I'm not sure what I want to eat, though," she said.

He smiled at her and took a swig of beer. It was cold, refreshing.

"Take your time," he said.

She smiled, took a drink straight from the bottle.

"You have cute eyes, you know?"

"Thanks," he said. "But no, I don't know."

"I can't believe nobody told you, you got nice eyes."

He shrugged.

"Well, you do," she said.

He nodded.

"You nervous?"

"A little."

"Don't be. I don't bite."

He laughed.

"That's good, that's good, honey. Oh, this waitress is giving me the stank eye, so I'd better order. The game, darling. Yes, extra hot."

"So tell me about yourself," Black said.

"What's to tell? I'm from Mexico City and when I got here in the . . . anyway, when I got here I couldn't work, at least not real work. No papers, you know? So I did a few odd jobs for cash. The usual restaurant work at half the pay an American would do it for."

"No taxes though, right?"

She shook her head, unsure if he was being funny.

"No, baby, there's always taxes," she said.

He laughed.

"Anyway," Sweet Girl said. "I got tired of the humiliation so I became a stripper."

"How long ago was that?"

"Long long time ago."

"But you look so young."

"Right answer, papi. So what about you?"

"I been around here so long I'm part of the landscape."

She laughed.

"And what do you do?"

"I'm a painter."

"My father was a painter too," she said. "He painted most of the houses in Mexico City."

"That's a lot of houses. But I mean I'm an artist."

"I was kidding. This painting pays your bills?"

"No," he said, explaining that he also did odd jobs. She listened attentively, but he got the sense she wasn't really paying attention.

"Sounds like you could make more money as a male stripper," she said, when he'd finished speaking. "Have you ever thought about it?"

He shook his head when he realized that she was serious.

"No," he said. "I don't think that's for me."

She shrugged and looked hurt, and he wondered if he sounded judgmental, but thought, Ah, fuck it. The rest of dinner passed in an easy silence. Now that they had spoken, scoped each other out in a way, they both knew less about what they wanted from each other. There was sex, there was definitely that. But there was more, Black sensed it, but he was unsure about its shape. He wondered if Sweet Girl knew.

"Here," she said, pushing her nearly full plate toward him. "I'm not really hungry."

He shook his head.

"No. I got my own."

"This will only go to waste."

"You can take it home. Eat it later."

She shook her head.

"No," she insisted. "You eat it."

"Thank you," he said. He was still hungry. If he was going to pay for dinner, he might as well pig out. Actually, he thought, I can't afford to pay for dinner. Shit. He hoped she had money on her. She should since she had come here directly from work.

Picking up his fork, he moved hers to one side. Reconsidering, he put down his fork and used hers. She smiled, although he didn't see it because he didn't look up until he had finished the food. He wasn't sure why he was ravenous or why the food tasted like all his fear and yet also like all his comfort. Contradictory and completely familiar at the same time. Finishing, he pushed the plate away and drank deeply from his bottle of beer.

"That hit the spot," he said. "Thanks."

Sweet Girl smiled.

"What was that?"

"Wild boar," she said.

He found that unaccountably funny. He laughed.

"You're silly," she said.

He sobered up.

"Is that bad?"

"No, I like it. Most men take themselves too seriously." She sounded sad.

Black shrugged. "Is that bad?"

She gave him a funny look and said:

"Not always. But sometimes for a girl like me it can be dangerous."

"I need to get out of here," Black said to her.

"Sure," Sweet Girl said.

"I'm kind of . . ."

"I know. I've got it, baby," Sweet Girl said, reaching for the check.

Outside it was cold and a wind was blowing ash from the brush fires around the street.

"Thanks for dinner, baby," Sweet Girl said.

"You're welcome."

They were standing by her car: a shiny silver Honda Civic. Silence. Street sounds. The wind.

"Reminds me of my spaceship," Black said, cursing himself as the words came out of his mouth.

"Is that what you call your car?"

She sounded shy and coy again. The Sweet Girl from the strip club. That irritated him a little. He smiled tightly.

"Where is your car?" she asked.

He pointed to the Blackmobile and she smiled.

"What?"

"Looks like Big Bird," Sweet Girl said, brushing hair from her face. She looked away and then back at him. Her arms were crossed against the cold and she shivered.

"I'm going for a walk," he said. "Do you want to come with me?"

She glanced at her watch.

"I do, but I have to be somewhere. Don't worry about me. I'll be fine. See you soon?"

"Fine," he said.

She could detect a sulk in his tone. She put her hand on his arm.

"It's not what you think," she said.

He nodded. Not waiting for her to get in her car, he set off down Hollywood Boulevard, heading west. Past the other strip mall that held more Thai restaurants. Past the fenced-in lot that housed a beat-up motor home and statues made by the artist who lived there. Past the public bandstand that the club next door had turned into its dance floor. Past the Hollywood Motel with its 1950s look and its revolutionary promise of telephones, hot water and televisions in every room. Past Espresso Mi Cultura. Past Pier One Imports.

And on and on.

Studios. A school. Endless strip malls. The Pantages Theatre with the limo stop opposite that had a limo impaled on a pole, though it wasn't as tall as Black's spaceship. Past the decaying and crumbling sex shops and nude bars, the stars on the sidewalk hiding their shame under grime and windblown trash—and now ash. Just before the neon renaissance of the Egyptian Theatre and Ripley's with the T-Rex on the roof roaring in purple neon, Black paused by the string of gift and trinket shops selling useless knick-knacks to mostly midwestern tourists: the men in shorts and Hawaiian shirts, white socked feet in Birkenstocks, and women in frumpy summer dresses or khaki Gap shorts and sandals. There was the occasional reluctant and inevitably overweight child or two, whose excitement with this no man's land's legends of muggers and drug dealers was enough to overcome the embarrassment of parents who were pointing out everything from the pub with the British name to the number of Starbucks franchises in such a small area.

Black ducked into one of the gift shops when a passing police car slowed down to watch him. He hated the police, the jackal snout of their hoods. Scavengers.

The shop had a full complement of trashy trinkets: model cars with surfboards on their roof racks, crystal necklaces, glass bong pipes, I ♥ LA key rings. Black stopped browsing to study the snow globes lounging next to the collection of American flags. Some of the snow globes commemorated 9/11. Firemen holding up an American flag amidst the detritus of Ground Zero in the same pose as the Vietnam memorial. He picked one up and studied it.

He shook it.

It rained, not snow, but tinsel in red, white and blue.

He put it back on the shelf and wiped his hand against his trouser leg, feeling dirty. What next, he thought, a holocaust snow globe with a Giacometti stick figure rising out of the lip of an oven that rained ash when shaken? He was shocked to see a couple next to him picking up six.

"These are great, huh?" the woman gushed at him.

"Yeah, great," he said.

He left the shop and continued down Hollywood Boulevard toward Grauman's Chinese Theatre. Outside the Roosevelt Hotel, waiting for a light, he wiped his hand across his face and then looked at his hand. Nothing. The ash drizzle had stopped except for a few big pieces. Maybe the wind has changed direction, he thought. He wondered what time it was.

"Excuse me," he said to a man passing, intending to ask for the time.

"Get a job," the man snarled.

Black shrank back as though he had been struck physically. Muttering under his breath, he headed back to the Palms. The Blackmobile was parked in front where he had left it.

Gabriel dozed on the roof.

a donkey.

And an old woman waiting patiently for the lights to change at the corner of Olympic and Alameda, just a block short of the Spearmint Rhino Gentlemen's Club. He pulled up alongside, smiled and said hello. She ignored him. If she was an omen, he thought, then she's probably a bad one. As if to confirm this, the donkey let out a steaming pile.

He stopped abruptly under the overpass, satisfied when he heard Gabriel fall from the roof of the bus and hit the ground with a grunt. Gabriel stood up, head lost in the shadows near the top of the bridge, and with one flap that sent dust flying everywhere, took off.

Black pulled off the road and parked. He felt constrained, like there was a band across his chest and he needed to feel free, to gain release. Already the erection that had begun stirring over dinner with Sweet Girl was full blown and hard. He needed to do something. He sat there and tried to imagine Iggy or Brandy naked while he masturbated, but he couldn't find the release. Instead he took off all his clothes and stood there for a moment feeling his body fill the night. Reaching into the back of the Blackmobile, he took the bag that held Iggy's wedding dress and wig. After she'd found it in the spaceship, he had taken to carrying it around with him. With a sigh and gentle swing of his penis, he headed off into the night.

thirty

Warm soap.

Maybe detergent. The smell left him pining for home. Familiar yet full of delicious warmth, like a stranger's leg pressing against his in a bus sometime, somewhere. Turning around in a circle, he tried to determine its source. He set off on foot down the rail tracks heading east. Crossed Santa Fe, crossed San Pedro and stopped there, behind the junkyard abutting the River. After a while, he realized the smell was coming from the wedding dress he carried. A second later, he realized he was still naked. Ducking into an abandoned warehouse, he pulled the dress and wig on. Wandering around, he decided to rest, perched in an empty window frame.

He didn't know how long he'd been there, having lost all track of time, but he became aware that a small group of people had gathered below the window. They were holding candles and reciting their *Hail Mary*s. Everywhere, there was the smell of soap. He felt both an old and inexplicable terror, and something akin to the sublime, and he searched for meaning in the folds of the dress; the way light between hills reveals valleys, or maybe rivers: or some such truth.

And something else.

There was sadness. But this sadness wasn't a turning, wasn't a leaning into healing. There was no tight-lipped hope in the face of it. This sadness was like a dandelion blown into the wind. Not the prelude to a new beginning, but a dispersal into parts so small that there was nothing to hold on to, no way to find them all.

Yet somehow, they filled the world.

Death is the mother of beauty; hence from her,
Alone, shall come fulfillment to our dreams
And our desires . . .

—Wallace Stevens

ray-Ray was stuck.

Black stood next to Iggy as the paramedics tried to get his heart started, but the "wet" had taken its toll. The lead paramedic looked up at Iggy and shook his head.

"His lungs are completely atrophied, ma'am. There's nothing we can do," he said.

Iggy nodded. She held on to Black's hand as Ray-Ray was wheeled out on the gurney, face covered by a white sheet. The paramedic was talking into his radio: "Ten-four, ten-four. One male, African-American, DOA."

When the room was clear, Iggy collapsed into a chair. Black said nothing, but stood by the window a shadow away from the supplicants outside. Watching a woman writhing in ecstasy, he wondered how death and the miraculous could coexist so easily. The lights in The Ugly Store were dim, and the moa cast a dark ugly shadow across the floor. Black turned away from the window, crossing to the bar where he began to make two cups of hot, sweet tea. He didn't know what else to do.

"He was going to die anyway," Iggy said. "I told him. Tried to help. You know?"

"You more than any of us," Black said, bringing two steaming mugs over. He sat down opposite her and took her hand in his. She squeezed it. Smiled.

"You are a good man, Black."

"No," he said, shaking his head. "No, I'm not."

"Hush, Black," she said. "Let me believe it."

He smiled uncomfortably and took a sip of tea. God, it tastes so good, he thought as its warmth spread through him.

"What happened exactly?" Black asked.

"I'm not sure myself. I mean, one minute he was fine, you know? Going about on his stilts, serving customers, trying to get the regulars to play that game with him."

"The Chandler game?"

"Uh-huh. Anyway he took a tray with coffee and muffins to that table," she pointed, "when he just collapsed. I thought he was goofing at first, but then I saw blood from a small cut on his forehead and I realized that he must have tripped." As she spoke, her finger was turning in the air. Tracing an arc, then returning to begin again, as though she were dialing an invisible rotary telephone, as though it was containing the words. As though it could. Black couldn't take his eyes away from her hand. "I called out several times, but he didn't get up," she continued. "I walked over to him. I thought he would say something funny, like a quote from Chandler, but he just lay there, struggling to breathe. Not gasping, just this horrible wheezing sound and something that sounded like a whistle, like something was caught in his chest. I called 911. I wasn't afraid. I was just confused. Anyway, he opened his mouth and I thought, Ok this is it, the moment of final wisdom, or the spitting up of the things stuck in his throat. But he just closed his mouth and that was it."

"What was?"

"His death. One moment he was trying to breathe and the next he was dead. I guess the holy books are right, death does come unannounced."

Her voice was no more than a whisper. Black took her hand and squeezed it. He wasn't sure why. Maybe he saw someone else do it, though he couldn't think when. And in all honesty he probably did it more for himself than her. The mention of holy books had reminded him of being a pastor. Putting it out of his mind, he said:

"Are you going to be okay?"

She nodded.

"Yeah."

Pause.

"It's just that the look on his face, his eyes, like he was begging for help. For it to stop. Ray-Ray died like that, eyes wide open in fear."

"Ssssh," he said. "I never know how to act in the face of death. It's like a desert or an ocean. Any emotion seems like an attempt to reduce it," he added.

Pause.

"More tea?" she asked him.

"Yes, please," he said, passing his cup to her.

She went behind the bar and soon the room was full of the hiss of steam and the desperate gurgle of heating milk. Conversation was impossible so he contented himself with watching her and listening to the warm sounds. When she came back to the table, she put a steaming mug before him. He drank gratefully, but carefully. They didn't speak. She returned to the counter, slid the glass door open on the display case and helped herself to a slice of chocolate cake.

"God," she said, stuffing her mouth. "Death always makes me hungry. Want some?"

He nodded. She cut two thick slices of cake and came back to the table, passing one to him.

"Didn't you just have a piece of cake?" he asked, digging into his own.

"What? Are you my personal trainer?"

They ate quickly, almost furtively. Was it embarrassment or fear?

"Do you know why you began wearing my wedding dress?" she asked finally.

"No."

"It's symptomatic of a deeper illness, Black. The not knowing, I mean. The blindness of it."

"Yeah? Maybe you're right. But you're ill too."

She smiled.

"That's why we eat chocolate cake."

"Well, then, here's to chocolate cake."

thirty-two

Insatiable.

The hunger of fires ravaging hillsides. Just that.

"How do you know which is which?" Bomboy asked Black, as he watched him mix up several batches of his special paint remover.

"I line them up in order as I mix them," Black replied.

There were five batches.

"Skeleton, muscles, flesh, skin and clothes," Bomboy said, counting them off.

"Yes," Black agreed. "Except in the reverse order."

"Oh, yeah."

There was a police car parked on the bridge, lights flashing. Two policemen lounged against it, watching Black.

"Who are they?" Bomboy asked, pointing.

"Cop One and Cop Two? Oh, they're just there to make sure I take Fatima down," Black said, following Bomboy's finger. He waved at the policemen. They ignored him. He had been served with an order to remove the painting by his usual nemesis, the LA City Council. At least the Army Corps of Engineers had laid off this time, he thought. The policemen were there to ensure his compliance. Black went back to mixing. He opened a tin of turpentine and stirred some into the last mix.

"Hey, man! Are you supposed to be smoking near that stuff?" Bomboy asked, as Black bent over the mix, cigarette dangling from his lips. "I thought it was flammable."

"So's your fart. Never stopped you," Black said, giving the mixture one last twirl before emptying it into an insecticide spray unit. Agilely he rappelled up the wall and began to squirt the painting, smiling unaccountably as paint began to run down the wall in black tears. As the sun began to set, Black finished and began to pack up his equipment. The policemen came down from the bridge.

"Hey! What are you doing?" Cop One demanded.

"Packing up. It'll be dark soon."

"But the woman is still up. All you've done is take her clothes off and remove the dove and the gun."

"I know. This stuff takes time. It has to be taken down layer by layer. Probably take a week," Black said cheerfully.

"No, no, no!" Cop Two said. "The order was to take it down before the kids came back to school. That's tomorrow."

"Really? I don't remember that. All I remember is that I had to take it down. I went to City Hall and they said I could do it layer by layer."

"Did you tell them it would take a week?" Cop One asked.

"I might have forgotten that detail."

"I should arrest you now," Cop Two said.

"Why? I am doing my best to comply with the order,"

Black said, sounding as obsequious as possible, and yet smirking at the same time.

Bomboy laughed so hard he began to choke on his cigarette smoke.

"And who are you, sir?" Cop One asked him, as Cop Two stepped away to talk into his radio.

"He's nobody," Black said.

Cop Two joined them again.

"They say we should let him go," he said to Cop One. "They'll send a sandblasting team over tomorrow. This painting will be off the wall in a matter of minutes."

"Before the kids come to school?" Cop One asked.

Cop Two shrugged.

"I don't know. It's not my business. We're done here."

"I've got kids," Cop One grumbled.

"Yeah, me too," Cop Two said.

They began to walk away.

"Good night, Tweedledee and Tweedledum," Black said.

"What did you just call us?" Cop One asked, turning and walking back toward them. Bomboy stepped away from Black. Before Black could answer, Cop One punched him hard in the stomach. Black collapsed with a loud grunt and threw up, just missing Cop One's shoes by a fraction of an inch. Both cops laughed.

"Did you see anything?" Cop One asked Bomboy.

"Like what? Where?"

"Good man."

Still laughing, both cops left, heading for the bridge and their car.

"Are you okay?" Bomboy asked, bending to help Black up, but Black shrugged him away.

"Thank you so much for helping me!"

"What was I supposed to do? These are the men in blue."

"You weren't such a coward when you chopped up those women and children back home."

"I'm leaving," Bomboy said. "Fuck you and your shit!"

Left alone, Black collapsed face first into the dirt before the wall. He rolled over onto his back and wiped his mouth, breathing raggedly. After a long time, his breathing settled down to an even rhythm. It was dark now and the only light came from the streetlights across the River, by the school. They reflected off the white screen of the wall, lighting Fatima in a ghostly, otherworldly glow. Still he lay there, staring up at the naked Fatima. She smiled at him. He smiled back. He got up and walked over to the wall and kissed her feet. Smiling he stepped back. He didn't know how long he stood there just staring up at her, losing time. Then he heard her call his name, talk to him.

"Yes?" he said, looking up at her face. "Take my clothes off? Now? Okay."

He stripped down until he was nude. He had a hard-on again. Hard to splitting. It hurt, but he ignored the pain and folded his clothes carefully. Using them for a pillow, he lay down and stared up at Fatima.

"Now what?" he asked. "Must I?"

He sighed and bent his dick back between his legs, forming a mock vagina. He touched himself. The way Sweet Girl had at the club, with a wet finger. He came in minutes. Spent, he lay there staring up at Fatima. She was smiling happily. Just then he heard the loud thud of Gabriel's wings above and felt the blinding searchlight of his gaze.

"Fuck you, Gabriel!" he shouted.

"You down there," a voice from a police helicopter called. "Put your clothes on."

Black sat upright, grabbed his clothes and ran for the shadows, chased by the determined halo of the spotlight.

He thought he could hear Fatima laughing.

thirty-three

Old; an upright piano.

It was inclined against the concrete wall of the River, caught on the edge of a tire protruding from a drainage gate like a black rubber tongue. Black leaned on it, smoking a reefer, watching the contractor the city had brought in to sandblast his painting off the wall at work. Iggy sat on top of the piano, legs crossed. The contractor had drawn a grid over the painting to focus his efforts, making sure to start with the crotch. Iggy watched the fifty-foot woman disappearing in squares, like a Hershey bar eaten by a careful child.

Still.

The schoolkids and even their teachers pressed their faces against the chain-link fence of the schoolyard to watch. Those who had gotten to school early were rewarded with Fatima in all her nudity, not this fast vanishing figure. And for years after, those boys and girls, even when they grew old, would never be satisfied with any love they had, because they, like Black, became infected by the

desire for Fatima. And even though they would never
member the name of it, this desire, it would fill every pore
in their body and drive them crazy.

Iggy was staring hard at Fatima's face. Liberated as it
was from the yashmak. It was her first good look at it.

"Did you know that you gave her your face?" she said to
Black.

"What?" he said.

"Yes, look. That's your face."

He looked. Iggy was right. He had given Fatima his
face. He wondered what it meant. Probably nothing.

"Huh," he said.

"Come to think of it," Iggy said. "With the exception of
the vagina and the breasts, she looks exactly like you."

"Trick of the light," he said, smiling.

"How can you smile at a moment like this? They are
obliterating your work," she said.

Black shook his head. "Everyone who saw that painting
will always carry it with them. Do you think the Chumash
are gone because the Mission settlers wiped them out?
History is everywhere here; if it weren't they wouldn't be
trying so hard to hide it. As for my painting? It will haunt
that wall forever."

"The ghost of a painting?"

"It's like this piano, Iggy. See how it looks broken?"
Black said, bashing the wooden and ivory keys down hard.
Apart from the dull knock of wet wood, it made no sound.
Iggy watched Black's energetic display, thinking he looked
stupid. In the distance, loud and annoying, was the hiss of
high-pressured sand blasting against brick.

"But see this, this is Beethoven's *Moonlight Sonata*,"
Black said.

His playing changed, if he was playing at all. Instead of the percussive bashing of his previous performance, Black was running his fingers over the cracks between the keys, skin barely touching wood. His eyes closed and his head rolled back and in that moment, Iggy felt she was in the presence of something important, though she would be hard-pressed to explain what—except to say, silence. The hiss of the sandblasting had stopped. Even the hovering helicopter seemed to have muted itself, hanging there in the clear blue sky with all the control of a dragonfly skirting a pond's surface.

It took Iggy a while to realize that Black had stopped whatever it was he had been doing. The sound of the sandblasting was back, as was the dull thump of the helicopter above them.

Black laughed.

Iggy stared off at the painting.

The top half of it was gone, but the woman was still there, at least from just below her hips. Black followed her gaze, looking at what was left of Fatima, trying to figure out the importance of this enigmatic woman. He knew he would never solve the riddle, but for now, he thought he knew what part of it was.

Iggy jumped down from the piano.

The contractor had knocked off for the day. Hanging there, in the setting sun, were Fatima's legs, from the knees down. Without the face or body, this wasn't Fatima: just the legs of a once fifty-foot-tall woman. The image was a cipher too big for Iggy to solve. She turned back to speak to Black but stopped when she saw him staring at the painting, tears running unhindered down his face.

"I'm sorry," she said, putting an arm on Black's shoulder. Black shook it off.

"No," he said, raising both arms up, palms out. "You don't understand. She is still so beautiful."

There was such awe in his voice, Iggy felt she was intruding on something she couldn't understand and wasn't necessarily meant to see. So she left him there, thinking Black was like someone who hadn't shown up and yet was looking for someone who was someplace else. Iggy paused on the bridge and looked back. Black was still facing the wall with the painting, swaying arms raised in worship.

An iroko the wind could not uproot.

d enny's?"

"I swear to God, there's this Denny's," he pressed on. "Downtown, near Union Station. They make the most amazing steak."

"Denny's? You sure know how to excite a girl," Sweet Girl said.

Black grimaced into the receiver, partly from the shame of it and partly because he could hear the loud music of Charlie's in the background. Denny's was all he could afford. And even for that he'd boosted money off of Bomboy. But there was also the knowledge that he didn't really want to meet Sweet Girl. He had to. There was no part of this that was desire anymore. What little there had been died somewhere between the night she jerked him off in the club and the night she gave him head at his place. What drew him still was an overwhelming sense that he had to burn this obsession out.

"What do you say?" he asked.

"If I'm not too tired when I get off, we'll talk."

"So I should call back?"

"Yeah, baby, why don't you."

Voices in the background, a man's demanding a lap dance. Sweet Girl's, conciliatory. She came back to Black.

"Listen, honey, I've got to go. Call me later."

He slammed the receiver home, but it was an impotent gesture. She'd already hung up. He pushed his fingers into the coin return slot. There was never anything there and he didn't know why he bothered but he did. He was in the cathedral of Union Station, one of the few places that still had working phone booths. He loved it here, but didn't come often enough. The station house was truly like an old Spanish mission, with its high vaulted ceilings that made him yearn to paint. He could turn it into his own Sistine. The old wood of the ceiling beams, the cracked and aged leather of the seats, the polished Mexican tiles on the floor and the high windows and white speckled paint all gave it a heightened sense of the sacred. Even at its busiest there was a hush here. There were some advantages to a town with little use for public transport, he thought.

"Nice, isn't it? I like coming here, reminds me of the quiet back home," Gabriel said from the vaulted ceiling. He was a pigeon again, and Black let out a sigh of relief.

"Fuck off, culero!" It wasn't a shout, it was a whisper, but harsh, like the grind of a train's brakes on the track. Black was sure not to look up.

"So, taking Sweet Girl to dinner then?"

"You shouldn't eavesdrop."

"Well, you know. I'm bored. Usually when I appear I get to dictate a holy book or two, but you are boring. Fatima, the one interesting thing you had going, is gone."

Black grabbed hold of his left arm. It ached like a broken wing.

"Cheapskate, though. I mean, Denny's? You're right next to Chinatown. Everything is better in Chinatown even if it is cheap," Gabriel said.

"Shut up, shut up, shut up! I don't know why you don't shut up!" Black yelled.

A couple of people turned to look at him. Nobody seemed particularly bothered though. It was downtown LA, the haunt of the crazy homeless.

Gabriel laughed.

Black ran out of the station. He stood outside huffing for a while. It might be a good idea to return to The Ugly Store. Hang out with Iggy. He glanced at his watch. It was ten p.m. and a strong wind had picked up.

thirty-five

Sacrifice.

That was all he had to look forward to. Bartering something precious for something that may not be worth anything, a game for fools and the pious.

Entering The Ugly Store, he instinctively looked to the bar to see Ray-Ray. Remembering he was dead, he walked to Iggy's office. She looked up as he came in. She was sitting with her back to the door while a Korean woman Black had never seen before cleaned the metal rings on her back. From the smell he guessed the woman was using surgical alcohol.

"Hey, Black."

"Hi, Iggy. Couldn't help looking for Ray-Ray just now," he said.

"I know. I miss him too."

He sat down.

"Hey, Black, do you mind? I'm kind of having a personal moment here," Iggy said, grabbing a T-shirt and holding it against her bare chest.

"I'm sorry," Black said, not moving.

Iggy turned to the woman and spoke to her softly. She nodded and packed up her bag and stepped out, closing the door behind her.

"Okay, Black, what's so important?" Iggy asked. "And don't tell me you've come to cry about Fatima."

"I went by there earlier. She's all gone."

"I know."

"Who was that woman?"

"None of your business. Now tell me what it is."

"I wish I knew. I have this feeling that I am inside myself and yet outside myself at the same time."

Iggy shook her head.

"Black, I don't have time for your bullshit."

"I thought you loved me?"

"I do love you, but I don't have time for your bullshit."

"But, Iggy, I am suicidal here."

Iggy laughed.

"I don't mean to be harsh, Black, but you're not suicidal. If you were, you would have killed yourself by now. No, I think you're too much of a coward to kill yourself, but what's worse is that you're also too much of a coward to live."

"I thought you were the psychic? Can't you tell me? Read my aura or something?"

"Aren't you an artist? I thought Fatima was the vision to save you?"

"I thought so too. Maybe she just reminded me of my mother."

"You always blame your mother for your life. What about your father?"

"I never knew him, I only dream about him. It's hard to blame a dream."

"Yeah?"

"Yeah. In the dream we were always in a living room. The same living room, only it was no living room I knew. Anyway, we would be there, him, me and my mother. My mother and I are always drowning in that living room, but my father has his back turned to us, looking out of the window. No words are ever spoken. Just him, looking out the window."

"I'm sorry."

"Why?"

"Because although I want to feel compassion for you—no, that's wrong, I *do* feel compassion for you. But I don't believe you know what it means to be sorry."

Black looked away.

"I need you to save me, Iggy."

"Why? Why should I save you? How come you can never save anyone?"

"I don't know."

"And what is the cost of saving you?"

"I don't know."

Iggy touched his face.

"I wish I knew what it took to make you happy, Black. But even you don't know that. For what it's worth, though, I think that the answer lies with Fatima and what she means to you. But I suspect you know that already."

"And Sweet Girl," he said.

She said nothing.

"I'm sorry, Iggy. I'm so sorry," he said.

"Turn around for a second."

He spun around in the chair. Iggy stood up and pulled her T-shirt on.

"Can I turn around yet?" he asked.

"Sure," she said.

He turned around.

"Aren't you going to ask me how I am?" she said.

"How do you mean?" he asked.

"Look at me, Black."

But he couldn't meet her eyes.

"Sometimes I think you've lost your soul. Ask me how I feel about Ray-Ray's death. Ask me how I feel about the stuff in my life. Just ask me about me."

He raised his eyes hesitantly.

"I didn't mean to hurt you," he said.

"I know. But your apology is still about you. About your wanting me to make you feel better."

"So what do you want?"

"I want you to leave, Black, to leave. Forget the rent, forget the past, just move on."

"But I don't want to."

"But I want you to. Don't you get it?"

He said nothing. Looked away again.

"Look, things are complicated right now."

"It's always complicated with you," she said.

"I know. I don't know," he said, his voice a whisper. "I'm afraid, I guess."

"What time is it?"

He glanced at his watch.

"Ten-thirty p.m."

"Damian's band is playing here tonight. It's a late gig, starts about midnight and goes on all night."

"Sounds good," he said, voice flat.

"I think you should come tonight, for the band. One last bash, eh? Then move on," she said.

"Whatever," he said.

"Send Suji in on your way out," she said. Even though her tone sounded final, there was a note of kindness in it.

"Sure," he said, opening the door.

"Black?"

"Yeah?"

She threw a goodoo doll at him.

"For love, for protection, for success, for healing," she said.

He rubbed the goodoo's clay body with a thumb. It felt cool to the touch.

"Thank you," he said.

"Maybe somewhere, sometime down the road, you know?" she said.

He closed the door behind him.

fingers on skin.

That was the sound and Black followed it downstairs to the café of The Ugly Store. He wasn't expecting Damian Thrace's band to be set up yet and he was right. Walter Henry, the percussionist, was tightening the skins on his djembe and congas with a small metal hammer, eyes closed. The entire operation, done by touch, by feel, made Black think of ritual, of sacrifice, as though Walter were speaking to the gazelles—if indeed they were gazelles—who had given their hides for this sound, for this sacred communion. A couple of other band members, whom Black recognized as the saxophonist and flautist Rakim and drummer Jo-Jo stood drinking tea and waiting for the room to fill up. Black walked over to them, thinking, Why is it that I can remember details about people and things that have nothing to do with my life and yet remember nothing about my life?

"Hey," he said, putting out his hand.

"Hey, brother," Rakim said, shaking his hand.

"Hey, black," Jo-Jo said, pulling Black into a half hug.

"Glad you guys could come out," Black said. He didn't know either of the musicians personally and now that he was here talking to them he felt slightly foolish, but they were both easy and friendly. He stood next to them for a minute then sauntered over to smoke by the door. There was a guy he didn't know standing next to a small table behind which Iggy sat with a cashbox. She was doing brisk business selling tickets, and the room was filling up.

"Black," she said as he stopped beside her.

"Iggy," he said, passing the cigarette she was reaching for. "Drew a big crowd."

"Told you it was a good idea."

"You did. Who is this?" he said, indicating the guy standing next to her.

"Oh, this is Leland. He's with the band. Protecting their interests, I guess," Iggy said, indicating the cashbox. Black nodded and she went back to selling tickets. Ten minutes and two cigarettes later, the music began.

At first it was a whisper. Just Damian: Joooooooooohnnn Cooooooollllltrane. Just like that, like breath teasing skin. Everything in the café stopped, everyone leaning forward to hear. There it was again, that whisper, warm, lush like warm wet tropical rain, and Black relaxed into it. There was seduction to it and it felt like Damian's calls were fogging up the windows, fogging the air thick enough to trace a message like, *Help, I am drowning here but I love it, help*. And as the lushness of Damian's voice backwashed, like a tide returning to the band, Walter's finger began to mark the beat on the rim of the djembe, the sound like a knife chopping through onions and tomatoes and ginger and garlic to the wooden board beneath, chopping; and behind him Jo-Jo spread oil over his snare's face with the sizzle of brushes and the high snap of hot cymbals and spreading, and Walter, licking his fingers and holding down the skin of the djembe with the heel of one hand, peeled the notes off with the wet finger, each one as sharp as a paper cut. And flowing back on the sound of Rakim's tenor, and Damian singing, the notes mixing until there was no Rakim, no horn, no Damian, no voice, just this spreading ripple of sound, not this note or that one or this instrument or that, not even this player or that singer, there was just sound, like an umbrella over it all and something else, the soft erasure of chalk on blackboard and Black was disappearing into it, diminishing and turning to smoke and the call and the fall and the all of it and he wanted to push against this thing but there wasn't anything, no provocation, just this poised vital ocean and the tactile feeling, this sweet decline and thoughts that were all slurred and blurred like the lights on a freeway disappearing from view as a spaceship rose into the open arms of sky, into the dark sky of memory, and there was forgetting here, everything you wanted to be and were and still Damian's crying, hollering and there was a shape, maybe remembrance, and the desire, oh, the desire, and Black was pulling back and even this was jazz and even now he was falling and there was the smell of fresh bread which is a lie 'cause no one he knew baked and the smell of bread, fresh bread turning to toast, and across the table the heaped hope of pancakes and butter waiting and waiting and then as Taylor caressed and teased notes down the spine of the bass, fingers weaving strings like an old African griot singing his lineage as he wove it all into a tapestry and when this was not enough, he picked up the bow, he sawed through the peg leg, cutting to another place and Black felt tears on his face and wondered what and why and shit, shit, shit, but Damian had latched on and he wouldn't let go and Black wanted to testify, to let it all out, let it come and a choked sob broke from him and he turned and fled, out of the door, out of The Ugly Store.

thirty-seven

Saffron sky.

The floating blue-black mirror of it reflecting fires burning for miles and miles. And smoke like an offering, rising, and then falling, like the breath of a continent, or penitents showering humiliation on themselves in the face of the sacred.

Black stood on the street in front of The Ugly Store and took a deep breath. Fear is only a limitation, he told himself. In the busy artery of the street, he felt there was no way to hide, and no need. The city had swallowed him up. It would shelter him from harm. Just then a police car passed and he stepped back into the shadow of The Ugly Store's door. The tall grass covers the antelope, he thought (remembering an old proverb that Bomboy had told him), but the hunter's bullet still finds it.

"Black!"

JUST HANGING.

The white T-shirt wore the slogan and a facsimile of an actual photograph of a lynched black man. Black couldn't believe Bomboy was wearing it. He was across the street at Pedro's taco stand. In his hand was a large burrito dripping sauce onto his arm. Black's eyes followed the thin trail as it disappeared behind Bomboy's elbow, thinking that his face looked uncannily like that of the half deflated raptor on the roof of the stand.

"Hey, culero! What the fuck is the idea with that shirt?" he said.

"Why don't you shut the fuck up?" Bomboy said.

"Even you have to know how offensive that shirt is," Black said.

"This?" Bomboy said, stretching the shirt with both hands and glancing down at it. "This is just a joke."

"How can that be a joke?" Black demanded.

"You're right, Black. *You* are the joke," Bomboy said. "Go hang with that."

Black shook his head.

"Now who's the loser?" he asked.

Bomboy took a bite of his burrito and spitting detritus at Black, said:

"Whatever. See me? When I came here I had nothing. Now I have a Lexus, an apartment and I can send money to my people. What of you?"

"You seem lost in this country. Like this is where your journey ends," Black said.

"But *you* have nothing," Bomboy said, spitting at Black's feet. "You don't even have shame. Without your shame you have no people, without people you have no lineage, without a lineage you have no ancestors, without ancestors you have no dead and without the dead you can never know anything about life. All you have is ash. And you know what happens to ash when the wind blows. It is I who pity you.

I may be many things that can be despised, but I am still better than you because I know my shame. My journey will probably end here, but your journey hasn't even begun."

Black lit a Marlboro and blew smoke into the already smoky air. He had no response. Instead he looked at his watch. It was nearly one in the morning. He should call Sweet Girl. Smiling at Bomboy, Black walked to his van and disappeared into the night.

She was laughing when she answered the phone.

"Hey, Baby," Sweet Girl said.

"Hey," Black said.

"What's up?"

"I wondered if you were done?"

"Yes, you still want to meet at Denny's?"

"Yes," Black said, his voice taut.

Sweet Girl picked up on it immediately.

"Just tell me where it is and I'll meet you there in about half an hour or forty-five minutes."

Black gave her directions. He'd called from the phone box outside the prison, about three minutes from the Denny's. He figured he would kill some time before going there, so he headed for the river. As he sat on the concrete lip smoking, he thought it was strange how he was always chasing this River in some way. Its flow, its line, its energy, its alchemy. Soon, though, his mind turned to Sweet Girl and their conversations.

"You have cute eyes," she'd said to him.

"You're one of the few men who has seen me. Who has looked me in the eye while I danced naked," she'd said.

"Your eyes," she'd said.

"I don't mean to interrupt," Gabriel said, "but have you noticed that you use red a lot in your work?"

Black couldn't see him at first, but when he strained he could just make out Gabriel's fifteen-foot silhouette across the river. He was smoking a cigarette. Black wondered why he could hear the angel so clearly from so far away.

"I could sound distant and crackly," Gabriel said, sounding like a cell phone with bad reception.

Black didn't waste time wondering how Gabriel knew what he was thinking. He said nothing, though, other than to mumble under his breath: "You're not real." Over and over.

"Red says a lot about you humans. The whole story of your miserable species unravels along the river of that color. The blood you are made from, the bloodline you belong to, the blood in your veins, the blood of your sacrifice and redemption . . ."

"You sound jealous," Black said.

"It doesn't help to get into arguments with an angel, you know. Just ask Kant," Gabriel said and laughed deeply.

"Time I was gone anyway," Black said, getting up and heading for the van. He and Sweet Girl would be arriving at the same time. This was good. He didn't want to seem too eager.

■

"The same as him," she said to the waiter, sliding into the booth opposite Black. "Am I very late?"

"No," he said, smiling shyly, "I was early."

The old Hispanic waiter in soft, worn running shoes

walked away, writing hard on the order pad, face furrowed in concentration as if trying to push the pen through. Black watched him for a minute. There was something about old men like this, they reminded him of good things, but he didn't know what. Maybe something like a poor man with very little but who would split whatever he had and give you a feast. Black's attention returned to Sweet Girl, as she adjusted her hair while looking into her compact, unself-consciously, with the air of a woman who is beautiful and knows it. She snapped it shut and returned it to her handbag.

"What'll it be?" It was a woman's voice.

Without looking up, Black said, "We've ordered. Thank you."

"I don't think she's a waitress," Sweet Girl said, smiling at the old woman who stood by them. The woman stank and Sweet Girl was doing her best not to be rude and show her disgust. Black looked up.

"What do you mean?" he asked.

"What'll it be?" the old woman repeated. "Money or death." She added this last part as though it clarified everything.

"I don't understand," Black said.

"I'm a fortune-teller," the old woman said, tone exasperated. "Do you want your fortune told?"

Black didn't, but he looked over at Sweet Girl. She smiled.

"Can't do any harm, right?" she said.

"Not if you pick money," he said.

Sweet Girl turned to the old woman.

"How much?"

"Five dollars."

"Five dollars!" Black said.

"Okay, two then. But only because the lady is beautiful," she said.

Black paid up. The old woman took Sweet Girl's hand in hers and squinting against an imaginary light, she stared off to the side of Sweet Girl's head.

"What are you looking at?" Black asked.

"Ssh!" the old woman said.

Sweet Girl made a face and giggled. The woman let go of Sweet Girl's hand and wiped her own hand over her face.

"Your energy is good. I think you are a good person," the old woman said. "Do people say you are a good person?"

"Yeah!" Sweet Girl said.

"And people always take advantage of your goodness, don't they?"

"Oh, my God!" Sweet Girl said. "This is too freaky."

Black yawned.

"I see a lot of money coming your way," the old woman said. "Right here in your aura," she added, gesturing. "Of course I am color-blind and it could just as easily be death."

Black laughed.

"I told you it was a scam," he said.

The old woman rounded on him, eyes glittering.

"If you don't believe me, then give me two dollars for your reading."

"I got it," Sweet Girl said, handing the woman two dollars.

"You're enjoying this, aren't you?" Black said.

"Hell yeah," Sweet Girl said.

The old woman folded the bills somewhere into her tent-like clothing and grabbed Black's hand with her dirty claws. She dropped it.

"You're a crazy mothafucker!" she said, backing away.

"Hey!"

"No, you're crazy and no good," the old woman muttered, backing away. "No good!"

The old man who had taken their order came over.

"Hey, Gladys," he said, and though he meant to reprimand the old woman, his tone was gentle. "Are you bothering the customers?"

"No, Tony, they paid, honest, look," the old woman said, showing him the money.

"You have to leave now, Gladys," he said, steering her toward the door. "Sorry," he threw back at Black and Sweet Girl.

Black looked rattled. Sweet Girl put her hand over his.

"Are you okay?"

He nodded. Lit a Marlboro. Fished a small bottle of brandy out of his shirt, poured generous shots into both their coffee cups.

"It's okay."

She sipped the coffee.

"Whoa, papacito, are you trying to get me drunk?" she asked, smiling.

"Maybe," he said, pulling the bottle out again and taking a generous swig before passing it to her. She shook her head. He took another swig. He looked bothered.

"Easy, mi rey," Sweet Girl said. "She was just a crazy old lady. You don't believe that stuff, do you?"

He blew smoke into his coffee cup, watched it swirl

over the surface of the dark liquid like mist over a lake. He took a sip.

"When I was a kid I used to read comics a lot. Silver Surfer. The X-men. There was this comic book that had a young boy in it. He had these aliens come down from outer space. Small little beings. And they saved him, turned him from a nerd to a hero," he said.

Someone banged in covered in soot. He sat at the bar. A couple of policemen followed. They looked tired, eyes bloodshot. They sat at a booth in the back. They seemed to be casing the diner.

"So?"

"So I was maybe eight. Anyway I built a landing platform out back, in the yard. Nothing really, just some packed dirt and a strip of plywood painted with a runway. I set up my flashlight as a beacon, leaving it on every night for weeks."

"Did they come?"

"No, but it cost me a fortune in batteries. We moved soon after. My mother and I, because my dad left and we couldn't afford the house."

"I'm sorry."

"Anyway," Black said, "I'm sure they came. I am sure they did. I just wasn't there to meet them."

Sweet Girl smiled and squeezed his hand.

"Of course they came, baby. Of course they did."

He was suddenly angry. He couldn't tell if she was mocking him. He wanted to hurt her, be cruel. He pulled the bottle out again. Took another swig.

"I'm a crazy fuck, you know?" he said.

"No, amorcita. I know crazy. You're not."

"I am and don't argue with me, you bitch," he said, but his words lacked the venom, the power, and they both knew it.

"Corazón," she said.

Just then the old waiter brought them their food.

"Enjoy," he said.

"Thank you," they said.

"If you need anything, just call," he said.

"Thank you," they said.

They weren't that hungry anymore, but they ate. They ate in silence. In the parking lot they could see the fortune-teller. She was staring right at Black.

thirty-eight

The red of flames reflected.

And this. Soft and white, like a butterfly, a flake landed on Black's hand. He stared at it for a moment and then looked up. The sky was full of the flurry of snow. Bracing himself against the wind that was whipping everything into a frenzy, he leaned back and laughed. Snow, in Los Angeles, and it seemed to mitigate what was usual here: sorrow and loss catching in the city's heart like tumbleweed. Snow and a red sky; he liked it. Black closed his hand around the flake in his palm and felt the papery crumple of it. The realization came slowly. It wasn't snow, but ash from the brush fires blown in by the wind from the neighboring mountains. Just like Los Angeles, smoke and mirrors, and in this case, ash. He shook his head.

Sweet Girl watched him for a minute, enjoying the sheer abandon of his joy. It was infectious. They ran around the Denny's parking lot squealing like children at play, watched by the confused policemen of the K9 unit, their dog's unbridled desire filling the lot with barking, and the ash swirling about them like a snowstorm. And there was something about the moment—the antiseptic lights that lit the parking lot like an ER, the traffic passing in a dull throb just beyond its wall, the Denny's sitting in the middle of the lot like a postcard diner, the new wing of Union Station hunched over it on the slight rise like an inquisitive worm—everything, that made it seem like they were caught inside a snow globe, lost among the bric-a-brac on someone's mantelpiece.

Panting, Black came to a stop, leaning against his van. Sweet Girl fell into his arms. She kissed him, long and hard, pulled back, smiled at him and said:

"You realize all the cars are covered in soot."

He laughed and stood away from the van, brushing at his clothes. He swayed.

"Easy," Sweet Girl said.

"I think I had too much brandy," he said.

She smiled.

"Your place or mine?" she asked.

"I'm closer," he said.

"Your car or mine?"

"We're leaning against mine."

"Then let's go, papitito."

Sweet Girl hesitated before the open door.

"What is it?" he asked.

"I think I'll follow you. I don't want to leave my car here," she said. "I sat in a lotta laps for it."

But they both knew that wasn't the reason. She still didn't trust him completely. They turned out of the parking lot and waited for the lights on the corner of the rise, Black's van trembling against the strain like an old man, Sweet Girl following closely. The Denny's fell away into the small dip behind them, and the parking lot was empty apart from a lone police car, slowly being covered in ash and looking as forlorn as a scarf forgotten on the seat of a fast moving train, or a glove, dropped in the street.

As they drove up Cesar Chavez, there were children in the streets, laughing and darting around the flakes. Parents watched them carefully from their places at Pedro's taco stand or leaning against storefronts. Even Bomboy was out standing in the middle of the street, hands held up to catch the ashy snowflakes, eyes closed, wearing for the first time a plain black T-shirt turning white with the fall.

The drive was slow as the street was full of people luxuriating in the snow. Somehow music had been introduced. There was a mariachi band at one end, and several parked cars with custom sound systems that were blasting music at their loudest. People were dancing—together, alone. Men in white shirts turning gray in the snow, dark blue jeans with razor-sharp creases, cowboy boots and white Stetsons stood in a group in front of the panaderia. They were passing several paper-bagged forties back and forth, watching, laughing, leering. A circle of women and a few men danced on legs unsteady from alcohol. One woman broke away from the circle, stood confused for a second before squatting by a tree, right there on the street. She rejoined the circle and began dancing again, skirt tucked into the back of her tights. No one told her. No one seemed to mind. Teenagers in baggy shirts and jeans that desperately held on to the backs of thighs as they slid down fashionably stared stonily at the parade of people from their perches on the hoods and roofs of their cars. Children squealed in and out of the snow and the crowds. Older couples danced with all the elegance of a past remembered romantically, content in that moment to be eluding death. There was the air of carnival about it, which meant the threat of an unbridled violence hovered over everything, becoming a thing that collected in the corners and under the cars, blown there by the inclement wind.

Parking across from The Ugly Store, Black waited while Sweet Girl pulled in behind him and got out before leading her across the street. The faithful, still spread out over the sidewalk in front of The Ugly Store, had now built a shrine. A life-size Virgin of the Guadalupe stood in the middle of a sea of flowers and candles, and spreading like a shock wave around her, people kneeling and saying the rosary.

"This place is crazy!" Sweet Girl said, sounding excited. "What is going on?"

"These people," he said, pointing to the faithful and the statue, "believe the Virgin has been appearing on the roof of my spaceship."

"You really have a spaceship?"

He pointed. At first she couldn't see it through the thick flakes of falling ash but then there it was.

"Black!" she said. "That is just far out!"

"Yeah?"

"Yeah. You don't know?" she said.

"Know what?"

She glanced behind her as a drunken man bumped up against her. "Hey, mama, let's dance," he said. She pushed him hard and the man fell back into the street, promptly falling asleep. She turned back to Black.

"I love aliens," she said. "Always have. Remember *The Twilight Zone*?"

"Yes."

"Well, ever since then."

"Let's go inside," he said.

He paused in the foyer of the store, leaning against the moa's case. The place was packed and the band was still playing an upbeat standard, but he couldn't make out what it was. On the far side of the room, he saw Iggy leaning against the door of her office. She looked at him blankly, like he wasn't there, then her eyes alighted on Sweet Girl and she smiled. Sweet Girl smiled back and it seemed to Black like the two women spoke to each other. Iggy motioned them over.

"Where was all that ash coming from? Is that part of the street parade?" Sweet Girl asked as they crossed the room to Iggy's office.

"Have you watched the news lately?"

"No, why?"

"There are brush fires eating up the whole state."

"Oh," she said, sounding disappointed. "Still, the parade seems nice," she added, perking up.

"There is no parade. Just a bunch of people going wild because of the ash."

"Gotta love LA," she said.

"Yeah, gotta love it."

Iggy had seen them coming over and ducked back inside her office. She was sitting behind her desk as they came and she rose to meet them, sailing out from behind the desk to kiss Sweet Girl on both cheeks. It was quite the display, and Black was confused by it.

"So," Iggy said, holding both of Sweet Girl's hands in hers. "You are Sweet Girl. I have heard so much about you."

"But Black has told me nothing of you," Sweet Girl said, looking at Black with wide eyes.

"Really?" Iggy said, her voice thick with delicious danger.

"Iggy, meet Sweet Girl. Sweet Girl, this is Iggy," he said, adding, "Iggy is my landlord."

"And an old friend."

"And an old friend," Black agreed.

"How good of a friend?" Sweet Girl asked.

"Oh, nothing like that," Iggy said, waving them both into chairs. "Sit, sit. Can I get you anything?"

Black and Sweet Girl remained standing.

"Actually, no, Iggy. We just wanted to say hello," Black said. He was uncomfortable and wanted to get out of Iggy's office.

"Quite an interesting place you have here," Sweet Girl said. "Nice music."

"Thank you, thank you."

"Lots of dead things," Sweet Girl said, noting the stuffed owl on Iggy's desk.

"Yes," Iggy said, stroking it. "Well, you know what they say. Death can only haunt the dying, not the living."

Sweet Girl looked at Black and made a face. Black shrugged.

"You're not dying, Iggy," he said. "Are you?"

"Well, of course I am, and so are you. But not Sweet Girl here. No, she is a pure one, you know, living inside her joy. Compared to her, you and I are the walking dead."

"I think we should go," Black said, steering Sweet Girl for the door.

"Bye, it was nice to meet you," Sweet Girl said, following Black.

"Yes, it was," Iggy said.

As they made their way up the stairs to his room, Sweet Girl rolled her eyes.

"What a weird woman," she said.

"She grows on you," he said, stopping by the door of his room. "Well, here we are."

He opened the door, but Sweet Girl hovered on the threshold.

"Aren't you going to show me your spaceship?"

"What? Now?"

"Pleeze?"

Nodding, he led her out onto the roof, and helped her up the ladder, making her leave her pumps on the roof. She went first and he could barely keep his balance, he was staring at her ass so hard. And he was hard. Like with Fatima. Sweet Girl was laughing nervously.

"Shit!"

"What is it?"

"I got a run in my panty hose."

He smiled.

"Are you sure this thing is safe? It's swaying around a lot."

"It's safe. Built to withstand earthquakes," he said. But he *was* worried. The wind was whipping the spaceship about like a loose branch. He secretly hoped the screws and bolts would hold. He should have taken care of that.

Sweet Girl pulled herself into the ship and sat in the open door watching him come up. As he got nearer, she spread her legs and flashed him, smiling. He laughed. Sitting side by side in the open doorway, they looked out through the snow-ash flurry covering Los Angeles. He took another swig from the bottle of brandy and handed it to her. She took a swig, grimaced and passed it back.

"I wonder if you can make snowballs out of it?" he said.

"No, stupid," she said.

They sat there for a while swaying in the dark, and Black hoped Gabriel wouldn't show up.

"Tell me about your family?" Sweet Girl said.

Right then the only thing he could think of was his dying mother. Him holding her over the toilet, feeling her bones through the thin fabric of her nightgown, feeling the weight of her, which was as light as a bird's, holding her while she heaved, sweat filming her, leaving the acrid aftersmell of medicine on his hands. And after he wiped her and helped her back into bed, he would return to clean the toilet: lift the seat, and with wet tissue, wipe the spatter marks away. Wipe them clean. Then flush the paper. He never told her, never knew why he did it. But he felt some kind of love in that, he guessed.

There was another memory. On hot nights, when the fever burned too hot in her, he would go into her room to wrap a wet blanket around her, but she would be masturbating hard and furious and fast, her legs splayed wide open, fingers peeling the pink and brown of her, a smile on her face, and she wouldn't stop, even when she could see him standing there not knowing where to look, wanting to and not wanting to, nauseous from his own curiosity. And then he would flee, chased by her maniacal laughter and loud groans.

But he couldn't tell Sweet Girl any of that.

"Why don't you tell me about your family," he said instead.

She pushed against him and stood up. "You know, I don't talk about my family. They betrayed me when I needed them most, because I was different. They disagreed with my life choices, said I was unnatural and threw me out.

What is more unnatural than throwing your child away, cutting yourself from yourself?" she said.

He stood up and squeezed her hand.

"How did you get this up here?" she asked.

"It's a spaceship," he said.

The wind hadn't let up. If anything it had gained velocity. It was tearing at the branches of the trees and was blowing even more and more ash down on the city, and from the ship they could see that Cesar Chavez looked like a bomb had gone off in the vicinity. The ash was nearly an inch thick, but still people were dancing in the street. The ship was swaying so badly it was hard to stay upright. Sweet Girl leaned into him.

"Are you sure this thing is safe?" she asked him.

"It's okay," Black said.

She smiled.

"I trust you. So does it fly?"

"No."

"Not yet anyway," she said. He looked pained. "I'm just kidding," she added.

"I know."

She peered into the dark interior of the ship.

"Does it at least have a light?"

He flicked the switch on and immediately regretted it as the light picked up the board with the photographs. The alcohol was clouding his reason and he'd forgotten about them.

"Wow," Sweet Girl said, walking into the ship. "It's beautiful."

She could stand upright and not hit her head against the roof, though it was a tight fit. Then she saw the board and the photographs. She walked over to it. Studied herself. Touched the photos. He wanted to say, Don't worry, it's not what it looks like. I can explain. But the truth was, he couldn't. Maybe she could.

"Black," she said, and her voice was tender.

He didn't answer.

"How long have you been following me?"

He didn't answer. She studied the board intently.

"This is amazing," she said, and there was a kind of awe to her voice.

"You're not freaked out?"

"Hell yes, I'm freaked out. But something else too. I feel loved. Is that crazy?"

It sounded crazy to him, but he said nothing.

"I feel like if you went to all this trouble, you must really like me. Love me even."

Black didn't think he loved her. He wasn't even sure he liked her. He was just drawn to her. Sometimes that was all there was. An inexplicable draw.

"I guess," he said.

"Let's go back to your room," Sweet Girl said.

As they descended, it seemed as though they were moving through a strange landscape. The city of angels had become the city of ash and wind. There were fires burning on the side of the road. A few stores had their windows broken and people were making off with loot. Police helicopters crisscrossed the sky, lights picking up every movement down below. Media copters flew close by them, waiting like buzzards for the action. And yet the whole city seemed to be waiting, the wind the only thing with a clear intent.

Black wondered when the shift occurred—when things changed from celebration to frenzy. And there was something else too. He crossed the roof and looked down, amazed to see a long line of candle-bearing pilgrims filing down the street toward The Ugly Store. There were already maybe two hundred standing in the River of the street, gazing up at the spaceship, holding on to lit candles, while the wind whipped the flames about and showered ash on everything. But this River was more ash than water, the dead sludge of it relieved only by the candles, giving the impression of a river of fire.

The crowd was singing. "Amazing Grace."

"This is too cool," Sweet Girl said, and not for the first time he wondered if she was high.

Back in his room, Sweet Girl asked for a robe so she could get comfortable. She changed right there in front of him, leaving only her G-string on. She walked around the room, touching things as though she couldn't quite believe they were there. Or maybe she was making sure she was there, that the last time hadn't been a dream. The sewing machine. A bolt of cloth laid out on the worktable. She saw a bundle of women's clothes—panties, garter and hose—next to the bolt of cloth. She held them up with an inquisitive smile.

"Is this part of the long story from the last time?" she asked.

"I use those for the costumes," he said. "For my models," he added. They both knew it was a lie, but she moved on.

She took Iggy's wedding dress from the hanger behind the door and held it up against her and giggled.

"Where did you get this? It was here last time."

"I'm fixing it for a friend."

"You are the perfect man," she said, returning the dress

to the hook behind the door. She came over and kissed him. "Tell me you can cook."

He shook his head.

"Sorry. But I do have alcohol. The brandy is finished, but I think I have some whiskey."

"Sure."

The empty bottle reclining in the dustbin reminded him he'd finished it. He held it up.

"Sorry."

"That's okay. You've had enough anyway," Sweet Girl said. "You can be my intoxicant."

She was leaning back on the bed and motioned him over. He went to her and she pulled him down onto her chest, her robe opening slightly. His lips found a nipple and his tongue flicked over it.

"Yes," she said. "Like that."

His tongue moved down, drawing a circle of moisture and air from her breast down her stomach. She arched up fluidly but wouldn't let him take off her panties. She pushed him back on the bed and pulled his pants down.

"I'm glad you're glad to see me," she said, and burying her face in his crotch, she parted her lips and took all of him in and he shuddered. She smiled around him. This was pleasure. She looked up and followed his gaze to the lingerie set on the cutting table.

"Wait," she said. She crossed the room quickly and came back with them.

"What's this?" But he sounded hopeful.

"Put these on for me, bombóncito."

He looked at the stockings and garter belt.

"For me, papi. I told you I was a lesbian."

He nodded. He liked it. It felt so wrong, it felt so right.

He tried to pull the stocking on and nearly put a hole through them.

"Here," she said, voice gentle. "Let me help you."

He lay back and let her dress him. He liked the feeling. Of being dressed, of the cool nylon against his skin.

"I want to fuck you," he said.

She came up on all fours.

"Fuck me from behind," she said.

He tried to pull her panties off, but again she stopped him.

"No, leave them on. I like it that way."

He nodded and pulled them aside. The only light came from the kitchenette and they were in shadow. She took him and guided him in. He hesitated when he felt the resistance.

"Yes, papi, right there, fuck me in the ass," Sweet Girl said.

But this wasn't the moist softness he wanted. This hard muscle was him. He couldn't become her this way. He knew this thing, this intimacy he craved wasn't about love, or even sex, but about filling himself. Shrouding himself in the body of another. He felt himself grow limp.

"What? What is it?" Sweet Girl asked as she felt his erection soften.

He pulled away.

"What is it? Is it me?" she asked. She sounded defeated. Quiet.

He shook his head. He was kneeling behind her, his penis drooping on his thigh. She reached up and pulled his face up by the chin and stared into his eyes. The look he saw in hers shamed him.

"Is it because I am a stripper? Will it help if you pay me?" she asked.

And then the tears came. He cried like a thing wounded. His body shaking. Hands over his eyes. Mouth open. Saliva trails holding the two halves of his jaw together. She stared at him. Confused. Angry. Ashamed.

Getting up, she left him there on his knees and made her way to the bathroom. I have a good heart, he wanted to say to her through the bathroom door, afraid that if he didn't do something she would leave. He even tried to get up, but something had taken his voice, his will, it seemed, and he flopped forward onto the bed. When she came back he was sitting on his haunches, body flopped forward, face buried in the mattress, arms like broken wings beside him on the bed. She picked up her clothes, pulled on her dress and turned to leave. He wanted to move, to stop her, but he couldn't.

"Please," he managed.

She stopped at the door and turned. She hesitated at the door before walking over to the stereo. She put on the first CD she saw: Miles Davis's *Kind of Blue*. Searching for the right sound, she stopped on "Blue in Green."

"Come," she said, pulling him by the arm as the music filled the apartment. "Come."

Obediently, like a child, he stood up. Followed her to the center of the room. She stood facing him. He was naked except for the garter belt and stockings. She took her dress off, so she was only wearing her panties. She put his arms around her neck, hers around his waist. She pulled up to him.

"Dance with me," she said.

"I don't know how," he said.

"Sshh," she said. "I'll teach you."

thirty-nine

Ond this was all.

A man and a woman. Naked. Two naked people. Cling-ing to each other. Dancing. Moving as slightly as a breath over lace. And night. Nothing more. Or this too. As they danced, he remembered a castle in Disneyland with a swan in the foreground. Outside, a gentle Los Angeles mist was settling over what was left of the night.

forty

Night's River.

And though he couldn't see it from the bed, he knew it was there, just beyond the street and the darkness and yet it was the darkness. He could sense Sweet Girl breathing next to him. They had danced and when the song was over, still they had moved together for what seemed like forever. There was no lust in it, only comfort. They had lain in bed and he'd rubbed her feet and then just held her as they drifted off to sleep. The way a couple old to each other, old together, might. He thought about how she had made something inside him give way. He made to get up and go to the bathroom and noticed she was staring at him. It freaked him out.

"What are you doing?" he asked apprehensively.

"Just watching you sleep."

He took her face between his hands and pulled her to him. In that moment he felt nothing but a deep tenderness for this wounded, beautiful woman. He kissed her deeply. She stroked his face.

When he got back from the bathroom, she'd slipped on his shirt that was too big for her and went to the bathroom too. When she returned, she sat on the edge of the bed.

"What is it?" he asked.

Sweet Girl smiled tentatively. Black looked so innocent, so vulnerable in nothing but the stockings and garters.

"You're not a violent man, are you, Black?" she asked.

"What is going on?"

"You're not, are you?"

"No. I don't think so. Are you going to tell me what this is about?"

"I'll show you, if you promise to be cool."

"Sure."

Sweet Girl stood up and pulled up the tails of the shirt. She didn't have any underwear on. But there was something else too, and it took Black a full minute to realize what it was. Sweet Girl had no vagina, not that he was expecting one, but he was expecting a penis and there wasn't one of those either. There wasn't anything. There was just a kind of bandage—no, more like flesh-colored tape—where her genitals should be.

"What is this?" Black asked, but he didn't look away.

Sweet Girl put her hand on the tape and pulled it away and shook her legs about and fluffed her groin. A penis, complete with balls, appeared. Black stared mouth open as if he was watching a magic show. It wasn't a big penis, but it was a penis regardless and dramatic nonetheless.

"No fucking shit!" he said.

He slid off the bed and sat on the floor. But he didn't take his eyes off of Sweet Girl. He looked up at her. She had danced on his lap, yet he had never felt a penis, not once, and he realized that somewhere in his mind he had actually convinced himself that she was a woman. Out of sight indeed, he mused. He wished he could get angry. He wished he felt something like rage. But all he felt was an overwhelming relief and curiosity.

"Are you okay?" Sweet Girl asked.

He smiled and shook his head.

"Is that really a dick?" he asked.

"Yes," Sweet Girl said.

He got up. He wished he had some whiskey now.

"Thank you for showing it to me. I'm not sure I'm ready, but thank you," he said.

Sweet Girl just smiled.

"You know I'm not gay," he added. His voice was hard.

Sweet Girl laughed. Deep in her throat. Mocking.

"I'm not gay either. Well, not in that way. I'm a woman, honey, this tackle is just a little inconvenience, okay? I am all woman. And if I'm gay, it's because I'm a lesbian."

Black laughed.

"Are you going to sit, negro? You're making me nervous," Sweet Girl said, patting the bed beside her.

"How did you do that?"

"This?" Sweet Girl said, tucking her penis back. It seemed to fold into the scrotal sack. She pinched the tip between her buttocks. From the front there was no sign of a penis. She put her arms up in the air and twirled round three times, and each time, Black saw no penis. Sweet Girl laughed and opened her legs, letting her dick drop.

"Can you show me how to do that?" Black said, sitting next to her.

She took his hand in one hand, and with the other stroked him on the cheek.

"You are so sweet," she said. "I knew you would be, but,

well, let's just say no one has been this gentle, this under-standing and curious."

He smiled. Her prattling was making him nervous, making him tense. He wanted her to shut up and just show him.

"So you'll show me?" he asked.

"Sure. There are two ways to do this."

"Yeah?" Black's voice was heavy and breathy.

"The tuck was what I just showed you, easy. To hold it in place, all you need is a pair of tight panties. Takes a few seconds."

Black licked his lips.

"And the second?" he asked.

"The other way is taping. Or what I like to call, tuck, duck and tape," Sweet Girl said, laughing. The joke was lost on Black.

"There are several ways. The basic way is to wrap the ball bag around the penis, tape it several times, then pull up, like in the tuck, then tape the tip to the inner side of both ass cheeks. Because I strip, and because I am small, I pull the penis into the shaft, smooth the ball bag over it and tape it. That way I get to wear G-strings."

"What about your balls? Where are your balls?" Black asked.

"That one is easy, rey. You suck the balls into your stomach like this. . . ."

Black watched her balls disappear.

"They're in your stomach?"

"Yes, touch the bag if you don't believe me."

Black leaned forward and touched Sweet Girl's scrotal sack. He'd never touched another man's genitals before. It felt strange; like the dried skin of a mango, yet smooth.

Technically Sweet Girl was a woman, so this didn't count as a gay experience, he told himself.

"It feels smooth, but wrinkly," he said.

"Smooth because I wax it. Nothing I can do about the wrinkles, except maybe botox, but that would be expensive and painful."

"But where do the balls go?"

"Same space in your stomach they were before you grew hair down there."

"Can you show me?" he asked.

"On you?"

"Yes."

"Come here."

"I can't suck my balls into my stomach, though."

"Try lying flat on your back, feet on the floor, then push. They will vanish."

"Is there another way?"

"Sure. I'll just push them in. It's gonna feel strange, but it won't hurt, I promise. Okay?"

He nodded, not taking his eyes off his crotch, as she gently pushed his balls up inside him.

"You got tape?"

He pointed at the cutting table.

"Hold this," she said, passing him the loose bit of skin, while she crossed the room and fetched the tape. Tearing off a one-inch piece, she tacked the loose skin of the scrotal sack down. He looked at the piece of tape.

"That doesn't look big enough. Look—it doesn't cover it," Black protested.

"Honey, you are so not gay! It's just there to hold it while I work on the rest, okay?"

Sweet Girl then pushed his penis back into the folds of

skin around it. It was difficult at first because he was hard, but she pinched him. The sharp bite caused him to lose the erection. He stared in wonder as she pushed it back into the shaft and then tucked it all under his empty scrotal sack.

"I could tell when I seen you, your dick was small," she said as she worked. "Big men usually have small dicks. Otherwise it would feel like a bull fucking you. God don't want nobody getting hurt, honey."

Carefully she tore a bigger piece of tape and applied it. Black laughed. His dick had disappeared. He was free. He stood up.

"Is it too tight?" Sweet Girl asked. "You need the blood to flow."

He stood there. It was strange, but he could feel his penis in the empty space where it once was at the same time as feeling an incredible void. An emptiness. He wanted to cry. To laugh. He didn't know what he wanted.

"Here, honey," Sweet Girl said, passing him her panties. "Put these on."

He did. Without a murmur, without a thought. He just did. A part of him wondered whether his lack of a penis made him more gentle, acquiescing? Is this how women felt? This is not the time to ask those questions, he thought. Not now, when nothing was clear. Not when he could barely wrap his head around it. He took a deep breath.

The tape pinched. The feeling was hard to describe; like the pull of nearly healed stitches. Not painful, but tender. The remembrance of flesh. He was afraid of this feeling, but couldn't stop enjoying it. Like when he picked at the scab of the wound on his face. The way the dried blood and new skin had pulled, before opening with a sting, fresh blood beading the rawness.

"How do you feel?" Sweet Girl asked.

He wanted to say something. Say, Help, I can't breathe. I am suffocating. I am claustrophobic. I can't feel my penis. Get this tape off me. It has gone for good. Who am I? What am I? He wanted to scream, to push against this feeling like a small death. The way he imagined spilt honey spreading over a dying ant must feel, bliss, breathlessness and the onset of terror. He swallowed hard, dug his fingernails into his palms and looked in the mirror. He was a girl. He began to cry. Sweet Girl clapped her hands and laughed.

"You look hot," she said. She got up, her dick swinging between her legs and walked over to the door. Okay, maybe not swinging, he thought, but definitely punctuating like a fat period. She came back with Iggy's wedding dress and helped Black put it on. Black slipped the blonde wig on. Then Sweet Girl slipped into an old suit of his. They stood side by side in front of the mirror.

"I guess you're my bitch now," Sweet Girl said.

There it was again. The mocking.

"I knew you wanted to be a woman. I knew it from the moment you walked into Charlie's," she said.

He could feel the tide coming in, the waves wrapping over his head, so near yet so far away. He took a deep breath against the drowning. He wanted Sweet Girl to shut up. He wanted to make her shut up. He wanted to kiss her. He wanted to be her bitch. He loved her. He despised her.

"Come," she said. "Sit."

He sat and she began to apply makeup to his face: blue eye shadow, pink rouge, black eyeliner and red lipstick.

Below them in The Ugly Store, Damian's band had struck the opening chords to Coltrane's *A Love Supreme*. He loved that song, loved the way Damian covered it. He knew it was their signature end piece, and he guessed it was all building to a head.

"Ta-da!" Sweet Girl said, holding up her compact for him to see. He looked like a 1940s German whore from a bad B movie. He hated her. He hated himself. He couldn't differentiate. How did she end up as the man, dick swinging in his pants, while he was now the bride, her bitch?

And she was smiling. The same smile from the club. And he knew he would never find this thing, this becoming that he wanted. It was a grace far beyond anything he had in the face of it. He had nothing to give to the dark angel of it. Nothing. And they all knew it: Bomboy, who didn't know what it was he knew; Iggy, who knew things about him he couldn't even guess at himself; Gabriel, an androgynous pigeon-angel; Sweet Girl, this man who was more woman than he would ever be. Watching her now, in his suit, it dawned on him that she was more man too.

Raul, below, on piano was already off to a spirited solo, while someone banged on a tambourine. Black seemed to watch his left fist hit Sweet Girl, even as part of him registered the music. He knew it was him, but it wasn't. He felt rather than saw her surprise, her shock, her fear. Then he was hitting her again and again. She was a small woman and his blows had her on the floor. She wasn't crying out, though, she wasn't begging. Tight-lipped and grunting, she was fighting back; each move between them punctuated by Rakim's harmonics on the sax like a hundred Pharoahs, Sanders that is; nails raking across his face, legs kicking at his crotch, but Black was safely out of reach beneath the tape. She, on the other hand, wasn't, and his knee to her dick caused her to double up. As she went down on her knees, she staggered back.

"Black," she gasped. "Why?"

Aaaaaaaaawwhhhh, Rakim's horn screamed.

But Black could only hear the roar of the blood in his head. Sweet Girl got to her feet just before he reached her and fell back against the worktable with all the pigments, sending a rainbow-colored cloud up in the air. As Black closed the distance between them, she scrabbled behind her for anything she could use to defend herself. Her fingers closed around a can and without looking she swung at him. It held turpentine and the liquid caught Black in the face and chest, and he screamed from the sting to his eyes. He backed off and wiped furiously at the liquid, the chemical dripping all over the dress. Squinting to try to see, Black took another swing at Sweet Girl, but his heart wasn't in it anymore. He'd never faced anything in his life and this time would be no different. Sweet Girl dodged the blow easily, but still afraid, she ran to the worktable. Black approached, half-blind, arms held open in a gesture of peace, of surrender, but Sweet Girl swung at him, the tip of the heavy sewing scissors she had found on the table sinking into his chest, just above his heart. She wasn't strong or determined enough to do much damage, although when she pulled the scissors out the wound bled; one jet that sprayed her in the face, then a slow leak down the front of his dress. She was crying as she watched the turpentine diluting the blood into a red blur. Black was crying too, tears and deep soul-wrenching moans. His makeup had run, and when he caught a glimpse of himself in the mirror he shrank back from the hideousness of it.

I'm a monster, he thought, and it reminded him of that night he had been raped under the bridge.

And Walter was off on a percussion solo, the rest of the band silent, only the fast rhythm of the heart-sounding congas. Each slap and smack on the tight hide hitting like a punch against night, each beat winding it all up.

"Black, baby, I'm sorry," Sweet Girl said, coming toward him, scissors still in hand. He backed away and crashed through the door, out into the corridor. Sweet Girl followed, calling for him, still holding the scissors like a vampire stake. Stumbling down the corridor toward the staircase that led to the roof, Black looked like a deranged and psychotic Miss Havisham, dragging a long train of white death behind him, the gossamer hide of a dead angel.

Once on the roof, he stumbled toward the ladder that led to the spaceship. He was still bleeding, though not too badly, and was half-blind from the turpentine. Grabbing hold, he relaxed against the rusting metal as his body pulled itself up, almost from memory, the climb feverish.

"Black!" Sweet Girl screamed from the roof, finally dropping the scissors, watching with fear as the wind whipped the cocktail sausage of a spaceship around like it would tear it up and throw it into the darkness and the River. Inside the spaceship, Black lit a cigarette and blew smoke out. He spotted the board with Sweet Girl's pictures on it.

"Oh, my God," he said. "Oh, my God."

And Damian's voice was back, singing softer than a cat running across a wooden floor, the crowd in the bar, the crowd outside the bar, all quiet, all holding their breath.

Black couldn't stand to be in the spaceship with her

another moment, so he popped the skylight. He didn't care if Gabriel was there. He was too far gone to be afraid anymore. It was really dark and he didn't want to be alone; the dark and the swirling ash made it look like the sky was alive with ghosts. He hesitated for a moment then stepped out onto the roof of the spaceship.

The spotlight from a helicopter picked him up.

The crowd of the faithful gathered below screamed in ecstasy. There she was, the queen of heaven, perched on the roof of the spaceship.

Below, in the club, the music had risen in volume, Damian's voice tapering off as Rakim blew his horn again, as though calling down the walls of Jericho, blew that horn in octaves too high and too low for human ears, blew harmonics like he was speaking another language.

The wind was whipping the train of Black's dress in every direction, and fluttering in the wind the way it did, the train made him look like he was flying, or rather, hovering, above it all.

And below, Taylor's bass thumped the chorus behind Rakim, throbbing with the excitement of a heart about to explode with all that joy and all that wonder, throbbing, *A Love Supreme, A Love Supreme, A Love Supreme.* Picking up the note as Rakim's sax died, Damian's voice called the changes with just the bass now, his voice holding all the water that had flowed across this land and all the water to come. *A Love Supreme, A Love Supreme.*

Outside The Ugly Store, below Black, in the street, the faithful picked up Damian's call, hundreds of voices chanting: *A Love Supreme, A Love Supreme,* a few calling: "Mother, mother," all of them beholding their queen in the pure light of the helicopter's spotlight, too far away to see the blood, too blinded by faith. Behind the Virgin, the night sky was a mixed hue of reds and pinks. Her face, glowing in the light from the helicopter searchlight, was ghostly, haunting.

The singing was growing louder and louder and pilgrims kept coming to join the crowd, swelling their numbers. Black, looking down, thought that the River of the street would soon be overflowing with people. The wind, growing even wilder, attempted several times to snatch him from his perch and dash him to the ground, at the feet of the adulating crowd. The faithful kept coming and coming, as though blown there, like the ash. He could make out Iggy in the street below. She was looking up at him and he knew she recognized him. An old woman, face awash with rapture, grabbed on to her arm.

"Isn't it wonderful?" she shouted. "She brought us this miracle, you know," the woman went on, one hand collecting the falling ash. "Snow in Los Angeles."

Black could hear her; he could hear everything; feel everything: the heartbeat of the faithful, the band in The Ugly Store, Sweet Girl on the roof screaming. He was sobbing and he raised his hands to rail against the night. The faithful in the River below cheered and began to sing another song. The police helicopter circled, washing him in a halo of light that seemed only to increase his appeal. He saw Bomboy come up to Iggy. He was pointing at Black and whispering. Iggy shook her head and said something to him.

It was all dance.

And wind: howling through the city, tearing souls from their moorings and casting them into the primordial swirl of making and unmaking. The crowds ran first this way and then that. The police arrived in droves and in well-rehearsed synchronized movements herded the crowd first this way and then that, clubs and boots reinforcing old lessons.

And the city burning with the red of flames held in a sky black with love and ash, and the wind, the wind.

"Oh, God!"

He wasn't sure if he had said it or if it was coming from the crowd, or if Damian was calling from the bar, but he could see several people pointing up at him, their expressions a mix of awe and fear and he wondered if Gabriel had appeared behind him. No. He smelled the burning and looking down realized that he'd dropped the still lit cigarette and it had caught on an edge of the turpentine-soaked dress. He stamped his feet trying to extinguish the fire, but the turpentine was an accelerant, and the flames enveloped him.

A woman on fire.

And the wind tore at the train of the wedding dress until it became a billowing sheet of flame trailing away behind Black, until it ripped the burning cloth free. The floating train hovered in the ash-heavy air for a moment, like a phoenix, all flight and fire, even as Black flailed dangerously close to the edge of the spaceship. Another updraft caught the train of lace and it sailed away, still burning. Set free it floated over the crowd, heading for the River. It sank from view.

Adrift on night's River.

Leavened.

This blue light here and trembling with knowledge beyond measure; also love: perhaps. It falls with the sense of a wingspan, but is gone just as soon leaving only the memory of it; and like this River, it is never the same twice.

Last night's regretful rain is now only ash.

And maybe this too.

Here, on the edge of morning, perched on the lip of a bridge, hunched in the solitary sadness of a gargoyle, a woman picks petals from a flower, dropping each into that endless flow, her whispers holding it all like prayer: he loved me; he loved me not. In the river below, an angry dog barks as it swims for safety unaware of the petals falling like gossamer, like promises not kept. But there are no scriptures here in this city of angels where every moment is a life lived too fast, where the spines of freeways, like arteries, like blood, circle in hope. Permanence is this River and with piety's conviction we make a home here.

There will never be no more River.